TEMPTATION

— CLUB X #1 —

K. M. SCOTT

The Club X Series, a scorching hot new erotic contemporary romance series by New York Times bestselling author K.M. Scott.

Cassian March, the public face of Tampa's most exclusive nightspot, Club X, has a great life. Women, sex, and money are his for the taking, and no man indulges his desires more. Life is short, and he plays hard. He lives by only one rule—never let a woman get close.

Olivia Lucas needs a job, and if that means working at a club that specializes in making members' wildest fantasies come true, then that's what she'll do. A girl's got to pay the rent, right? She never expected to fall for the gorgeous owner of Club X, though, but a man like him would never go for someone like her. Or would he?

Temptation is a work of fiction. Names, characters, places, and events are the products of the author's imagination. Any resemblance to events, locations, or persons, living or dead, is coincidental.

2014 Copper Key Media, LLC

Published in the United States

ISBN-10: 1941594042
ISBN-13: 978-1-941594-04-9

Cover Design: Cover Me, Darling

Adult Content: Contains graphic sexual content

To my wonderful friends and assistants,
Kelley, Erica, and Lea.

You not only make my job easier,
but you make me laugh every day.
Thank you for being there.

Contents

Chapter One

Olivia

The large, manila envelope sat on the coffee table with the ticket to the next chapter in my life. After nearly six months of being unemployed, it was time to join the ranks of the working again. I knew that. But after being out of commission for so long, all that was running through my mind was pure, unmitigated fear.

Whoever said a degree meant a sure job must have been living in a different century. I'd done everything right. After four years of college, I'd graduated magna cum laude from a good school with a degree in management in hand ready to conquer the world. Unfortunately, I hadn't realized thousands of others just like me had the same plans, many of whom had attended even better schools and had a jumpstart on me with even better internships than mine.

So after five years dedicating myself day and night to climbing the corporate ladder at the nation's newest sports apparel company, the fine folks who sat in cushy corner offices at Premier Sports decided to promote the other guy to regional sales manager of the northeast and gave me a pink slip. "You know how it is, Olivia. The economy just isn't what we hoped it would be. Best of luck."

Best of luck. Nice. So Tony Galente and his lovely wife and three kids moved to Boston while I got a weak excuse for being fired and stayed right there in Tampa. Picking up the envelope, I thought about the frigid New England winters and muttered, "I hope he freezes his ass off up there."

Printed in big letters, the name of my new employer stared up from the envelope at me. March Enterprises. The real name on the envelope should have said Club X. I'd lived in Tampa all my life and never once had I heard of any club named that, and I'd spent my fair share of nights celebrating everything from birthdays to bachelorette parties to my friends' promotions. But my friend Jake had and thinking he was helping me one night while he was on a partying binge had mentioned my name to one of the owners who was looking for an assistant to the main owner. That he was entirely too vague on the particulars of Club X made me uneasy, but he'd assured me this was a job I'd be perfect for. All I had to do was find a way to be okay that Club X was, as Jake termed it, "the kind of place I was in desperate need of," whatever that meant.

Well, as they say, beggars can't be choosers, and this beggar had just about depleted the last of her savings. Whatever Club X might be, I needed this job.

So I sat there with a potential job offer in my hands, unsure of what exactly the owner at Club X would want me to do but sure I couldn't turn it down. Slowly, I slid the lone piece of paper out to again see merely a paragraph telling me that if I desired, the job of executive assistant was available. All I had to do was interview at two that afternoon. Reading between the lines, I knew they wanted to see if my in-person style was as impressive as my qualifications on paper.

"So they want to see you, Olivia. Time to show them what you got."

Standing on shaky legs, I walked into my bedroom and checked out my interview look in the mirror. A navy blue business suit, white blouse, and navy three inch pumps said I was a confident businesswoman, even if my insides were shaking like jelly. I smoothed a few stray red hairs back into my bun and took a deep breath. I could do this.

I had to do this.

Arriving much earlier than I'd planned, I parked my 2005 Subaru Impreza across the street from an enormous warehouse and checked the address on the paper, sure I'd made a mistake. Jake had told me Club X was a bar and entertainment complex. Looking out my driver's side window, all I saw was an huge building that resembled an old factory. My GPS said I was in the right place, though, so I sat back and listened to music for ten minutes, hoping my interview jitters would calm themselves soon.

As Katy Perry's Roar played like an anthem for my interview, I watched for any sign of life in the building I was supposed to enter in just minutes but saw no one.

The warehouse was five floors and took up half an entire city block. Unlike other factories, though, this building had few windows. In addition, there was no neon sign alerting potential patrons that Club X even existed there. Perhaps that was why they were looking for an executive assistant to the owner. Someone needed to clue these people in on basic marketing techniques.

The song ended, and I checked my phone for the time. 1:48. Time to head in. One last quick look in the rearview mirror to check that I didn't have lipstick on my teeth and I was ready to go. Stepping out into the warm May sun, I took a deep breath and made my way to the building.

Unsure of which door to enter through since all the doors looked like the basic industrial strength steel variety, I turned the doorknob on the one closest to the left side of the building and hoped I wouldn't have to try too many and end up being late for the interview. Luck was with me and the door opened into Club X.

I tried to calm my shaking legs, stepped inside, and stared with wide eyes at the scene in front of me. Open to the ceiling two floors above, the room was enormous. A solid glass bar ran the entire length of the far wall on the main floor, along with tables and chairs that took up most of the room. At the opposite end of the room was a huge space, I suspected for a dance floor. Craning my neck, I slowly turned around and tried to see the floors above but in the dim light I could only see walkways and staircases leading from level to level.

"Ms. Lucas?"

I turned at the sound of a deep voice saying my

name and saw a man coming toward me. Over six foot, he was well-built yet lean, like every muscle in his body was trained to work at peak performance. His hair was dark brown and short, and as he came closer I saw his eyes, a brilliant blue color framed by dark lashes. His grey business suit was obviously expensive and tailor made to fit his well-proportioned body. In fact, everything about him screamed money. And sex. Definitely sex. Like the kind of sex that left you boneless on his silk sheets with him still inside you after fucking you better than you'd ever been fucked before.

Extending my hand to shake his, I smiled and tried to keep myself composed as I introduced myself. "I'm Olivia Lucas. It's very nice to meet you, Mr…?" I left my statement hanging because there hadn't been a name on the letter they'd sent.

His piercing eyes studied me intensely before he spoke and his voice flowed over me like silk. "March. Cassian March. Welcome to Club X."

He surprised me by pronouncing the Roman numeral ten for X. "Oh, I hadn't realized the X was the Roman numeral. My friend had called it Club X, as in the letter x," I admitted, feeling a blush cover my cheeks at the mention of Jake's mistake.

He studied me again, his gaze unwavering as it held mine. "That happens a lot. The club's secretive nature lends itself to the x name, but I originally opened it up with the intent of calling it Club Ten but with the Roman numeral. You'll find many of our patrons think like your friend does. Perhaps it's time I did the same."

His voice dropped, and I hoped he wasn't already

disappointed in me even before I had the chance to show him I was as good in person as my qualifications were on paper. Pressing a smile onto his very kissable lips, he held his arm out to lead me to his office and I followed him, enjoying the view from behind even as I silently scolded myself for not focusing on what was important. Checking out my new boss's incredible ass wasn't keeping my eye on the prize, no matter how hot he looked in that suit.

Guiding me into his office at the very back of the building, he sat down behind an enormous glass desk and extended his arm once again, this time to offer me a seat. As I tried to relax, he picked up the phone and called someone to alert them I'd arrived. Instantly, my anxiety ratcheted up more than a few notches as I hadn't realized this would be a group interview. He shuffled papers around on his desk, seeming to look for something, and I told myself I could handle this. An interview with five or even ten owners was the same as an interview with one owner, right?

As I looked around at his minimalist designed office, a younger man responded to his call, and I guessed he was in his mid-twenties. He took his place next to Cassian and began to talk to him, and I noticed my potential new boss looked similar to this second man, even though this younger man had lighter hair and brown eyes.

"We're just waiting for Kane. He's the third owner of Club X," Cassian explained in a voice that signaled his impatience at the fact that this other man hadn't appeared yet. "While we're waiting for him, let me introduce you two. Stefan, this is Olivia Lucas. She's here for the job as my assistant. Olivia, this is my brother, Stefan March."

The one I pegged as the younger brother wore jeans and a white T-shirt with the club's logo, which showed off his arms full of tattoos that covered from his wrists all the way up to where his shirt began and a bigger, more muscular body than his brother's. The man clearly saw the inside of a gym and often. He carried himself far more casually than his brother too. And if Cassian screamed sex, this man oozed it, like the sweetest honey drizzled on the tip of your tongue. Sandy brown hair slightly longer than his brother's shorter, more professional haircut gave him a carefree look, but there was no escaping the fact that he was as intense as his brother, just in a different way.

With a gorgeous smile, he slid his dark brown gaze over me and nodded. "Nice to meet you, Olivia. I manage the day-to-day operations of the club, unlike Cash, who spends all his time in this office dressed in suits meant to smother a man."

"It's nice to meet you, Stefan," I said with a smile, unable to remain purely businesslike in his presence. In just seconds, I'd warmed up to him more than I imagined I'd ever warm up to his brother.

"You're going to love it here," Stefan continued. "And I promise if my brother works you too hard, all you have to do is come find me. I'll make sure this doesn't become a nine to five grind."

Something in the way his eyes continued to focus on everything below my neck told me he would live up to that promise if I let him. I tried not to look too enchanted by him, even if I instantly felt attracted to him and his warm personality, because even as we began to get to know one another, I sensed disapproval in Cassian's face.

Out of the corner of my eye I saw someone approach the office, and turning my head, I saw a third man much bigger than either Cassian or Stefan but practically Cassian's twin, except for his very short hair. Dressed in black pants and a long sleeve black Henley that only accentuated the darkness of his cropped hair, he instantly intimidated me. The polar opposite to Stefan, this man said nothing and appeared unhappy at the prospect of meeting me at all.

"Kane, this is Olivia Lucas. She's here for the assistant job. Olivia, this is my brother, Kane."

Extending my hand, I shook the third man's hand and said hello, but he said nothing back. His jet black hair and blue eyes gave him a striking look, much like his brother's, but Kane's demeanor frightened me with its coldness. Backing away from me, he seemed happy to have the introductions over, and I felt pretty much the same about him.

I also noticed how Cassian's voice caught slightly when he said Kane was his brother. They looked around the same age, but they weren't twins, so what were they if calling him brother was so awkward?

"So Olivia, maybe I should tell you about who we are and what we do here at Club X," Cassian said with a smile, using the letter x for the first time in the name. "I handle the business of running this place, while Stefan handles the operations. Kane handles the security and performers. Together, we own the biggest private club in the city."

He stopped talking, and I sat waiting for him to

continue, my gaze focused on his very attractive face. Chiseled features with masculine lines, his look was very much one of a man of power. He merely stared back at me and appeared to wait for me to speak, creating an odd silence I was sure wasn't going to bode well for my chances at getting the assistant job.

Thankfully, Stefan spoke up. Pushing on his brother's arm, he said with a broad smile that made my uneasiness disappear, "Cash, Jake obviously didn't tell her what we do here. I think you may have to be a bit more detailed."

Detailed? Cassian grimaced at his brother's suggestion, but with a slow nod, he agreed with Stefan and continued, this time explaining more about what exactly Club X was.

"Club X is a private club that serves as a nightclub and a place that caters to our members' fantasies. People pay to join and have the choice of merely coming here to enjoy the best nightlife the city has to offer or, if they choose, having us provide the necessary requirements to fulfill their fantasies."

He said those words as if he were describing how to water down patrons' drinks. Fulfill fantasies? Was he talking about sexual fantasies?

"I can see by your expression that you're a bit surprised. Please feel free to ask whatever questions you may have," Cassian said in a deep, reassuring voice I already liked hearing.

Struggling to form an intelligent thought, I asked the first question that came to me. "Are we talking BDSM? I know it's all the rage these days."

A slow smile spread across his gorgeous mouth, but it was Stefan who spoke up to answer my question. With a chuckle, he said, "No. There are dozens of places on the West Coast that handle that. We're more unique here at Club X. Imagine this. A woman wants to be wined and dined, but her husband has no interest. She comes to us for a night she'll remember for the rest of her life. We give our members what they want."

"So, no sex? Just dinner and conversation?" I asked, pretty sure that's not what he meant.

With a twinkle in his eye, Stefan cocked one eyebrow. Shaking his head, he said, "No. If that's all they want, that's fine, but we find that our members tend to want experiences that will stay with them forever, and that usually means sex."

"Oh." I had no idea how I was supposed to respond to that. I was no prude, by any means. I got my freak on from time to time. It's just that I wasn't sure what I was getting into with the March brothers and Club X.

I did need a job badly, though.

"Think of us as matchmakers for very particular people," Cassian said with a smile, "matching them with experiences they've only dreamed of."

"I don't mean to ask all the wrong questions, but is this legal?"

Thankfully, my question didn't sound as silly spoken out loud as it did in my head. All three men smiled, even Kane, and Stefan answered, "Nothing wrong with that question, Olivia. Yes, it's entirely legal. It would only be illegal if we were providing men or women paid solely for sex. We're not doing prostitution. Just fantasy fulfillment."

I wasn't sure fantasy fulfillment was strictly legal either, at least the way they did it, but I let that go for the moment. "Where does this all happen? I mean, this building is huge, but much of it seemed to be the nightclub I saw when I walked in."

Cassian looked to his left. "I'll let Kane explain that part."

His face serious once again, the biggest brother stared down at me, making me feel small and vulnerable. Something in his piercing blue eyes unnerved me, and as he spoke, I couldn't help but look away. His voice, even deeper than Cassian's, came out in a rasp. "The upper three floors have rooms to accommodate fifteen members in total. Most nights all the rooms are reserved well in advance. If a fantasy requires more than one room, then that's what we give them. For a price, of course."

Looking at Cassian, who'd quickly become the only brother who didn't make me nervous, I asked, "May I ask how much all this costs?"

"Basic membership is five thousand, with gold membership at ten. Platinum members pay twenty thousand, but with that membership comes a number of perks, such as top shelf liquor and the ability to jump ahead of other members in the reservation line. We also work very hard to accommodate platinum members'...wishes."

The way he hesitated before saying the word wishes made me think there was much more to what those platinum members received for their twenty thousand dollars. My curiosity piqued, I continued with my questions. "How much does each fantasy fulfillment cost?"

Cassian folded his arms across his chest and leaned back in his chair. "It depends on the type of fantasy the member wants to pursue. Just as with the memberships, there are basic, gold, and platinum level fantasy packages. Fantasies in the basic package level take less than two hours to stage and don't include anything sexual. They cost anywhere from two thousand and up, depending on the extras required. Gold level fantasy packages take between two and four hours to stage and can include sexual components. The gold package level costs from five thousand and up, again depending on the extras required, such as alcohol, costumes, and additional people. Platinum level fantasy packages require more time and preparation, so they're more expensive. Often, they need up to eight or even ten hours, and that level almost always involves sexual fantasies. The platinum package level starts at ten thousand and depending on the extras required, can cost twice or three times as much."

As I struggled to keep my face from showing exactly how shocked I was at what I'd just heard, I mentally wondered who the hell Club X's members were and how they afforded these things. If what Kane had said was the truth, then there were a lot of people in my hometown living out their fantasies and paying through the nose to do so. No doubt Jake had paid with his father's money, but I had to wonder—which level membership did he have?

"Wow. I've never heard of anything like this," I admitted quietly, sure I sounded like some sheltered soul who'd never truly lived a day in her life.

Pleased with my response, Cassian smiled warmly and nodded his head. "We saw a niche we could fill and we've been lucky enough to find a receptive audience in the Tampa area. I want to assure you, Olivia, that your job would involve none of the actual operations of the club but merely assisting me in my part of running our business. Unfortunately for you, I'm the owner who has the least exotic part to deal with."

His self-effacing way of saying he was the purely business part of the club charmed me, even if he hadn't meant to, and whatever reservations I had about the job evaporated under his appealing gaze. "Thank you, Mr. March. I'm sure the job will be challenging and fulfilling."

Stefan threw his head back and laughed out loud, and I thought I even saw Kane crack a smile as I spoke. "Mr. March? That's got to go," Stefan said, elbowing Cassian next to him.

"You can call me Cassian or Cash, whichever you like, Olivia. We'll be working closely, so Mr. March seems incredibly formal."

"Even for Mr. Suit and Tie it's too formal," Stefan joked. "Just call him Cash. It's what we call him. Leave Cassian for business meetings."

Cassian opened up a folder on his desk and pushed a stack of papers toward me. Looking down, I saw they were part of a contract.

"Take a few minutes to think about what we've discussed, and feel free to consult legal counsel before you sign the contract we require. There is a non-disclosure agreement that you should be aware of barring you from discussing anything you see or learn as my assistant concerning the club's business practices. We'll leave you to read over the contract, and when I return, we can discuss anything you aren't sure of."

Before I could say another word, they filed out of the office one by one and left me there with a stack of papers I knew I should have an attorney look at before I signed a thing. I began reading the contract, all the while knowing that I couldn't afford to visit a lawyer, much less say no to the job.

I read every word of the contract, but it wouldn't have mattered if it said I had to wear a French maid's uniform while I worked and couldn't get benefits until I got down on my knees and begged. The salary was more than I'd expected and would help me finally get out of the hole I'd been in for far too long. Finding nothing suspect in the dozen or so pages of the contract, I sat back and waited for Cassian to return.

He needed an assistant, and I needed a job. It was a match made in heaven.

Chapter Two
Cassian

Following Stefan and Kane out of my office, I met them in the bar area to give Olivia some privacy while she read over the extensive contract I required all employees sign. Although we'd just met, I liked her and wanted her to accept the job, mainly because I'd gone long enough without an assistant.

In a low voice, Kane said with a grin, "I always love it when you say what we do here is legal. You're the only one of us who could pull that off. There's no way anyone would believe that coming from Stefan or me."

"Yeah, well, we'd never get anyone to come in here as my assistant if we told them we had to pay off the cops and grease the politicians to stay open, especially someone like Olivia there."

"She's a cute one, even in that suit," Stefan said with a predatory smirk, betraying how much he liked her already too.

"Don't even think of it," I warned my little brother whose inability to keep his hands off the employees had led to more than one legal mess I'd had to clean up.

"You're not talking about that non-fraternization business in your contracts, are you? What's the point of running a place like this if we don't get to enjoy ourselves sometimes?"

Kane rolled his eyes and shook his head in disgust. Unlike Stefan, my half-brother never bothered with any of the staff, despite the fact that he dealt with the more erotic areas of the club and had more than ample opportunity to try out the dancers, even if it violated the non-fraternization clause of our deal.

"No, I'm not talking about the fact that you're supposed to keep your hands off the bartenders so I don't have to deal with another problem that will cost us more money to keep another girl quiet. That non-disclosure clause requires lawyers to enforce it, Stefan."

"Then what are you talking about? She's hot." He peered over my shoulder into my office and grinned. "Have you ever noticed how few good looking redheads there are in the world? She's definitely in the hot redhead category. I usually don't like red hair with brown eyes, but they work on her. Why shouldn't I see if she wants to get together?"

Intentionally making my voice stern, I answered, "Because I said not to."

I saw in Kane's eyes that he instantly understood my point, but Stefan's cock was doing the thinking for him, so he didn't seem to comprehend the sharpness of my scolding. "Are you saying she's off limits, Cash? That sounds like a challenge to me. I bet I could have her begging for it in no time."

Taking a step closer to him, I leaned hard against his

shoulder to warn him. "I'm saying she's not to be touched. Are we clear?"

Stefan looked over at Kane as if he couldn't believe what he'd just heard, and when he didn't find an ally in him for his conquest, turned back to face me. Putting his hands up in surrender, he shrugged. "No problem. I was just having a little fun. That's all. I had no idea you'd decided she was yours. Take it easy, Cash. You won't find a problem with me. You might want to try showing her you like her, though. My guess is that she has no idea since you act like all the fun in you is trapped in that suit and tie."

I looked back at Olivia as she sat in my office examining the contract I hoped she'd sign. Unlike Stefan, I didn't make it a practice of sleeping with every woman who worked for me. My previous assistant had left because she'd gotten married and her husband had thought little of her working in a place associated with other people's fantasies. I could understand that. I'm not sure I'd want any wife of mine spending her workdays surrounded by what we dealt with here.

Stefan hadn't been wrong in his assessment of how attractive Olivia was. He may not have found redheads sexy more times than not, but for me, redheads were always hot, no matter what color eyes they had. Fiery and hot-tempered, there was nothing sexier than a redhead, and a smart one like Olivia was the best type of woman there was.

Jesus, I sounded like my horny younger brother.

I didn't need to troll the club for potential girlfriends. My personal life was better left right where it was—

separate from my business life. I didn't date women who were members of the club, especially those who enjoyed the fantasies we provided. That had disaster written all over it. I lived by the old adage "Don't shit where you eat".

Women were easy to come by. I didn't have to spend my time at work picking them up. If only I could convince Stefan of that fact.

"So you think she's going to work out, Cash?" he asked, shaking me from my thoughts.

"She'll be fine. She's got great qualifications and she seems easy enough to get along with. As long as she can handle the place, I don't see a problem."

"I wonder if she'll take advantage of the unique benefits package we offer," Stefan said with a grin.

Kane looked moderately interested in his idea, probably because it was he who organized that part of the business. I wasn't sure allowing upper level employees like our assistants to become members automatically was a good idea, even though I'd had Olivia checked out thoroughly before she walked through the door. She had no bad habits, no addictions, and decent credit, except for the past six months, so even if she wasn't an employee she'd likely been eligible to become a member. I just hoped letting her wouldn't encourage that shitting where we ate thing.

"You know what I think about mixing business with pleasure, little brother," I chastised, hoping Stefan would get the hint that whatever would happen with Olivia wouldn't involve him at all.

"That it makes us millions of fucking dollars a year?

Stop acting like you aren't intimately involved in this business of ours, Cash. I don't care if you've never taken advantage of the pleasures Kane and his people offer upstairs. You benefit from the mixing of business and pleasure every day of your life, and just because you dress like some stiff doesn't mean you can divorce yourself from who we truly are."

Kane winced, his expression almost one of pain at Stefan's choice of words, but I let his little lecture slide for the moment. Just because I was part owner of Club X didn't mean I had to be like him.

"If there's no objection to Olivia, I'm going to offer her the job," I said definitively. I didn't think there'd be any opposition to her, but as equals in the business, I had to legally give my partners a chance to express their disapproval, if they had any.

Silently, Kane shook his head, and when I looked to his left at Stefan, he pretended to think of a reason to argue against my hiring of her but just shrugged his shoulders. "You know what I think. I think you shouldn't waste time getting her to join you upstairs. You're not seeing anyone seriously now, so there's never been a better time."

Turning to walk back into my office, I leaned in toward Stefan and whispered, "I've told you before what I think of you getting involved in my personal life. You made that mistake once and I forgave you. Don't make it again. I can't promise I'll be as forgiving the second time."

Before he had the chance to give me some bullshit answer that would likely irritate me, I left him standing with Kane and rejoined Olivia as she finished reading her contract. Taking my seat behind my desk, I adjusted my suit coat sleeves and waited for her to ask whatever questions she had about her new job.

I studied her, remembering how the background investigation on her had said she was twenty-seven. Something in her face showed an edge that gave her a more mature look than one I'd expect in someone her age. I liked that. I didn't need some doe-eyed girl who needed direction at every turn. I needed an assistant like Kate had been for me—competent, intelligent, and supportive. Watching Olivia, I hoped I'd found that in her.

She seemed uncomfortable as she hesitated for a moment before looking up from the papers in front of her. "I'm sorry. Do you have a pen?"

Sliding one toward her, I touched her finger with mine, noticing instantly how soft her skin felt as she slid the pen from my grasp. She smiled her appreciation and with no more hesitation, signed on the bottom line to become my new executive assistant.

A little surprised by her lack of questions about the position, I guessed she likely was in as much debt as the investigator had reported. Still, I felt uncomfortable beginning our working arrangement without some discussion of her possible concerns.

"Olivia, you have no questions?"

Taking a deep breath, she exhaled slowly. "I have a lot of questions. Like can you give me some history on the club? I tried to find out about it, but you've been very successful in keeping this place under the radar."

"No problem. Originally, my brothers and I bought

into Club X with two other investors, one of whom was a silent partner. The other wasn't as silent, but when the first one decided to offer his part in the business, I believe because he was getting married, the other man chose likewise to give us a chance to buy him out and we did. That was just a few months ago, but in truth, we've been running the club by ourselves for a little over five years."

She smiled politely, and I prepared to tell my usual lie so she didn't bolt out the door before she even got to give the place a chance. "I suspect you're concerned about the legality of all this, despite my explanation before. I can assure you that the police know about this place, and in fact, some even are members."

Olivia nodded her understanding and smiled. "Thank you. It makes me feel much better knowing that."

When she smiled, she looked more like a twenty year old. Her brown eyes lit up her entire face, and the apples of her cheeks got a pinkish color to them that gave her a sweet look. As long as she could handle the job responsibilities, she could look any age she wanted to. "Please feel free to ask me anything that's on your mind. It's important that you feel comfortable here, Olivia."

"Okay, then here goes. On page four there's a paragraph after the non-disclosure section about my responsibilities concerning the press. Is this something that I should be prepared for?"

"Yes and no. Because the club has been around for a while, the press usually approaches one of us if there are any questions. However, that doesn't mean it can't happen with one of the club's employees. We tell all our people that the standard answer of 'No statement' usually suffices. Just let me know if you're asked any questions, and I'll take care of it."

Nodding, she smiled as she attempted to hide her uneasiness. "Okay. On page seven the section about becoming a member…" She knitted her brows and looked away as she lowered her voice. "I don't have that kind of money. I mean, you don't have to worry about me being a gambler or drug addict or anything like that. That's not why I'm a little shy on cash now. It's just that I've been out of work for a few months, so thousands of dollars right now isn't something I can do."

Her cheeks blushed a deep red now, and I saw in her eyes her pride made her hate the words she had to say, so I quickly worked to belay her awkwardness. "It's fine, Olivia. Upper level employees are given memberships free of charge. It's entirely up to them if they choose to take advantage of them or not."

Why I said that I had no idea. I'd never cared one way or the other what employees did concerning membership to the club before. And why I'd said it that way, almost implying that she shouldn't take advantage of everything the club offered, made it seem like I didn't want her to.

"Oh, okay. Thank you."

Quickly, I moved to change the subject. "Were there any other questions?"

She thought for a moment and then smiled warmly. "Just one. Nowhere in the contract was any mention of what hours I'd be working. I know you're obviously here in the daytime, but it seems like your business is primarily a nighttime one."

Amused by her observation and the lack of attention to that point in the contract, I chuckled. "I'm here every day from eleven am to midnight. You may choose any eight hours within that time that you like. If I need you for something at a particular time, I'll let you know."

"Every day?" she asked, her eyes wide.

"I'm here every day. I guess you can call me a workaholic. You won't have to be. Monday through Friday will work fine, unless there's an event I need you for."

I wasn't sure why, but I wanted to add that she could stay late any night. Never once had I even thought that for any of my assistants, but something about Olivia made me want to be more like Stefan. It was wrong. I knew that. I'd worked damned hard to make Club X a success, and that didn't include fucking around with the people who worked under me. Our lawyers had enough on their plates dealing with the problems Stefan's libido caused for us. I didn't need to add to them.

Olivia staring at me jarred me from my daydreaming. Quickly, I pulled the contract toward me to pretend to examine it, giving myself time to regain my composure. After a few moments, I looked up and said, "If there are no other questions, you can begin tomorrow. Sound good?"

Nodding, she smiled like she was relieved. "That sounds great. Thank you so much for the opportunity. I'm looking forward to learning all about Club X."

She extended her hand to shake mine, and I enjoyed the warm and welcoming feel of her skin. As I escorted her out, I couldn't help but notice she really was quite stunning.

Maybe hiring her wasn't such a good idea.

I watched her wave back at me as she opened the door to head out into the sun and heard Kane behind me mutter, "She's a lot different from Kate. Are we going to lose her when she gets married too?"

The last sight of Olivia faded as the door closed, and I shook my head as I continued to stare at where she'd just stood. "I don't know. I didn't bother to find out if she was with anyone."

I heard him turn away as he said, "Maybe you should have."

* * *

By midnight, I was ready for a diversion. A full night of my mind wandering to my new assistant when I should have been hard at work had been frustrating, and I wanted nothing more than to start acting like myself again. Cassian March didn't spend hours fantasizing about any woman, especially one of his employees, no matter how hot she was. Thankfully, it didn't take much to make the real man I was come back again.

My phone rang as I drove back to my condo providing me with exactly the distraction I needed to get my mind off Olivia. Pulling into my parking spot, I picked up my phone to see Cheri calling, as if the Universe had seen me acting like some oversexed boy and sent her to remind me of exactly what I was.

"Cash, it's Cheri. What are you doing, baby?" she cooed into the phone.

"Just getting home."

"I can be there in fifteen minutes. Why don't you take a shower, don't bother with putting clothes back on, and have a glass of Cab Sav waiting for me?"

The memory of my last time with Cheri sent a jolt through my body, making my cock stiffen in anticipation. Blond hair, blue eyes, and nearly six foot with legs that seemed to go on forever, she was built like she'd been made especially to please a man. A little vapid, she didn't offer much in the brain department, but then again, I wasn't looking for an intellectual discussion tonight. I really didn't give a damn about what she thought about much of anything. What I wanted tonight was someone to fill up the spaces in my mind occupied with fantasies I shouldn't have with the reality I could easily have again and again.

Thinking Cheri's offer was exactly what I needed, I closed my eyes and still said, "I don't know. It's been a long day."

The phone fell silent and I could almost hear her pouting. I pictured her perfectly shaped lips brushing against her cell phone as she considered what words she needed to say to convince me.

"Cash, you know you want to. I can hear it in your voice. You're dying for something to take the edge off after a long day running that club of yours. Don't deny it."

"You're very persuasive, Cheri, but I don't know. Maybe I just want to relax tonight."

"Baby, in fifteen minutes, I can be there and you can be feeling like you haven't felt since the last time we were together."

Any other woman saying that would sound ridiculous, but when Cheri promised a night of pleasure,

I knew she'd deliver. The girl was one-of-a-kind. Running my free hand over the front of my pants, I closed my eyes and remembered the last time we were together. If it was possible, my cock grew even harder at the memory of her on all fours and me fucking her from behind on my balcony. Never a quiet lay, she took it to the next level that night, screaming my name over and over as she came. My neighbors must have loved that show. Thankfully, I couldn't make it to the next condo association meeting. Taking a deep breath, I said, "I'll leave the door unlocked. Let yourself in."

She quietly moaned. "And do you know what I'm in the mood for tonight, Cash?"

I could only imagine. Cheri's sexual appetites tended toward the wilder side compared to most of the women I knew, with role play one of her favorite pastimes. While I normally enjoyed the idea of tying her up or her in that schoolgirl outfit she liked to wear, I wasn't sure I wanted anything that involved tonight. I wanted to fuck Olivia out of my system, not put on some sex show. Some nights just called for the basics, and tonight was one of those nights.

Turning off my car, I stretched my legs at the thought of what she might want. "I have no idea."

"I've been aching to fuck you in your shower again. Do you remember that time? My legs were tired all the next day. I don't think I've ever had sex for that long in my life." Her voice practically purred in my ear.

The time she and I fucked in my shower I nearly blacked out from the sex. The woman knew how to fuck, no doubt. I hadn't planned on doing anything that required that much exertion tonight, but if this was what the Universe was sending me, who was I to turn it down?

As the memory of Cheri riding my cock until the two of us practically melted into an exhausted heap of sated flesh danced through my mind, I made my way toward my place, thankful the Universe knew me so well.

"Be here in fifteen, but I think we'll have a replay of our time on my couch instead. And don't be late or I'll find someone else to spend my time with," I said sharply, not exactly teasing. Cheri liked a strong hand to guide her, and I was more than happy to oblige.

Only a fool would turn down such a gift.

Chapter Three

Olivia

"I can't believe you guys never told me about Club X! What am I? The ugly stepsister?" I said jokingly while I handed Josie and Erin glasses of wine as we settled in for a night of celebration for my new job.

"We did. Don't you remember?" Erin said in their defense. "It was that time when Jake offered to help us all get memberships."

I narrowed my eyes to faux angry slits and studied her expression to see if she was kidding. Her dark brown eyes stared back at me, telegraphing she was telling the truth. I didn't remember Jake ever offering to get us into Club X, though.

"I have no recollection of that, ladies," I teased, doing my best lawyer voice for Josie.

Erin looked to her right at her, who sat on the arm of my couch smiling. "Would you like to help her remember?"

Josie loved her job as an insurance fraud investigator and even though we teased her about the fact that she acted like one twenty-four-seven, she took every opportunity to tease us right back. "My pleasure, Ms. Andrews. Now, Ms. Lucas, do you remember the night Mr. Richfield and the two of us sat here discussing how to celebrate your twenty-fifth birthday? I believe you were seated in the same place as you are now, not surprisingly since you're a creature of habit who never changes."

She took a breath in her interrogation, and I mumbled, "Harsh," at her assessment of me, regardless of how correct she was.

"Continuing on, Ms. Lucas. Now do you remember Mr. Richfield suggesting you go wild and really let your hair down?"

Her piercing blue-green eyes stared at me as she waited for my answer. To be honest, I didn't remember anything she and Erin were claiming. "Ms. Tellow, since Jake says that to me at least once a week, I doubt I'd be able to remember the time he said that nearly three years ago."

"It was a week before your birthday, and he told all three of us he could get us into Club X. If I remember correctly, and I'm sure I do, you declined his offer while the two of us eagerly jumped at the chance to join."

Erin nodded her agreement. "Ringing any bells, Liv?"

"No, but now I feel like the odd man out. So you two have been going to Club X all this time? What's it like?" I asked, unsure if I really wanted to know but too curious not to ask.

"In. Fucking. Credible," Josie said as she slid down onto the couch cushion next to Erin. "Some of our best times have been at Club X. Now I've never taken advantage of the top floors, but someday I will. I'm telling you ladies, when I think of a fantasy I can't make come true in my regular life, those Club X folks are going to come in damn handy."

I looked over at Erin, the more reasonable of my two closest friends, but she had that same wide-eyed look that told me she'd enjoyed my new workplace too.

"What?" she asked, throwing her hands up in the air. "You're looking at me like you're surprised. I'm not allowed to have any fun?"

"No, it's just that I always considered you the more sensible of the two of you."

"Yeah, well, sensible or not, that club you're working at is the hottest place I've ever partied. You should see the men there, Liv. Oh my God!"

"Nice. So why haven't I heard you guys talking about this place before now?"

Erin and Josie turned to look at one another, and then Josie made a gesture to zip her mouth closed. "It's like Vegas, baby. What happens at Club X stays at Club X."

The two of them burst into laughter, and for the first time since I'd met them years before on our high school track team, I felt like an outsider. Everybody I was close to knew all about Club X but me. It was sophomore year when I didn't qualify for regionals and they did all over again.

"It's okay, Livy. You haven't missed anything you would have liked. You like a more refined kind of place," Erin said trying to make me feel better but only making me feel worse.

Emptying my wine glass, I swallowed my pinot noir and shook my head. "You're right. I don't like to have fun much anyway. I was too busy working my ass off to get canned before I could even get vested."

I knew I was slipping into the pool of self-pity, but I didn't care. I may not be the kind of girl who swung from the chandelier, but I wasn't the model for the front of Old Maid cards either.

"Oh, Livy. Erin didn't mean anything bad by that. It's just that you tend to be more straight-laced, you know? We just thought Club X was too low brow for you since you showed no interest in Jake's offer. You're more of a wine and cheese party kind of girl."

"I guess that's supposed to make me feel better, Josie?" I asked with more emotion in my voice than I'd intended.

Erin leaned over to give my knee a sympathetic squeeze. "I'm sorry. We're both sorry. It's all water under the bridge now, though. You're going to be part of the inner circle of Club X, so whatever stories we have are going to pale in comparison to yours. I've heard the men who run the place are sexier than all hell. Are they?"

I thought about Cassian and Stefan March and had to agree. Both were definitely sexy. And Kane? While that mad, bad, and dangerous to know vibe wasn't what I liked in a man, I could certainly understand why some women would be all over him.

"I don't know, Erin. They were very nice," I teased as I pretended to play coy.

"Nice my ass," Josie butted in. "I saw that Cassian March one time at a hospital benefit Sebastian and I attended last year. The man oozes incredible fuck. I swear if I hadn't been in a relationship, I would have made my move on him. I bet he gets freaky when that Italian made suit comes off."

"I remember seeing his younger brother one night at the club," Erin added. "No suit for him, but I can tell you that man can definitely fill out a shirt. He was wearing this button down look that fit so perfectly I swear he had it painted on. I like my men more muscular than Josie here, so he's my kind."

"His name is Stefan," I said, liking that I could at least feel like I knew them in a different way than Erin and Josie. "He's really sweet."

"You like him! I see it in your eyes, Liv. Tell us everything that happened!" Erin squealed.

I stood from my seat to head into the kitchen for another glass of wine and to escape the probing stares of my two best friends. The non-disclosure agreement I'd signed just hours before weighed heavily on my mind already. I knew it probably wouldn't have violated anything if I told them about meeting all three brothers, but I wasn't going to be able to keep my cool about Cassian and Stefan if I didn't get my feelings under control.

Gulping down some wine, I took a deep breath and walked back into the living room to find them waiting for me to explain. Sitting down, I balanced my glass on the arm of my favorite chair and shrugged. "There's nothing to tell. I met all three brothers in my interview. I'm going to be Cassian's assistant, but I had to meet with the other two also. They were nice."

Josie pointed her finger at me and cocked one perfectly shaped dark eyebrow. "You're holding out on us, girl. I know. I deal with witnesses all the time who have that same face you have on right now. Spill it or we'll never let you have any peace."

"Yeah and don't leave any of the details out," Erin added.

"There's nothing to tell. I swear. Yes, Cassian is very good looking. Yes, Stefan is funny and hot. The third brother, Kane, is a little scary for my taste, but he's definitely got a sexy vibe to him too. Other than that, I don't know what to tell you. No one asked me out or bent me over the desk while the other ones interviewed me. It was just a boring, run-of-the-mill interview. I swear."

Both women had leaned forward in anticipation of hearing all my salacious details, but now they sat back crestfallen with a look of disappointment on their faces. I must have looked like I told the truth because Josie didn't appear to want to grill me anymore.

"I've never heard of the third brother, Kane. What's he do there?" Erin asked, almost as an afterthought.

"He's in charge of the fantasy part of the business," I explained, suddenly realizing there was something I could tell them that I hadn't. "Oh, I forgot! I get a free membership to Club X, and that includes the fantasy stuff, not that I'll ever use it, I imagine."

Josie's and Erin's jaws dropped. It was one of the rare moments in our friendship that I, Olivia Lucas, got to shock them instead of them shocking me. It wouldn't last, but for the time being, I basked in the limelight of being cooler than everyone else in the room.

"So what fantasy do you plan to have them fulfill? You know what they say about you quiet types—still waters run deep. And dirty. I know you have some deep, dark desires inside that business suit look you sport," Josie said with a wink.

"Oh, I love this! Liv, you have to do the fantasy thing. It costs a fortune, and you get it for free," Erin said.

"I don't know, guys. It might not be a good idea if I want to keep my job. You shouldn't mix business with pleasure. You know, no shitting where you eat."

"You have a scat fantasy?" Erin asked, her eyes huge with shock.

I couldn't help but laugh when Josie elbowed her for being so dumb, splashing wine down the front of her shirt. "No, I don't want someone to shit on me. Jesus, Erin! What the fuck? I'm boring, remember?"

As she grabbed a napkin off the coffee table to blot the wine, she tried her best to explain. "Well, Josie said your kind runs deep and dirty and then you mentioned shitting. I just thought…"

"Well, don't."

"In all seriousness, Liv, they wouldn't offer you the club's services if they didn't expect you to take advantage of them," Josie said in her legally solemn voice. "I think it might be good for you too."

"Why do I get the feeling you two spend your time pitying me, like I'm some nun or something compared to you guys?"

"How many dates have you had since you and Mark broke up?" Josie asked in her interrogator voice, making me feel like any answer I gave would only validate their sad opinion of me.

I didn't want to admit that I'd had just a handful of dates in nearly a year, and only one of them had included any sex whatsoever. And that hadn't been anything to write home about either. Quietly, I admitted, "A few. You know how it is. When it doesn't click, there's no point in going any further."

Josie turned to look at Erin, and they both gave me their best pity faces. "Honey, you're twenty-seven years old and you spend more time in this apartment alone than any healthy woman should. You're gorgeous and you could have any man you want. You just choose not to. I know the whole Mark thing was tough, but there are more fish in the sea and you need to put your pole back in the water," Erin said, her voice full of sympathy.

"I think you have your sexual metaphors mixed up. Seriously, I'm fine, guys."

Shaking her head, Josie frowned at me. "You're not fine, but I think you might have a good chance at fine if you find some happiness at this new job and take the chance on their fantasy services."

"I don't know," I said, lying. I knew all too well I didn't want to get involved in any fantasy business at Club X.

Erin tilted her head and smiled. "We're not saying you have to try to fulfill a fantasy of having sex with an entire soccer team or anything wild like that. Just try something small that feels good. Will you at least consider it?"

I was never going to see an end to this conversation

if I didn't agree, so I forced a smile and nodded. "I'll think about it. Good enough?"

"That's all we're saying," Josie answered. "Just keep an open mind, okay?"

"I will. And if I ever come up with something I think Club X can make come true for me, I'll consider it."

* * *

Opening the heavy steel door to Club X, I paused as my eyes adjusted to the dim light of the club. The place was quiet and deserted, but I suspected the three owners were nearby. Unlike the day before, I took a good look around my new workplace, imagining my best friends having the time of their lives there. The club was really just a large space lined on the side with metal walkways to the upper floors and an enormous bar on the main floor, but I envisioned when it was filled with people and the lights were flashing to the beat of the music it transformed into the place my friends had bragged about.

I waited for someone to come out and greet me, but after a few minutes no one had appeared so I decided to investigate a little around the main floor. The bar looked like it was made of glass and seemed to go on forever down the left side of the room. Reaching out, I ran my fingers over the top of it and felt the coolness of glass. Above me, hung from the ceiling, hung frosted curved pendant lights. Behind the bar was more glass in shelves and refrigerator doors. Bottles of red, blue, and even a neon green liquor sat on the shelves that reached what looked like ten feet in the air. Craning my neck, I wondered how the bartenders reached the top shelves and the liquor up there to make drinks.

"You came back, so I guess my brothers didn't scare you off. Good. I bet you're thinking you can't imagine how anyone gets to the top shelf stuff, aren't you?"

I lowered my head and saw Stefan standing next to me. Dressed in what I imagined was his usual look, he wore a black Club X T-shirt and jeans and looked incredible. His hair looked tousled, as if someone had been running their hands through it in the heat of passion just moments before. I imagined it was entirely possible that had actually just happened, likely with one of the many women he had in his life. He had a look that said he was rarely alone and liked it that way.

"You must be reading my mind. I could barely reach the third shelf, much less those all the way near the ceiling."

He smiled warmly and pointed to a silver button behind the bar. "See that? They're moveable levels. All the girls have to do is step on them and press the button to reach the highest shelves."

"Cool. They must have great balance," I joked, picturing women pitching themselves off the levels by mistake.

"They have railings to hang onto," he said with a chuckle. "But I'd never thought of the balance problem before. I have no idea how the girls walk in four inch heels every night, but they do it and without falling."

I noted immediately how he referred to the bartenders as girls. "Are all the bartenders female?"

Stefan leaned his back against the bar and smiled. "Not all of them, but most. There are some male bartenders for the female customers, though."

I couldn't help but notice how incredible his body was. His muscular arms bulged out from underneath the cotton T-shirt, and I was sure his abs were washboard cut. Trying to act like I wasn't checking out one of my bosses, I quickly said, "I'm sure if I had to do their job in four inch heels I'd topple over. It would be a big mess."

His gaze traveled the full length of my body down to the floor and then back up again. With a twinkle in his eye, he said, "You'd be fine. We'd take good care of you."

Why was it whenever this man spoke, every word came out the way a man would sound when he was on top of me? As I looked away uneasily, I heard footsteps coming close and turned to see Cassian approaching us, his expression far more serious than his brother's.

"Good morning, Olivia. I see Stefan has already found you. Has he been explaining the workings of the bar?"

If Stefan sounded like he was always trying to seduce me, Cassian sounded like he was always working to control himself, especially when Stefan was nearby.

"Actually, I was telling her that I think she'd be a perfect bartender. She'd love working under me."

I could have sworn I saw a flash of anger for the merest moment in Cassian's eyes as he shot Stefan a glance at the mention of me as a bartender. Whatever his look was meant to telegraph, Cassian looked back at me with a smile that soothed the edge still present in his expression. "Let me escort you to your office and we can get started."

An awkward feeling settled in among the three of us, so I said goodbye to Stefan and followed Cassian toward the back of the building. Just as the last time I walked behind him, I couldn't help but check out the view. He may not have been all muscles like his brothers, but Cassian March certainly did fill out a suit well. I knew it was wrong, but something about how serious he was even as he stood there looking gorgeous was incredibly appealing.

Before he caught me checking out his ass, I silently chastised myself for acting like Josie and Erin and made a pledge that I'd be all business, just like he was. He stopped in front of an office right next to his and turned around to face me, his expression back to the serious one he'd worn when we'd talked alone the day before.

"This is your office. While it is separate from mine, they both adjoin in a meeting room through the door on the back wall. Feel free to make yourself at home. I have something to take care of, but I'll be back in a few minutes."

With that, he walked past me out toward the bar and I entered my new office, immediately impressed with how nice it was. No cost had been spared on the furniture or décor. A stunning deep red teakwood desk and black leather office chair sat in front of matching teakwood bookcases and file cabinets. Still modern like Cassian's desk suite, it felt warmer and far more luxurious. Two coordinating leather upholstered chairs were placed in front of the desk, and on the floor was a cream colored tile just like in his office.

It was the nicest office I'd ever had. Taking it all in, I couldn't help but admit I could get used to this.

"I hope you feel comfortable here, Olivia," Cassian said behind me.

Turning to face him, I nodded to show my approval. "It's gorgeous. Whoever picked out this furniture has great taste."

"I'll make sure to tell her. I'd have gone for a glass desk like mine, but the designer reminded me that you'd likely prefer something a bit more inviting. I'm glad you like it."

His face was so cool and emotionless, but something about the way his voice lowered when he said he'd tell the designer how much I liked her taste in furniture made me think there was a lot more to their relationship than simply designer and client. Maybe Mr. All Business wasn't just that, after all.

"We have a large party to get ready for Friday night. Kane has his part under control, but I need you to plan the event that will occur before they head up to the top floor. I realize you don't have experience in party planning, but not to worry. I'll walk you through this first event, and then you'll be fine for future ones. Sound good?"

"Sure. I'm ready."

"Great. Let's get started."

Chapter Four
Cassian

By the end of her first day of work, Olivia had settled in to her new position perfectly. A quick thinker, she was everything I wanted in an assistant. That I'd watched Stefan swoop in on her not five minutes after she walked through the door had started my day off pretty fucking rotten, but after that, I'd enjoyed helping her get her bearings while she assisted me with the annual Lady Godivas' party the local chapter of that not-so-secret sex society held each year at the club. I could have simply repeated what Kate had arranged the year before since the Lady Godivas had raved about the event then, but there was no better time than the present to initiate Olivia into my business.

As much as I hated to agree with Stefan, I did benefit from the mixture of business with pleasure. That didn't mean I had any plans to mix them with Olivia, though. I couldn't deny that seeing her in my brother's crosshairs rankled me more than I wanted to admit, however. But I knew from watching him create workplace disasters that whatever thoughts that may have crossed my mind as she and I worked together were something I needed to fight.

Still, when she blushed at my mention that the Lady Godivas would likely end up half naked by the end of the night, I couldn't help but be charmed. How long had it been since anyone had blushed around me? Certainly women like Cheri were long past the time when anything about sex made them nervous or uncomfortable. Watching Olivia's cheeks pinken charmed me, despite my jaded attitude and insistence that I wasn't going to allow myself to like her.

I left her to finish up the details of the party while I handled a far too curious reporter who obviously hadn't gotten the memo from her boss that Club X wasn't a potential story. Young, eager, and too cute for her job with long pale blond hair and big blue eyes, she waited in a red, skintight dress that screamed she knew nothing of professionalism. It did, however, clearly telegraph that she had heard what my club was all about.

I found Ciara Danson standing outside my office flirting with Stefan. For once, I didn't mind him thinking with his cock. In fact, I wondered if I should let him handle her inquisitiveness, but knowing my younger brother, he'd have her flat on her back on his desk in mere minutes and then we'd have not only unwanted publicity but another lawsuit on our hands.

Stepping between them, I eased her away from him and closed the door behind us. "Please take a seat, Miss Danson."

She sat down in a chair in front of my desk, letting her dress ride up on her legs until she was flashing me the tops of her thighs. Subtlety obviously wasn't Ciara's style.

Opening her blue eyes wide, she lowered her head and looked across the desk at me. "Please, Mr. March, call me Ciara."

"And please call me Cassian. I hear you're interested in our little club. I wish there was a story, but I'm sure Gary told you we're just your basic nightclub here at Club X."

Ciara leaned forward to show me far more of her breasts than I wanted to see at that moment. "Cassian, I may look naïve, but this isn't my first reporting job. You know as well as I do that Club X isn't just your basic nightclub, as you say, even if my boss agrees with you. I was hoping to get an in-depth look at behind the scenes, if you will, and I can't imagine anyone better equipped to do that than you. My readers at All The Rage would love to know all about you and your club."

Equipped. Hmmm... I couldn't decide if Ciara was offering to fuck me right there on my desk or really wanted to know more about the club. She wasn't my type—too eager for me—and I had no interest in giving her any in-depth information about the club, but she wasn't going to be put off easily.

As I began to explain once again that there was no story here, Olivia knocked on the door and walked in. Her eyes opened wide at the sight of Ciara's less than subtle body language, and she quickly turned to leave, but before she could Ciara began with the questions.

"Perhaps if I could speak to your assistant, Cassian, she could help me."

Olivia immediately begged off and I shouldn't have put her in the position to deal with a reporter so soon, but

I wanted to know how she'd handle it. If she was going to be a part of Club X, she'd have to learn how to master dealing with the press sooner than later, and if she failed now, at least I'd know and could begin looking for her replacement.

I stood from my chair and motioned for Olivia to take my place behind my desk. "Olivia, this is Ciara. She's from the website All The Rage and has a few questions about Club X. I'm going to let you talk to her."

Olivia looked shell-shocked but sat down and put on her prettiest smile for the young woman in front of her. As I walked toward the door, she said in professional voice, "I'm more than happy to help you, Ciara."

Closing the door, I listened as Olivia handled her like a pro. As I stood there, Stefan walked toward me with a confused look on his face. "What are you doing out here? I thought you were talking to that smokin' hot reporter."

"Quiet," I whispered. "Olivia's in there now with her. I'm listening to hear how she does."

"Trial by fire, huh? You must think a lot of her to let her run interference so soon."

"No time like the present. If she can't deal with Ciara, then she's no good to me."

"How the hell do you see only the glorified secretary you want her to be? You won't let me have her, but you won't make a move on her. What the fuck is that about?"

Sighing in frustration, I tried to hear Olivia but all I heard was Stefan. "That's being professional. You should try it sometime. Now go and let me hear how this turns out."

"Fine, but I'm telling you, you're missing out on this

one. There's fire beneath that cool thing she's got going on. I'd bet money on it."

Stefan was the last person I wanted dating advice from, so I waved him away and returned to listening to Olivia double-talking Ciara right out of a story. For every question she asked, Olivia had an answer that at first sounded like she'd given some tidbit of information, but quickly turned into nothing. She denied the truth of the club as well as any one of us would have, and I knew at that moment I hadn't made a mistake in hiring her.

I stepped back when the door flew open and Ciara stormed out, obviously unhappy about being so expertly handled. As I entered my office, Olivia stood behind my desk, her arms folded across her chest.

"Thank you, Olivia. I think you took care of that very well."

"Cash, I don't mind acting the part of the company woman, but next time could you please give me a little warning? Or was that the point—to put me on the spot and see how I would do?"

She was smart. Good. I needed that in the person who was to be my right hand. "You might say it was a test, but if it makes you feel any better, you passed with flying colors."

Stepping around the desk, she walked toward the door, stopping inches away from me. With a direct stare, she shook her head and smiled. "I've always been a good test taker. I think you'll find that I'm just as good an assistant as you need me to be. However, if you feel the need to test me more, just know I'm up to it."

She was all business, but damnit if at that moment I

didn't want to see if there was another side to her. Staring into her brown eyes, I impulsively said, "I think as a reward, you should join us for the Lady Godivas party. It would be good exposure to what the club is really all about."

Olivia gave me a smile that seemed just a bit forced, as if my offer had caught her off guard, but she quickly recovered and agreed to join my brothers and me at the party. I just wondered how she'd handle how wild those women got when they had a few drinks in them.

* * *

In the days leading up to the party, we worked side-by-side and my professional admiration for her grew by leaps and bounds. I'd underestimated Olivia from the moment I'd read her resume, mainly because of who had referred her. Jake Richfield hadn't shown himself to be someone whose opinion I'd normally rely on. Every time I'd seen him at the club, he'd had a different woman on his arm, each one cheaper than the last. Not that being a player was a problem for me. I didn't care who he fucked or how many females fell for his lines. But there was something cheap about him that never sat right with me. Maybe it was that black department store watch he liked to flash around like it was a fucking Rolex. Stefan liked him, though, which didn't help his case any in my mind. Nevertheless, I'd been desperate for an assistant after Kate left, and when Richfield mentioned that he had a friend who he was sure would be perfect for the job, I'd reluctantly agreed to check her out.

Pretty good on paper, Olivia's real worth became clear when I saw her on the job. It didn't take long for me to realize that she'd work out even better than Kate had. And unlike with my previous assistants, I began to want to know more about this woman who seemed all business but who'd caught the eye of not only one but two players in my club.

I didn't want to let Stefan know how interested I was in Olivia, but his comments about her and Jake Richfield led me to believe she was just friends with him. As for my brother, I didn't have to wonder what he thought about the woman I spent my days with. Every leer and nasty remark about how he wanted to get into her pants told me loud and clear. He bordered on sexual harassment on most days, but with her, I couldn't decide whether she should sue us or crack him across the face.

Or if I should.

At nine-thirty I found her behind her desk taking care of last minute details for the party. Stefan had received the guest list and Kane had the list of who wanted what fantasies that night. She'd handled everything with aplomb, so barring any drunken madness by the Godiva women, the night would be a good opportunity for Olivia to see the inner workings of Club X.

Still in her work clothes, she stood from her seat and straightened her black suit coat and skirt. Compared to the rest of that night's partygoers, she and I would look like the adult chaperones at a junior high school dance. We weren't there for fun, though. Tonight was as much work as anything we did during the day.

"Remember what I told you about these women? Just keep that in mind and you'll be fine."

"Cash, I'm not a nun. I swear I must be giving off the wrong vibe. First my friends are sure I'm the most boring person they've ever met, and now you're worried that some ladies getting freaky might make me faint. Trust me. I may not look it, but I'm actually capable of having fun."

There weren't more than a handful of people who could talk to me like that and get away with it, but Olivia had a way about her that made me overlook things I wouldn't in other people. "I was just trying to prepare you. You've never been here at night. Club X looks entirely different in the dark."

With a sly grin, she said, "Well, this sheltered girl who doesn't get out enough, according to everyone who knows me, is looking forward to seeing this place when the lights go down."

For a moment I studied her, seeing for the first time a sexiness I liked. "Okay. Let's go then."

I led her out onto the floor and checked with Stefan to see if all the Lady Godivas had arrived. "Are the ladies all here?"

"All good." Looking at Olivia, he smiled his best frat boy grin. "Hey you! It's about time you joined us out here. Ready to experience the hottest club in town?"

"I am," she answered with a chuckle. "I can't wait to see these women. We aren't talking naked women in long blonde wigs on horseback, are we?"

"No animals tonight, as far as I know. Kane would have mentioned a Catherine the Great," Stefan joked with a wink.

I hated how easily he drew out her fun side. With

almost no effort, he had her giggling and joking around. I'd spent hours with her each day, and not once had I seen the smile she gave him or the sparkle in her eye she got when he spoke to her.

It went against every principle I believed in, but after only a few days, I wanted to see her like she was with Stefan when only I was around. I wanted to bring out her playful sexy side.

"You two planning on hanging out down here, or are you going to head up to the top floors and catch the action?"

"I think we'll walk around down here for a while and then head upstairs. I want Olivia to get the full experience."

"Oooh, the full experience? Brace yourself, Olivia. My brother rarely spends any time out here once the action starts, so if he wants to show off the full experience, he must have something in mind."

Stefan was as subtle as a Sherman tank, and I looked over at Olivia to see her cheeks blush that cute pink color that was only more accentuated by her red hair. What I had in mind was showing off the club that took up my days and nights. If anything else occurred, though, I couldn't say I'd be unhappy.

I slid my arm around her and gently pressed my hand against the small of her back to guide her away from Stefan before he announced his opinion on what he thought were my favorite sex positions or how nice we looked together. His act may work for him, but I preferred a smoother style when I wanted a woman's attention.

"We'll see you later, baby brother."

Olivia turned toward me and with a smile said, "I thought there'd be music. Not that it's quiet in here with people coming in, but I just thought it would be more like clubs I've been to."

"It will be. The music starts later. Stefan likes to get our customers a little drunk before he lets them loose on the dance floor. Plus, people tend to have a better time if they can talk first. Then they get relaxed, get drunk, and tend to spend more money."

I led her to a lounge across from the bar beside the dance floor, still nearly dark for now. She sat down next to me on a red couch and angled her body toward me, and in the dim light of the wall sconce above our heads I saw a look of anticipation in her eyes.

"Cash, I thought the rooms upstairs were booked months in advance."

"They are."

"Then how do people spend more money here? You don't serve food, so the only items to buy are drinks and the fantasy rooms."

"Ah, I see your confusion. People hear about the rooms and other members' experiences and after a few drinks, they want to pay to have one of those experiences for themselves. The rooms may be booked solid, but at that moment when they're drunk and having a good time, they'll pay to reserve a room months later."

"Clever. You March brothers are quite the businessmen."

A few people passed by and sat down nearby on another sofa. Leaning in so they couldn't hear our conversation, I revealed the truth of my family's past. "Only Stefan and I are Marchs. Kane is our half-brother. We have the same fathers but different mothers."

"You and Kane seem close in age. I'm guessing it wasn't a case of a child by a second marriage since Stefan is younger than you two."

She hadn't said anything wrong, but I was surprised for a moment by her deduction. My hesitation in confirming her guess came across as being offended, and she quickly reached her hand out to touch my arm in a sympathetic gesture.

That look of anticipation that had been in her eyes just moments before was gone, replaced by worry that she'd overstepped the line of propriety with her boss just weeks into a new job. "I'm sorry. That was rude. I didn't mean to pry. Really, I didn't."

The feel of her touch on my sleeve made a rush of heat race up my arm. Shaking my head, I said, "It's okay. You weren't being rude at all. You're right. My father had an affair with Kane's mother right around the time he and my mother found out they were pregnant with me. So Kane is just three months younger than I am. Stefan is two years younger than us, even though he acts like he's more like ten."

"He's just more lighthearted than you, and especially Kane," she said with a smile, obviously relieved she hadn't committed a misstep. "Younger siblings get to do that."

"I guess. I just wish he'd act something close to his age sometimes."

"I think he relies on you for that."

Her delicate way of saying that I was the serious brother only reinforced what I suspected she thought of me—Stefan was the fun-loving one, and I was the somber one. Ordinarily, I didn't mind that. This was who I was in public. I wore my straight man role comfortably and left the frat boy antics to Stefan, who wore them like a second skin. Now, though, I wanted Olivia to like me as she did him, but I couldn't change who I was.

If she wanted someone like Stefan, she wouldn't want me.

I looked down at my watch and saw it was nearly eleven o'clock. The lights dimmed until the room was pitch black, and with the first beats of the bass from the DJ, the club exploded in light and sound. The glass bar and shelves behind it glowed in shades of neon blue and green lights, and the electronic light show lit up the dance floor, encouraging the Lady Godivas to begin their partying.

Olivia's mouth hung open as she watched the dance floor fill with women well on their way to having the night of their lives and the half-naked men they'd brought with them. The Lady Godivas never left their good time to chance, so they always chose us to host their parties and always made sure they had more than enough men for whatever their members desired.

Leaning close to her, I said in her ear, "Let's go to the second floor. The sound isn't as loud up there."

As the women and their guests gyrated across the dance floor, I took Olivia's hand in mine and led her up the metal stairs to a secluded area above the action. The acoustics of the building created a pocket where we could watch the party and still be able to hear one another speak.

We sat down on a black leather couch as the party kicked into high gear, neither one of us speaking for a long time as Olivia stared down at the crowd below. It didn't take long for the women to begin shedding their clothes and soon the only people fully clothed were Club X workers and Olivia and me.

"I didn't realize this kind of thing happened down there in the club. I thought..." Her sentence trailed off and she returned to watching the action on the dance floor.

I tried to conceal my disappointment, but it was likely written all over my face. I'd hoped the reality of my business wouldn't chase her away, both from being my assistant and anything else we might be in the future. "If this isn't something you're comfortable with, Olivia, it's better we find out now before either one of us gets too used to working with one another. I understand."

Her eyes grew wide, and she smiled as she shook her head. "Oh, no. I'm not uncomfortable. I want to see more of what happens here. Don't worry about me. I'm far more fun than I look."

I nodded, wanting to believe she could handle Club X—that she could handle the life I led.

CHAPTER FIVE

Olivia

I wasn't being entirely honest with Cash when I said I wasn't uncomfortable with what was going on one floor below us. Maybe if I was there with Erin and Josie watching half-naked men thrusting and pumping into a bunch of drunken women I would have been into it, but sitting there with Cash made the scene in front of us even more erotic than it already was. I sensed his gaze on me as I pretended to be engrossed in the action, watching me instead of the Lady Godivas.

The brief touch of his leg against mine, his suit coat lightly skimming my arm heightened the electricity in the air, making paying attention to anything but him impossible. He appeared so at home there in the middle of all this debauchery, like he'd lived this life forever, despite how serious he looked each day as we worked together. That man who was all business had vanished leaving one far more sensual in his place. Maybe it was the music and lights, or maybe it was the near sex show unfolding just one floor away, but that tiny spark that had flickered inside me since meeting Cash now grew into a flame of desire that threatened to consume me.

He leaned in and said, "Why didn't you ever try to become a member here, Olivia?"

I turned my head slightly and felt his lips brush against the shell of my ear. "What do you mean?"

"Your friends are members. Why didn't you ever apply to be a member?" he asked in a deep voice that made me want to close my eyes and simply enjoy the tenor of it against my skin.

His question took me back to that night Jake had offered to bring me to this very place and why I'd said no. It wasn't that I was frightened of what Club X may have been. The truth was far more mundane. "I was too busy trying to climb the corporate ladder. While everyone else was having fun, I was working thirteen hour days just to be sent on my way after a few years."

Cash said nothing in response, even as I waited for him to speak, so I turned my head and saw him smiling at me. "I hear in your voice that you're ashamed of what you just said. Don't be. An intelligent woman like you should never be ashamed of wanting to succeed. Leave the partying to those people who don't have a world to conquer."

I felt my cheeks grow hot as I stared back at his piercing blue eyes full of admiration. I'd never met a man who spoke about work like he did yet looked so incredibly sexy. At that moment, there wasn't a thought in my head about the corporate ladder or anything else but how much I loved the way he looked at me just then.

The music stopped and Stefan's voice over the loudspeaker interrupted our moment with the announcement that tonight was all about the Lady Godivas. The crowd below erupted into cheers and catcalls as he promised a party to end all parties. Cash's expression hardened, and he turned his head away from me. When the music began again just moments later, whatever had been between us had disappeared, leaving us as boss and assistant once again.

But I didn't want to be merely that anymore. I wanted to look into those eyes and see desire instead of last year's numbers and next year's projections. Each moment his gaze stayed away from me another chance to get to know him slipped away. My mind spun with how to get him back to where he'd been before Stefan had intruded on us. I didn't know him well enough to make small talk, but I wanted to say something.

Anything to bring back the man who'd shown himself for that brief moment tonight.

Unsure I should mention the top floor, I leaned toward him and blurted out, "I'd love to see the rest of the club. Can you give me a tour?"

If the music hadn't been so loud, the pounding of my heart would have been thundering in my ears as I waited for his response. The idea of seeing a fantasy room was exhilarating and frightening at the same time. My curiosity had been piqued the moment Cash mentioned the fantasy area of the club, and even if Kane's part in it was a little daunting, I still couldn't help myself from wanting to know more about it.

Cash turned back to look at me, surprised by my suggestion. "You want to see the rest of the club?"

Nodding, I smiled, hoping to see that man from just

a few moments ago return. "Sure. I wouldn't be much of an assistant if I didn't know all about it, although not knowing gives me plausible deniability just in case any more reporters come sniffing around. It's not technically lying if I don't know."

A slow smile spread across his mouth. "I like that. Okay, let's go visit the other parts of the club."

He stood and held out his hand. Looking up at him, I placed my hand in his palm and felt my stomach flutter when he closed his fingers it. His touch was light even though his hand was strong. I didn't know how I knew it, but whatever this was, it wasn't about a simple tour around a business.

We walked up the stairs past the third and fourth floors that seemed to function as private areas for club patrons to enjoy drinks and conversation outside the fantasy rooms. The sound of the music still filtered up to those floors, but it was far quieter than on the first two.

Each step we took hand in hand toward the top floor and those fantasy rooms was another step toward something new and exciting. I wanted to see more of Cash and more of the business he owned. As we stepped onto the stairs that would take us to the top floor, I wondered if he visited this part of Club X much. He hadn't seemed to be someone who would before, but now I could envision him making his fantasies come true in one of those rooms I'd only imagined until this moment.

Thinking about it made me jealous. It was irrational and silly, but I felt jealous. Would I see a room he always used or did he have a private room all to himself? Had he led many women up these very stairs to that room?

Silently, I chastised myself for being so stupid. What did it matter if he did? As a grown man who owned a club dedicated to making fantasies come true, of course he'd been to this floor and lived out many fantasies.

My mental tug of war made me pull my hand away as we reached the last step, and Cash turned his head to find my hand again. With a smile, he took it and looked up at me. "We're almost there. You ready?"

His voice was deep, but it held a hint of mystery in it, like he wasn't sure what lay ahead for us. I simply smiled and followed him, preparing myself for Kane's part of Club X. The ruler of this fantasy kingdom stood with his arms crossed leaning against a far wall. Taller and more imposing than Cash, he looked like he belonged here, like being downstairs would have been wrong for someone like him.

The noise from below barely made it to this top floor, and the muffled sound of the music seemed so far away now. The look of this area of the club was different too. No neon lights flashed here. Instead, dim sconces lit the way.

We stopped in front of Kane, who seemed surprised to see us there, and Cash gave him a quick nod. "Everything good?"

Kane nodded in return and gave us a small smile. "Get sick of the madness downstairs?"

I had the feeling he was speaking to Cash more than me. Cash chuckled. "I'm going to show Olivia the floor. I'm assuming most of the rooms are still empty."

"For now, yeah," Kane said in his usual raspy voice as he pointed toward the far end of the floor. "I have one room at the end busy now, though."

"Okay, we'll stay away from that one."

Kane narrowed his eyes and grinned. "They like to be watched, so feel free. And there's always the dancers, if you like."

I couldn't imagine where any dancers could be on this floor. The entire area seemed more like a suite of offices than a nightclub. As Cash led me away, my curiosity got the best of me. "What dancers? Where are they?"

"Kane handles this floor, which includes dancers in booths connected to each room."

"Like a strip club?"

"Not exactly. More like a private show for each room."

"Can I see?" The words tumbled out of my mouth, and I didn't care that I sounded almost childish in my enthusiasm.

"Absolutely." Cash continued walking and stopped at a door. With a smile, he said, "I guess you've decided against plausible deniability."

"I've always been a fan of knowledge over ignorance, so yes, I'm afraid from now on I'll have to actually lie about everything here."

"That's the spirit." The sexy smile slid from his face, and he winked at me. "Time for your education, Olivia."

A sparkle in his eye unnerved me for a moment, but I was ready. I wanted to see everything here. He opened the second to last door and escorted me in. It was dimly lit, even darker than outside the room, but I saw a couch and coffee table like would be found in a hotel living room. Was this it? It all looked very run-of-the-mill.

"Take a seat and I'll show you what happens when someone reserves a room like this one."

I continued to look around at the beige walls and average looking furniture as I sat down and waited for Cash to begin explaining how everything on this floor worked. Instead, he dimmed the lights even more and sat down beside me. The air crackled with excitement as the moments ticked by, but still he remained silent.

Turning toward him, I studied him as he sat with his arms spread across the back of the sofa and his legs open, the picture of confidence. This Cash was everything Josie claimed he was—sexy and sensual. And entirely fuckable.

As every erotic thought I could think of ran through my mind, I could have sworn the room began to close in around me. My heart pounded against my ribs, and the feel of his muscular thigh pressing against the outside of my leg made me want to know what the rest of him would feel like against me.

I struggled to form a coherent sentence, already nearly overwhelmed by this place, but thankfully he rescued me from my embarrassment. With a sexy grin, he said, "Olivia, meet the dancers."

His gaze traveled to the wall across from where we sat, and I watched as it raised to reveal a window. A soft white light slowly illuminated the space behind the glass, washing over the female who stood there looking out at us. Tall, blonde, and gorgeous, she wore a skin-tight black dress that highlighted every perfect curve of her body. I suddenly felt like one of the ugly stepsisters watching Cinderella step out onto the dance floor. Cash appeared unmoved by her, though.

Soft music filled the room, and just as I braced myself to watch some gorgeous woman strip right in front of us, a man appeared behind her, his hands cupping her shoulders sensually as he trailed his lips up her neck to nip at her earlobe. Was I about to see a sex show sitting right next to my new boss, a man I suddenly wanted more than I should?

My breath caught in my chest as the scene in front of me made taking any air in difficult. Jesus, I was as uptight as all my friends thought! They'd be conducting their own sex show with Cash right now, but all I did was sit there nervously watching for what would come next.

Turning to face me, he said in a low voice thick with sensuality, "Olivia, they'll do as much or as little as we want. What do you want?"

Cash's voice caressed my ears like silk gliding over my skin. What did I want? At that moment, I wanted him. I knew I shouldn't, but I did. I wanted him to kiss me like that man was kissing the gorgeous blonde—like I was the only woman he ever wanted. I wanted to feel his hands sliding over my body as he held me tight to him. I wanted to hear him moan as his desire for me made his cock ache with need.

But I was too timid to tell him any of this, so I mumbled, "I…I don't know."

God, I really was lame.

He stared at me, not with disgust like I felt for myself but with curiosity in his eyes, making me wish I was whatever he thought I was. Without looking away, he waved his hand, and out of the corner of my eye, I saw the man slide the thin strap from the woman's shoulder before he dipped his head to press a kiss onto the top of her breast. I didn't know where to look—at Cash or at the erotic scene playing out just feet away from me.

"Olivia, this is what Club X is. I need to know you're okay with this. I need to know this is something you'd protect for my brothers and…for me."

His blue eyes bored into me searching for the answer. All I could do was nod my agreement. This was so new and exciting that I had no words. I wanted to be the kind of woman he'd bring to a room like this. The kind of woman who excited him as much as he excited me.

With a sharp wave of his hand, the two dancers stopped their seduction and the lights dimmed to darkness behind the window. Had he misinterpreted my silence to mean I wouldn't protect him and Club X? Nervously, I asked, "Is something wrong? Why did you send them away?"

A genuine smile spread across his lips. "I had the feeling they were making you uncomfortable."

He did think I was some pathetic prude. "No, no. I was fine. I didn't mean to act like I had a problem with watching them. It was fine."

I wasn't very convincing. Cash just shook his head and continued to smile. "It's okay. It's not everyone's thing."

He did think I was a prude. I turned my body to face him and reached out to touch his arm. "No, I don't want you to think I can't handle what happens here at the club. I wanted to see everything tonight. I guess I just wasn't prepared for it. But that doesn't mean I can't handle it."

"I believe you, Olivia. Don't worry. Your job isn't in danger because of tonight."

A feeling of relief washed over me. At least the display of my inhibitions hadn't caused him to reconsider hiring me. That was important, but that he saw me as some kind of sheltered, uptight woman bothered me. Men like Cash March didn't want someone like that.

Someone like me.

He stood to leave and I followed him, past Kane who stood near the stairs and down to where Stefan watched the crowd of Godivas debauch the men who escorted them. They spoke about something I couldn't hear and Cash turned to me with a smile. "Enjoy yourself tonight. I'm going to head back into the office. If you need anything, come find me."

Then he walked away, leaving me standing there wanting to say, "Don't go. Stay here and let's get to know each other."

Instead, I just watched as he weaved through the crowd and vanished behind a group of Godivas. All around me were people having the time of their lives, the beat of the music pounding through the club like the rhythm of everyone's heart as they grinded against one another, and I felt like some kind of middle school dance chaperone. Josie and even Erin would have walked right back to that office and showed him exactly what they needed from him, but I couldn't. I stood planted in that spot next to the wall as if my feet were trapped in concrete.

"Having a good time?"

I looked up to see Stefan standing next to me looking

every bit the player he always did. At least he didn't think I was some inhibited school marm. "It's great," I said, hoping he didn't see right through my playacting.

"What do you think of these women? Wild, huh?"

"They look like they're having a good time. Can't blame them for that."

Stefan chuckled. "Just wait until they go upstairs. Kane and his men will have their hands full."

I let my mind travel to the thought of all these Lady Godivas living out their wildest fantasies upstairs in Kane's realm, and a twinge of jealousy nipped at me. I wished I could be like them. They seemed so free and happy. I wanted to be like that.

"From what I've seen, Kane can handle himself."

Nodding, Stefan gave me a wink. "We all can handle ourselves, each in our own way. You'll see that after you're here a while."

Pressing a smile onto my lips, I wondered what way Cash handled himself. As I stood there fantasizing about him handling me, his brother touched my shoulder. "I bet you're not as serious as you seem, Olivia."

A line of Godivas danced by us with their boy-toys, and I looked up at Stefan to see him grinning like a kid in a candy store about to binge on sugar. "Maybe I am. Somebody's got to be serious, right?"

He leaned down until his mouth was right next to my ear. As his lips grazed the side of my face, he said in low voice, "That's what Cash is always saying. Maybe one of you should try being less serious. Just a thought."

And with that he left me standing there watching as he and the rest of the Godivas and their men danced up the stairs to the fantasy rooms. I looked around at the bartenders and a few customers who already were too drunk to enjoy the offerings on the floors above and knew something had to change.

I had to change or I'd forever be boring Olivia standing by as the world marched by me.

Chapter Six
Cassian

Kane strolled into my office and took a seat in front of my desk. My half-brother rarely stopped in to see me, so I put my work aside and looked to see him wearing an uncommon grin as he sat leaning back, his right leg draped over the arm of the chair.

"Something on your mind, Kane?"

"Maybe. You look like you have something eating at you. Perhaps they're the same thing."

I took a deep breath and let it out slowly as I sat back in my chair. I'd just returned from a meeting with our accountant Mitch, who had once again reminded me of the financial ramifications of Stefan's constant need to fuck the women under him. Literally. Obviously, my frustration with my little brother was written all over my face.

"I just got back from the accountant's. Do you know what percentage of our income is now devoted to legal fees courtesy of Stefan?"

Kane shook his head. "You know I don't get involved with that part of the business. I leave that misery to you."

His dry humor wasn't helping me get into a better mood. "I'd willingly trade you my misery for your duties upstairs."

With a deep chuckle, Kane gave me a grin. "They're not your style. You'd be surprised at how dirty I have to get up there. You're not the strong-arm type, Cash."

"Don't tell me any more. I don't want to deal with the legal issues you cause too."

He laced his hands behind his head. "No legal issues from me. I know how to hide my dirt."

"Nice. Well, the answer to my question is nearly twelve percent. I'll tell you, I'm pretty fucking sick of paying for his sex antics."

"Stop him then."

Another deep sigh. "That's easier said than done. Each of us is an equal partner here. I can't just lay the big brother smackdown on him. I also can't trade places with him since I'm pretty sure he'd run our business into the ground. And I don't think asking you to trade places with him would work. It wouldn't be open season on bartenders, but I can only imagine what trouble he'd get into in your area."

Kane nodded his agreement. "Good point. My people need a strong hand to guide them. Letting him loose up there would be like letting a fat kid loose in a bakery. Hell, he's already tried to hit on a few of the dancers. If I hadn't made it clear to them they'd lose their jobs if I caught them anywhere near him, he'd have been all over them. Stefan's a lot more like our father than we are."

"Stefan's a fucking man whore. Our father was never

this bad. If he had been, we'd have dozens of brothers and sisters out there."

"Let's hope we don't," Kane said in a low voice, sending a chill down my spine. God, I hoped we didn't have any long lost siblings out there.

"I don't think you came down to talk about our brother's inability to keep his dick in his pants, so what's up?" I truly hoped Kane had something that would make my day better and not worse.

"I got an interesting request recently."

Kane infrequently bothered to give me the details of his part of the club, usually only when a member reserved a room for something wilder or more bizarre than what he was used to. I settled in to listen to his story, happy for a reprieve from my problems with my other brother. "Do tell. I can use a good freak show story, as long as this isn't going to involve the cops or more lawyers."

"Nope, this one won't get us into any trouble at all."

"Then hit me with it. Just tell me, is it better than the guy who wanted Siamese twins? That was fucked up."

Kane gave me one of his rare laughs before his expression turned more serious. "Yeah, Sheerer likes the weird stuff. I can't tell you how fucking hard it is to find Siamese twins willing to hang out with a guy like that. That put a dent in my budget that quarter. Thank God he's a platinum member. And I don't even want to imagine how much it would have cost if he wanted them to fuck him instead of just sit with him. No, this one involves your assistant."

In that moment, it felt like all the air had been sucked out of the room. "Olivia?"

"Yeah. You gave her a membership, so she wants to use it."

"What did she request?" I asked, my curiosity piqued more than I thought it could be concerning Kane's area.

"She wants a room and she wants to...how did she put it? Experience being out of control. It's just a basic level request. Nothing big."

"Out of control?" I repeated, stunned that my relatively proper assistant had even requested a room upstairs.

"Yep. It's no Siamese twins gig, but I thought you'd find it interesting."

I found it more than interesting. The idea of Olivia even approaching Kane with a request like this surprised me. After giving her the tour of the fantasy rooms, I'd felt like something had changed between us. We'd been getting to know one another and then within a few days, she was all business, as if finding out what the club was really about had changed her opinion of me.

"Did she ask for anything specific?" I asked, trying not to appear too interested.

"No. She didn't seem to understand how it all works. She filled out the request form, but she didn't include any details about exactly what she wants. I had the feeling she was a little shy about it all."

I input my password into my laptop and brought up my calendar. Typing in meaningless comments on a few random dates, I worked to look nonchalant. "So what do you plan to give her?"

Kane slid his leg to the floor and crossed his arms across his chest. "I have nothing planned as of yet. She reserved this Friday, so I have three days to figure it out. Any suggestions?"

He wasn't buying my disinterested act. When the hell did I become so goddamned transparent? "I have no idea. I don't get involved in your domain, remember?"

"I just thought you might want to be a part of this."

Obviously, I hadn't been as slick as I thought I'd been about how much I liked Olivia. I didn't want to see her get in over her head upstairs. "Take it easy on her, Kane. She's a nice girl. I don't know exactly what she's looking for, but don't go overboard and scare her off. I like working with her."

Kane's smirk told me he saw right through my cool attitude. "No problem, Cash. Maybe I'll hook her up with Samson. The ladies like him."

Samson looked everything his name implied. Giant with muscles and long blond hair, he was requested more than any other of Kane's performers. The Godivas had kept him busy for hours at their party, and he'd left with enough tips to fill a bank bag. Kane knew all this too. Nothing like a little brotherly ass busting.

"Samson sounds fine, Kane. He's experienced," I bit out, struggling to keep my cool.

"Yeah. He'll treat her right. Don't worry. I think she just wants to loosen up a little. Nobody knows how to loosen a woman up better than Samson."

Fuck. As much as I didn't want to admit it, the very idea of that Fabio type doing his phony seduction routine with Olivia made my stomach turn. And my half-brother's thinly veiled reference to Samson loosening anything on Olivia got under my skin. Kane had called my bluff, so I had no choice. I had to show my hand. "I don't think Samson is the man for the job. He might be a bit much. Olivia doesn't need that."

Kane raised his eyebrows in surprise. "You know what she needs?"

"She doesn't need your resident fucking gigolo, Kane. All she wants is a taste of our world, not enough to choke on as she tries to swallow."

Another rare smile brightened up his face. "Well, then what do you want me to give her? Are you thinking you want me to do it? You don't have to worry about that non-fraternizing clause. I'm not like Stefan."

The thought of him taking care of loosening up Olivia was barely better than Samson. My half-brother had a penchant for the rougher side of things, if his choice in piercings and the rumors I'd heard were any indication of his preferences. I couldn't imagine him having the patience needed to take care of a woman like Olivia. She didn't need Samson's heavy seduction or Kane's rough style. A woman like her deserved something more sensual, something I doubted neither Kane nor Samson excelled at.

I typed Olivia's name into my calendar for Friday night. "I think that might be unnecessary. Leave this to me. I'll take care of it. You said she reserved Friday night, right? Just make sure I know the time and what room you give her."

"I'm surprised, Cash. You never bothered to get involved when Kate took advantage of the fantasy rooms."

Looking up from my laptop's screen, I said, "Olivia isn't Kate."

Kane smirked. "No doubt. Kate knew how to have a good time. That's why her husband made her quit this job with you. From what I hear, he thought you were fucking her. I don't think you were, but I can tell you that girl knew how to party. Olivia, on the other hand, could very well be a virgin for all I know."

Kane's gossiping about my former assistant amused me. He said so little that when he did say something like that I couldn't help but imagine him like some Peeping Tom on the upper floors spying on our patrons as they lived out their fantasies. Maybe that strong, silent thing he had going on was all an act.

"I had no idea you knew so much about my assistants, Kane."

Leaning forward, he tapped his knuckles on the top of my desk. "Just takes a little paying attention. Kate was a good time. I liked her. As for Olivia, I get the feeling she's a bit more uptight. It'll be interesting to see how this all goes."

Closing my laptop, I shook my head. "I don't want her to feel like she's doing anything wrong, so don't say anything to Stefan so she gets scared off."

"Not a word, Cash," Kane said as he stood to leave. "I'll put her in one of the smaller rooms on the top floor so you two can have all the privacy you need."

He turned to leave, but I stopped him. "One more thing, Kane. Make sure you make it early, around midnight, and make sure she wears a blindfold."

Kane said nothing, but the look on his face showed

I'd piqued his interest. I had no intention of explaining what I planned for Olivia, though. That was between her and me now.

And then just as my day was looking up, in walked another dose of misery for me to deal with. Looking up at Kane as the two met at the door, one of Tampa's VICE squad, John Sheridan—or as we called him when he wasn't around, Shank—had a look on his face that told me anything I'd been worrying about with Stefan would be child's play compared to what he wanted to discuss.

"Kane, how you doing these days?" Shank asked as they shook hands, the question meant to be a thinly veiled reference to my half-brother's past run-ins with the law.

"Same as always." Looking over the policeman's head, Kane shot me a look of disgust. "Don't worry, Cash. I'll take care of things."

"John, what can I do for you?" I asked as he sat down in front of me and smiled that greedy, cop smile he always gave me.

"Just my usual monthly visit, Cassian. You know how this works."

Reaching into the file cabinet behind me, I grabbed the envelope Shank had come for. I handed it to him, and he slid it into his jacket pocket, as always. "I do, John. You know how thankful we are for your help."

Shank patted his chest where our monthly payment sat inside his coat. "I like working with you, Cassian. You're a real businessman who understands the way of the world. You've got a nice thing going here. I'm happy I can help to keep it nice."

Nice. I'd heard that word from Shank enough to know it meant he wanted something. Something more than the twenty grand we paid him every month to make sure Club X didn't get shut down. Hesitant to know what he wanted, I leveled my gaze on his pockmarked face and stared into his dark eyes. "What can I do for you?"

Expecting him to want something akin to a pound of flesh, I was surprised to hear his next words. "Did you know I have a daughter?"

I'd anticipated a different answer, and as worry ebbed from me, I shook my head. "No, I didn't."

Leaning back in his seat, he smiled and for a moment I thought I saw a proud father in the man who shook me down for protection money every month. "I do. Her name is Lorraine, after her mother, God bless her soul. It was just the two of us after my wife died, so she's my entire world."

Unsure of what to say since this John Sheridan wasn't someone as easily hated as the one I usually dealt with, I nodded and mumbled, "That's nice, John."

"I want you to give her a job here."

And there it was. The pound of flesh. Shank might very well have been the ugliest man I'd ever seen. Greasy, salt and pepper colored hair pushed back from his face allowed the world to see the ravages acne had left on his skin, and eyes like a snake's didn't add any good to the overall picture. If his daughter looked anything like him, there was no way she'd be able to be a dancer or a bartender for me. Plus, did I really want some relative of Shank's getting a bird's eye view of the inner workings of Club X?

But there was no way I could say no. Not if I wanted to keep our arrangement going. "You want your daughter to work here? Things get kind of rough here sometimes. I wouldn't want her to get hurt."

"I trust you. She's a good girl, a lot like her mother. She has experience bartending, so just tell Stefan he's got a new worker."

"Okay, John. No problem. I'm sure it will work out fine for her and us."

He flashed me that old crooked cop grin and stood to leave. "I knew you'd say that, Cassian. She'll be thrilled. I'll tell her to come over."

As he left my office, I just hoped she looked a lot like her mother too. If not, maybe I'd have to consider placing a bartender on one of the upper floors in a corner somewhere. But if she looked like Shank, I wouldn't have to worry about Stefan going after her. At least there was that.

* * *

Leaning back against the couch cushions, I closed my eyes and let Rachel do what she did best. For all the hassle and unhappiness she'd brought into my life on more occasions than I cared to remember, she did know how to suck cock like a champion. Ordinarily, I'd be enjoying it like I always did, my hand stuffed into her long black hair guiding her, not that she needed any help. We'd done this enough times over the years that she knew exactly how to get me off. There were no mysteries about her, no secrets to uncover. Rachel was what she'd been for years—someone to fuck. No more, no less.

Her hands danced over the tops of my thighs, gently

raking her long, perfectly manicured nails across my skin before she wrapped her palm around the base of my cock and squeezed. I'd always enjoyed that moment when her hand's motion let me know she was about to take me into her mouth and deliver a world class blowjob. I'd had every intention of enjoying it tonight, but as I sat there watching her slowly bob up and down in my lap, it just wasn't there.

I was barely there.

My hand slid from her head and landed on the couch next to my leg, a not-so-subtle sign I was bored. Rachel may have been self-centered and thoughtless most times in her life, but she wasn't stupid or blind, and I wasn't even trying to hide my disinterest.

She looked up at me as she slid my cock out of her mouth, those nearly jet black eyes questioning me before the words passed her lips. "What's wrong with you tonight, baby? Hard day at the club?"

"No. I've got other things on my mind."

Rachel sat back on her heels, but her hand never left my cock. Stroking it from base to tip and back again, she shook her head. "Poor Cash. Always so worried about everything. Let me guess. Another lawsuit from a disgruntled worker? You need a better screening system there."

I rolled my eyes at the veiled reference to my younger brother's sexual antics. Of all the people in the world, Rachel was the last one I wanted to discuss Stefan's indiscriminate fucking with. "No, it has nothing to do with a lawsuit."

Her expression showed me she didn't care why I was

distracted, just that I wasn't fulfilling my role in the play we acted out at least one night a week. As I looked down at her petulant face, I suddenly felt like I didn't want to do this with her anymore. It had been nice for a while, but I didn't want this.

"What's going on, Cassian? Is this about that thing again? I told you he meant nothing."

"No. I don't care about that."

Her hand stopped its movement against my skin, and as she let my cock loose, it smacked off my stomach. She stared down at it in its still rock hard state, her mouth turning down into a pout. "Then what? You're killing our good time here, baby."

I ran my hands through my hair while I tried to figure out what was going on with me. It had been a long time since just sex hadn't been enough, but now as Rachel worked to coax interest out of me with her mouth on the inside of my thigh, I just couldn't fake it. This wasn't enough.

The truth was that since hearing Kane say Olivia had reserved one of the fantasy rooms I couldn't think of anything but her. And the thought of one of Kane's guys taking care of her made me want to hit someone. After working with her for just a short time, I shouldn't have been jealous at the thought of Samson or even Kane being with her in any way, but I was.

I wanted to be the one with Olivia when she finally shed the mask of control, not my half-brother or one of our employees. That she was my assistant didn't make my desire for her easy, though. I'd religiously stuck to my belief that fraternizing with employees was a mistake none of us could afford to make, and now I was quickly becoming obsessed with the idea of doing just that with her.

"Cash, did you hear me?" Rachel asked in a voice full of irritation, shaking me out of my thoughts about Olivia.

I pulled up my pants and walked over to the bar for a drink. Pouring myself a glass of whiskey, I looked out the enormous window at the bay below my condo. The alcohol warmed my throat going down, and I took another swig before turning back toward Rachel now sitting in my spot on the couch.

"I think it's time we admit this isn't what either of us want, Rachel. We had fun. Most times we did. It's just run its course."

She stared at me for a long moment before that mouth that had given me so much pleasure in the past hitched up into a knowing smile. "Who is she, Cash? I've known you long enough to know when you're in love with someone. Remember? You used to look that way when we got together."

Turning back to look out the window, I took another drink, holding it in my mouth for a second before letting it slide down my throat. "I'm not in love with anyone. You forget who you're talking to. I don't do love. I do sex. Sometimes I do sex exclusively, but I don't do love."

"Yeah, right, baby. Don't tell me you weren't in love with me, Cassian March. I know you better."

I didn't want to have this discussion with her. She wasn't wrong. I had loved her. Up until just recently, I'd thought I still loved her, even after she tore my fucking heart out. I'd lied to myself and convinced some part of me that fucking her like I did would show her I didn't care anymore, but for a long time the spark she ignited in me still burned strong.

Not anymore, though.

Rachel padded up behind me and slid her arms around my waist. "I loved that look you get in your eyes when you're in love, Cash. I thought since I saw that look again tonight that you might ask me to come back."

Her words resonated through my body, but they meant nothing anymore. For the first time since we broke up, I didn't want her. Turning in her hold, I looked down at her beautiful face. "It's been over for a long time with us. You knew that better than I did."

"You never forgave me, did you? You forgave him, but not me. That's the truth, isn't it?"

"No. I never forgave him really either. I just don't have a choice in that."

We stood there silently until I saw in her eyes she understood this was it. "You'll be fine, Rachel. I imagine you already have a few on the hook besides me."

She ran her hand over my chest until it came to rest over my heart. "She's a lucky woman this one who's captured your heart. Any one of the dozens I've seen you out with?"

Shaking my head, I chuckled. "No. You wouldn't know her. She's not like you. She's not like anyone I've ever met."

Rachel laughed. "Really? You're doing the 'she's unlike anyone I've ever met' thing with me? I've known you since you were just that rich teenage boy with too much freedom and money to blow. I've met practically every woman you've slept with since we broke up too. I doubt she's unlike the rest of us, Cash. You like a certain type. I can picture her already. Tall, legs that go on forever, platinum blonde, or she might be the occasional brunette, but only if she has black hair like mine. Am I close?"

I shook my head at how wrong she was. "No. Not even close."

"So you've decided to fall for a dumpy girl with mousey brown hair? Really, Cash. Is this some kind of thing to show me you can go on without me?"

I took the last gulp of whiskey in my glass and pushed past her as she continued with her questions. She wouldn't get anything more out of me on this. For the first time since I was that teenage boy, I wanted whatever Olivia and I would be to remain private. No parading her in front of cameras for publicity at social events just to promote the club. No telling Rachel about her in some misguided attempt to make her jealous or show her I'd moved on. No showing her off to impress others.

No, Olivia was unlike anyone else I'd ever met. Intelligent, confident, and sweet, I wanted to protect her from the life I'd led all these years and the people I'd included in that life. Taking my seat on the couch again, I said, "Rachel, this has nothing to do with you. We had a good time for a while. Let's leave it at that."

For a moment, she got a look on her face that made me think she might actually miss me, but then it was gone, replaced by a perfect smile and a roll of her eyes.

"As you wish. You know your happiness has always been important to me."

"Thanks, Rachel."

She dressed and grabbed her bag. Walking behind the couch, she leaned over and gave me a kiss just below my ear before she whispered, "Be happy, baby. Maybe we'll be even better at being friends than we were lovers."

I didn't answer because I had nothing to say anymore. My mind was already past Rachel and onto Olivia and what would happen Friday night. Whatever the future held, I was about to break my cardinal rule I'd lived by since opening Club X. I just hoped it wasn't the biggest mistake of my life.

Chapter Seven

Olivia

By the time Friday came, I'd lost five pounds from worrying. The minute I pressed Send on the email to Kane to request a fantasy room I regretted it. I wasn't that type of woman, even if I'd always wanted to be. I was the timid girl afraid to send a man a drink in a bar even with my friends egging me on. I was the nose-to-the-grindstone bookworm who felt more comfortable around facts and figures than men.

But I didn't want to be that woman anymore.

That didn't mean I should turn into some Lady Godiva wannabe at my workplace. What was I thinking? I had to work with these men, and now they'd think I was some kind of oversexed woman who didn't have brains enough to shed her inhibitions in private.

Even worse, although Cash hadn't mentioned anything about my request, he'd seemed distant for the last two days. Or maybe it was just my being paranoid. I wasn't sure. I wasn't even sure I'd go up to the top floor at midnight like Kane had instructed me to in his email back to me.

The sound of the music pounding in the club outside my office made concentrating impossible tonight. Now I knew why I usually preferred to work my eleven to seven schedule, but the truth was I wouldn't have been able to get much work done even if it was dead silent outside my door. My mind raced with the implications of my decision to follow my friends' suggestions to let loose and enjoy myself. What if Cash found out? What would he think?

Who was I kidding? He already knew. That's why he'd become colder than Mr. Frosty suddenly. If only Stefan was my boss. He'd understand. The younger March brother wouldn't pass judgment on me. Hell, he'd probably join me. Instead, I worked for the owner who was all business, even though I'd tried in my own very timid way to let him know I liked him.

I stared at my laptop screen, realizing the truth. I was as pathetic as Josie and Erin thought I was.

"Olivia?"

I lifted my head at the sound of a deep voice and saw Cash closing my office door. He looked incredible in a black suit and sapphire blue dress shirt. Damn, he filled out a suit well!

"Yes?" I answered, my mind filled with how good he looked standing there.

"I'm going to be out of the building tonight. I know this is the first time you've chosen to work while the club is open, so if you have any problems, just text me."

"I don't expect to have any problems. No one even knows I'm back here. If I need anything, I can just ask Stefan since he'll be close by."

My suggestion meant to help Cash leave behind the worries of the job for one night caused him to frown. "No. I don't want you bothering Stefan. If you need anything, text or call me. Are we clear?"

"Oh…oh, okay," I stammered out, stung by his sharp rebuke of my kind gesture.

"Have a good weekend," he said, his voice back to its usual sexier softness.

I wished him the same, and as he turned and walked out into the club probably to some great date with a gorgeous supermodel, my heart sank. Even though I'd worried about him knowing what I planned for later tonight, some tiny part of me had secretly hoped it would have made him open up a little more and maybe show me he liked me too.

So much for my pie in the sky dreams.

* * *

I walked through the nightclub section of Club X in my tiny black tank dress and almost four inch heels, weaving through the crowds to the beat of dance music on my way to the stairs that led up to the fantasy rooms. Although I rarely dressed up like this, I liked how it felt when I saw a few male patrons check me out. They didn't know I was all walk and no talk, but it didn't matter. Tonight wasn't about impressing them.

Tonight was about me becoming the new and improved Olivia.

My legs shook almost uncontrollably as I climbed the stairs past the second, third, and fourth floors, avoiding the gazes of the throngs of people passing me. Each step I took moved me one step closer to my fantasy. I'd been pretty vague on my request form, only saying I wanted to experience not being in control all the time. I wasn't up for anything too freaky, but I didn't want to put too many restrictions on my request and end up having tea with some pathetic guy in glasses because Kane thought I was looking for something tame.

By the time I reached the top floor, it was nearly midnight and my stomach was completely tied in knots. My palms felt clammy too, and as I walked toward where Kane stood talking to some man, I nonchalantly wiped my hands down the front of my dress, hoping to dry them off a little. The men stared at me as I approached them, and I immediately wondered if this was the person Kane had arranged to spend time with me. Tall and very muscular, he wore his blond hair a little too long for my taste and reminded me of that model who'd been on all those romance novels my mother used to like to read. He seemed intensely interested in me, though, and I couldn't help but feel a little disappointed at the idea that my first venture into the sexier side of life would be with him.

"Olivia, I almost didn't recognize you," Kane said in an unusually pleasant voice for him.

I looked down at my dress and back up at him. "Yes, well, I thought I should..." I felt foolish explaining my choice of clothes and by the look on the mystery man's face, he couldn't figure out why I was boring them with the information either, so I let my sentence trail off into awkward silence. My brand new sexy life wasn't starting off well at all.

Kane pointed down the hallway I'd walked with Cash the week before. "Go to the last room on the right.

Be sure to follow all the directions on the card. Most important, have a good time, Olivia."

The scary owner seemed downright chipper tonight, but I had the feeling it was more amusement at me than a new outlook on life. I turned and walked through the crowd of already drunk partiers directly to the room, just as he'd told me to, finding only a note and a plain, white box on the table next to the ordinary tan sofa. Taking a deep breath, I sat down and opened the note card.

Welcome to your fantasy, Olivia. This night is all yours. For the next two hours, let yourself go. You want to experience not being in control, so you'll do as I desire. If you don't obey, I'll correct you once. The second time you make any mistake, our time will be over.

In the box, you'll find a blindfold. Put it on and wait.

Nervous but exhilarated by the promise of the evening, I opened the lid and nestled inside sat a black silk blindfold. Lifting it out of the box, I ran my fingertips over it, loving the cool, smooth feel of it against my skin. I took one last look around the room that resembled the one I'd sat in with Cash and put the blindfold up to my eyes, tying the ribbons behind my head to hold it in place.

And then I waited.

Without my sight, the sound of my heart pounding became my focus, but I listened to hear my companion for the evening approach, unable to make out anything outside this room because of the soundproofing. Every puff of cool air from the ducts overhead, every hint of my favorite perfume gently wafting the scent of vanilla and floral up from behind my earlobes became so pronounced. I felt vulnerable and on display, and I wondered if anyone stood behind the window waiting for the moment when the covering would rise and they could see everything inside the room. Straining my ears, I waited to hear the sound that would tell me the wall had lifted, but after five minutes or so, I stopped and let myself relax, as the note had told me to.

The door opening put every cell in my body on red alert. The person who entered said nothing, but I felt them standing there watching me. I sat ramrod straight, my heart hammering away in my chest, as I anticipated their first words to me. The air around us nearly crackled with excitement, mine mostly I imagined, but I wanted to think this person who'd spend the next two hours with me wanted to be there too for their own reasons.

As the door closed, I heard them move toward me, and then the first touch of their hands made my breath catch in my throat. Large and strong, the man's hands slowly caressed my upper arms, sending goosebumps all down my skin. A mixture of exhilaration and fear rippled through me. Closing my eyes, I reminded myself that this was what I wanted. I couldn't go on living life so safe that I never truly lived at all.

Unsure of how to act, I nervously asked, "What's your name?"

A deep voice whispered, "Shhhh," and he took my hand to guide me from my place on the couch. It wasn't even a real word he spoke, but it was an order—a command—that I was supposed to listen to, and I did willingly, loving how little control I felt already.

His hand slid down my back to the base of my spine as I walked, an unmistakable act of power. Our time would be governed by his rules, not mine. The thought of him controlling my fantasy excited me. What would he do? What would he want me to do? I'd only reserved the room for two hours, a basic fantasy, so there wasn't supposed to be sex involved.

But at that moment, I so wished it would be. He'd barely touched me, and I wanted him so badly. No, I wanted Cash, but for tonight, this man would be him, at least in my mind.

I sat on the barstool he'd led me to and sensed him move around me. His warm breath slid over the skin on my neck, making every hair stand at attention. Never before had I been so aware of another person near me. My hands ached to reach out and touch him to learn more about the man who already had such an effect on me, but I had the surest sense that wasn't allowed until he said it was.

He stood in front of me, and I imagined him silently watching me. I didn't know what to do or how to react. Fulfilling fantasies was his job, but this was all new to me. I licked my lips to moisten them as my nervousness made my mouth as dry as cotton and I heard him exhale. Then he touched my cheek and instantly I felt lightheaded. The pad of his thumb traced a line from just under my cheekbone to the swell of my bottom lip I'd just licked with my tongue and as his finger reached the corner of my mouth, his fingernail grazed my skin, sending a shiver down my spine as he moved his hand away.

I listened as the sound of his shoes hitting the floor signaled he'd moved around behind me. Tensing my muscles, I waited for him to touch me again, desperate to feel his skin on mine once more. My mind swirled with thoughts of Cash as the man there with me. For the first time, I let myself fantasize about him without fear.

This was a fantasy room, after all.

Without realizing it, I relaxed as I imagined what being with Cassian March would be like. Eyes closed behind the blindfold, I let my mind's eye create images of how he looked out of those expensive suits, his muscular body revealed just for me. As I enjoyed my private fantasy, the man behind me softly pushed my hair off to my left shoulder and pressed his lips against my neck. His mouth was warm and gentle on my skin, and an involuntary moan escaped from my throat when I felt his hand moved around to stroke the column of my neck.

I lifted my chin, needy to feel him touch me more, and deliberately his fingers squeezed my flesh ever so lightly. Fear spiked inside me at the fact that his hand, so big and strong, could crush my windpipe in one swift move if he chose, but his touch was gentle, if insistent. I was his to control, not hurt.

He moaned low and quiet near my ear, sending a shockwave straight to my core. I had no idea who he was, what he looked like, or even what he sounded like when he said my name, but at that moment if he had wanted me I would have willingly given myself to him. I knew it was foolish, but that didn't change how I felt.

His thumb rubbed against my neck, leaving a trail of heat wherever he touched. Then just as I thought I couldn't take another instant of his teasing touch, he moved his hand away and I heard him walk around me again. I sat there confused why he'd stopped. Our time couldn't be up yet.

Swiveling my head left and right to try to get a sense of what was going on, I caught a hint of his cologne. Vaguely familiar, I'd never smelled anything more delicious in my life. I wanted to fill my nostrils with that masculine scent as I buried my head in the curve between his neck and shoulder and pressed my lips against his skin.

He stopped my head with a gentle touch of his hand on my jaw. Every movement stimulated my senses because even though he never touched me harshly, there was no mistaking his control over me. Yes, I'd requested this fantasy and I knew this was all an act to him, but to me our time together brought out a part of me I'd never really knew existed. I wanted to give up the control I'd always thought was so important, and this stranger brought that out in me.

And then he kissed me, his lips soft and warm. They moved over mine like they knew exactly how to excite me. His strong hands cradled my face as our kiss deepened, nearly burning my lips with the heat between us. The first light touch of his tongue on mine made my pussy run wet. I wanted to feel that tongue slide over my clit as I slipped over the edge into a toe-curling orgasm.

My mind reeled between fantasy and reality. The person I wanted to do all these things to me was Cash, not this unknown man playacting because it was his job. Desire mingled with the truth, pushing it aside as his kiss deepened even further, his tongue eagerly gliding over mine.

Timidly, I reached out to touch the man who so easily brought out in me such sensuality that even I couldn't believe I wanted these things. He didn't stop me, so I pressed my hands against his chest, broad and hard under a dress shirt. My mind flashed back to what the man standing with Kane had been wearing. This was not him. A lick of fear tore through me. Was it Cash's brother there with me?

I ran my hand over the back of his neck and instantly knew it wasn't Kane I was touching. He wore his hair cropped to his head, and this man's hair was a little longer, just barely hitting the collar of his shirt. It felt as soft as silk as I slid the ends through my fingers. Who was this?

As I pondered this question, he moved back away from me until only his hands touched the tops of my legs. His thumbs traced a slow path down toward the inside of my thighs that seemed to fall open of their own volition. God, I wanted him to ease the ache he'd created in me.

I opened my mouth to speak, knowing he didn't want me to but needing to say something, but stopped dead when I felt his lips on my inner thigh. I gasped as he flicked his tongue against my skin, and I could have sworn I heard him moan my name. Slowly, he inched his way up under my skirt, so close to where I desperately wished him to be. He was so close I felt his breath on my…

And then I felt his finger slide through the front of my damp panties, tracing the cleft up to my needy clit. Leaning back, I moaned, "Oh," and waited, wishing more than anything he'd put his mouth on my pussy.

But he stopped, leaving me wanting as he stood up and leaned in to whisper so quietly I barely heard the words, "Goodnight, Olivia."

My emotions spun out of control, and before I could say a word, he left me sitting there aching and desperate for more. Tearing off my blindfold, I looked around for any sign of who my mystery man had been and why he'd left so abruptly before our reserved time was up, but I saw nothing. Walking to the door on shaky legs, I opened it to see the crowd of people in the hallway. Was the man who'd been with me one of them?

I hurried down toward where Kane had stood just a short time ago, but his post was empty so I couldn't even ask him who had been assigned to my room. Not that it mattered. Whoever it was, in my mind it had been Cash there with me.

Hours later, I lay awake in bed still strung out from my first time in a Club X fantasy room. Every inch of my body had been awakened, every sense heightened by a man whose touch thrilled me but whose face I'd never seen. I wanted more. I wanted to feel that sexy again.

My fingers slid slowly down over my stomach and through my folds as I replayed every moment of my fantasy coming true. Closing my eyes, I thought about the one man who'd filled my nights for weeks.

Cash walked into my office and closed the door behind him. Dressed in a black suit and red shirt, he looked more stunning than usual, if that was possible. His cool blue eyes focused on me as he walked toward my desk.

"Staying late tonight, Olivia?"

Another boss asking me that question would be perfectly normal, but something in his tone told me his interest in my schedule had nothing to do with the work I was busy with. Shifting in my chair, I nodded. "I thought I'd catch up on some work. You know, so I can begin ahead of the game on Monday."

He stopped in front of my desk and smiled. "Always so diligent."

God, he could have been reading one of my management textbooks in that voice and I'd want him inside me. I wondered if he knew how sexy he sounded, or did he simply always sound like a sex god?

I began to needlessly explain that I liked to begin the workweek fresh, like some overachieving nerd who didn't understand what to do when a gorgeous man came into her presence. I knew. I just wasn't sure enough to act on that knowledge with someone like Cassian March.

He rounded the corner of my desk and leaned down just inches away from me. "I think it's time for you to get off work, don't you?"

The room suddenly felt too small as he stared down at me with those stunning blue eyes. His face was so close to mine that all I had to do was lean forward just a tiny bit and I'd finally get to know what his perfect mouth felt like.

Instantly, I wished I could say something sexy—something that would make him hot like he made me—but he unnerved me so much my mind went blank and it was all I could do to squeak out, "Oh, okay."

Then he pressed his lips to mine in a kiss that took my breath away. The room swam around me. His lips were as soft as I'd imagined and he claimed my mouth with an urgency that belied that cool persona he wore every day.

He pulled away and licked his lips as if to taste me on

them. "I know there's more to you than just a great worker, Olivia. Time to show me who the real you is."

His mouth crushed against mine again as his one hand held me to him while the other slid up my thigh under my skirt. He moved fast, but stopping him was the last thing on my mind. More than anything, I wanted to feel him inside me, whether it was his fingers or his cock.

I stood from my chair, my skirt pushed up around my waist to reveal my panties drenched from how excited he'd made me. He leaned back against my desk and began to undo his belt, quickly unzipping his pants to show nothing but his rock hard cock.

All my thoughts of straddling him and riding that cock were suddenly pushed back in my mind in favor of taking him in my mouth and sucking him dry. I wanted to taste that gorgeous part of him more than anything. Dropping to my knees, I palmed the root of his shaft and wrapped my lips around the swollen tip, sucking him into my mouth as much as I could. He moaned loudly and buried his hands in my hair to guide me as I slid his gorgeous cock in and out of my mouth.

His skin was velvety smooth over his rock hard shaft, and he tasted faintly of salt and muskiness. Pure male. I cupped his balls in my free hand and looked up to see him staring down at me with a look in his piercing blue eyes that told me this was exactly what he'd had in mind. Over and over, I swallowed his cock, loving the sound of his moans as I inched him closer and closer to release.

I felt his hands tighten in my hair, sending delicious pain skittering across my scalp. Looking down at me, he licked his lips and grinned. "Slow. I want this to last."

Controlling my pace, he fucked my mouth slowly and

methodically, and I licked and sucked every glorious inch of him. I felt his sac tighten in my palm and knew he was just seconds away from coming. Keeping my gaze on him, I watched his eyes glaze over as his cock flooded my mouth. Gently, I squeezed the base, feeling it twitch as cum spurted out of him.

When he finally finished, I stood up to face him and he quickly moved to push my panties out of the way. "Straddle me, Olivia. I want to see you ride my cock."

My fingers slid through my wet pussy and over my swollen clit as the fantasy of fucking Cash played itself out in my mind. My orgasm hit at just the moment when he ordered me to ride him, and I plunged two fingers inside me just as the vision of him sliding into my body filled my mind.

CHAPTER EIGHT

Cassian

My time with Olivia in our fantasy room affected me more than I thought it would, and by the time I saw her at work on Monday, I wasn't sure I could hide that I wanted her. Even more, I wasn't sure I wanted to hide it, but I still wasn't convinced I should abandon everything I'd believed in for years. Shitting where you eat wasn't a wise business decision. I knew that, and still I had to fight the urge to walk into her office half a dozen times to see her.

From the moment she walked in that morning, I saw she was different. She had an air of sensuality that I hadn't seen before in her. Something in her deep brown eyes sparkled as we spoke about work. She wore this new sexiness well. I wondered if she had any clue it was me next to her just nights before in that room loving the smell of vanilla in her hair as my lips tenderly brushed her ear and my hands caressed her soft skin.

When she left the club that night, I had to know if she'd reserved another room. I'd never cared as much as to wonder if a woman would ever come back, except for Rachel. I'd cared far too much about her, and I'd paid for that mistake and likely would for the rest of my life. Now I found myself caring about what this woman thought—what she felt—what she wanted.

I'd pushed this side of me away for so long I didn't know if I could control it. I hadn't been able to in the past. Within mere days of meeting Rachel, I'd been consumed by her. Her perfume, the smell of her hair, the taste of her lips on mine became necessities in my life. Was I ready to be that man again?

Kane stood at his post on the top floor watching monitors as he always did, and I approached him knowing as soon as I asked about Olivia that I'd be showing him my hand. My half-brother played his cards close to the vest, and right now, I hoped he'd keep my business under wraps too. I didn't need Stefan knowing anything about what Olivia and I were up to.

"How's it looking tonight?"

He looked at me with suspicion, and I knew he saw right through my attempt to act like nothing was going on. Instead of asking me any questions, he simply nodded and smiled. "Same as always, Cash. Life never changes up here."

"Yeah. Same downstairs."

"How was your meeting with that scumbag Shank?"

"He wants me to hire his daughter."

Kane's eyebrows shot up. "For what? If she looks like him, all she'd be good for is guarding the door, and I don't need any more bouncers."

"I know. I know. I couldn't say no to him, though. Without his help, we'd have to deal with cops every night."

"Make her a bartender, Cash. Good thing is Stefan

won't want to fuck her if she's got her father's face. And when the ugly lights come on at the end of the night, it won't matter because everyone's stone drunk anyway."

I had to laugh at Kane's straightforward approach to the problem. I made a few more attempts at small talk, which he thankfully ignored, and then got straight to the reason I'd come up to see him. "Did she reserve a room again?"

"Who?" he asked with a vicious grin.

"You know who."

"I don't know. I'll have to look it up. I should be able to locate that information by tomorrow. Maybe Wednesday."

Leaning over his station, I leveled my gaze at him. "Is this your Stefan impersonation? Just tell me."

Kane let out a deep laugh. "Sorry, Cash. It was just too easy. Yeah, she reserved a room for this Friday."

I waited for him to tell me anything else I should know, but he wasn't going to make this easy for me. "Did she request anything…or anyone?" He stood silently, giving me a look that told me he was enjoying himself. "Jesus, Kane. Don't be such a dick."

"Old habits die hard, big brother. I didn't realize we were best buddies now."

He had every right to be an asshole with me. Never recognized by our father until right before he died, Kane had grown up without the comforts the March name offered. Not that Stefan and I were to blame for that, but I understood why he had a chip on his shoulder. Right now, though, that chip was causing me grief I could do without.

"So?"

"She requested the same room and the same guy. Same tame fantasy too."

That's all I needed to hear. A rush of happiness raced through me. "Thanks, Kane."

"You like this one, don't you, Cash?"

With a smile, I said, "So now we're best buddies?" Two could play this game.

Unlike Stefan, Kane had a great sense of humor, even if he rarely displayed it. He chuckled and said, "No. I was just curious. I don't think I've seen you react to anyone like this for a long time."

"It's not a big deal. Just keeping an eye out for her."

"If that's what you want to call it, that's fine. I'll go along with it. For what it's worth, though, she had a good time and seems like a new woman."

"Been spying on the rooms again, Kane?"

Sitting down, he leaned back in his chair and folded his arms across his chest. "I don't have to. I saw her earlier, and it's written all over her face. That woman is primed."

"Again acting like Stefan. Don't make this something it's not."

Kane shrugged and gave me an unconvinced smirk. "Whatever works for you. I just know what I see."

I turned and walked away before he goaded me into saying something I didn't want to. Playing games wasn't on my agenda. I much rathered thinking about Olivia wanting another night like I'd given her. And that's exactly what she'd get.

* * *

Seated behind her desk in a pale pink cotton dress, she looked more like she was ready for a picnic than working at organizing a birthday party with a Roman orgy theme one of the platinum members had reserved for the next weekend. Standing in the doorway to her office, I asked, "Olivia, are you planning to work late on another Friday night? It's already nine o'clock."

She flashed me a smile and nodded. "Yes. I have plans later, so I thought I'd work until then."

"Have something special to do tonight?"

Biting her bottom lip, she looked away for a second and then back at me. "Just something I've wanted to do for a long time. What about you? Do you have big plans this weekend?"

I shook my head and worked to keep my happiness at her answer hidden. "Nope. I'll be here all weekend. I'm thinking I'll work late tonight too, so if you need anything, just stop over."

"Okay, thanks! I already had dinner, but if I need anything, I'll be sure to let you know." Her tone not so subtly told me she had something better on her mind. As I made my way back to my office, I had to admit knowing the something better was me made her dismissal easier to take.

I busied myself with work, all the while distracted by the plans I had for her when we were together in that room again. While the silent act may have been entertaining for a night, I wanted her to know who was seducing her. Tonight I'd let her hear my voice, and if we had any future together, I'd know by her reaction when I said those first words.

The sound of the club outside my door made hearing much of anything difficult, but I felt the vibration of her door close just before midnight and knew the time had come. Opening my office door, I watched her head into the crowd and gave her a few minutes to climb the stairs and find the room. By quarter after, I figured she was ready and ascended the stairs to join her.

Like the week before, groups of people filled the hallway leading to the room she waited in, platinum members I recognized immediately as what I liked to call the fringe of that level. Clients since our early days at the club, they saw Club X as a refuge for their wildest fantasies and we graciously accommodated each and every one of them. Glad-handing as I made my way toward where Olivia sat waiting for me, I finally reached our room at the end of the hall, the same as last Friday.

I entered and quickly closed the door, wanting to push away the noisy remnants of the club's patrons who milled about outside. Whatever they planned to be that night, I didn't want them intruding on my time with her.

She sat silently on the couch, her back straight and chin high, looking confident but alert. Vulnerable in the same black silk blindfold as the first time, she turned to face me as the door clicked closed.

I saw by the way her lips parted slightly that she wanted to speak, but my admonition to her during our previous time together forced her to be silent. Not ready to give my true identity away quite yet, I reached out and ran my fingertip over the seam of her mouth, letting my touch linger on the corner. Her lips were soft and as I pulled away, she whispered in a voice I could barely hear, "I've waited all week for this."

Her words, tinged with shyness, nevertheless told me she was ready to feel more than she'd ever let herself feel before. I wanted to bring that out in her. I wanted to be the man who made her scream in pleasure like she'd never experienced before in her life.

That might have been a little premature. No matter how much I wanted her, I wasn't going to make love to Olivia for the first time in one of my club's fantasy rooms. She was better than that.

Taking her hand, I led her over to the bar stool on the opposite side of the room. She sat down, and I watched as she fidgeted with her dress, nervously tugging on it to cover her gorgeous thighs. Reaching out, I covered her hands to still them and placed them at her side, returning to slide one finger over the inside of her right thigh.

She jumped at the feel of my touch on her tender skin, and I heard her sharp intake of breath as I watched my fingertip trace a line up her leg under her dress. A gentle twitch of her skin and a soft sigh made my cock harden, and I worked to keep myself under control.

I moved my hand away, and Olivia straightened in the chair, gently squeezing her thighs together in a brief clench as she waited for me to make my next move. She was so responsive, unlike any woman I'd been with before. Each quiver, each quiet moan excited me more than I thought possible.

But I wanted more than just a response from her. I wanted her to go after what she desired.

Stepping in between her legs, I pressed the front of

my thighs against the chair and leaned in to kiss her, stopping just before my lips brushed against hers to inhale the delicate scent of vanilla. Her mouth melded to mine, pressing eagerly in a kiss full of need. Slipping my tongue between her lips, I leisurely teased the tip of her tongue as if I was flicking my tongue over her clit. Soon…For now, her tongue would do nicely.

She tasted like peppermint, and as we kissed, the fresh flavor filled my mouth, making me want more than just the polite making out she offered. I cradled the back of her head and held her fast to me, my mouth plundering hers as she wrapped her arms around my shoulders. Stroking my thumb against the base of her neck, I heard her softly mew into my mouth as she scooted her ass forward on the chair toward my rock hard cock.

I pulled away suddenly, and she made a sound like a tiny moan filled with disappointment. The corners of her mouth turned down slightly as she turned her head to search for my touch. Crouching down, I pushed her dress up and pressed my lips to the tender skin of her inner thigh. Lightly flicking my tongue over it, I heard the sharp intake of her breath and felt the quiver of her skin against my lips as I inched my way up her leg.

Whispering, I said my first real words to her in this room. "Relax. Let yourself feel good, Olivia."

Instantly, her body tensed and the gentle sound of her breathing stopped. I stood to watch her reaction, and after a long moment she let out a deep sigh but said nothing. Had she recognized my voice or was she just surprised by my speaking to her for the first time?

She was lovely sitting there, vulnerable but eager to shed her shy girl self and act on her true desires. Reaching out, I ran my hand over her hair and twirled a lock around my forefinger, stopping next to her ear with a gentle tug. She bit her lower lip and leaned toward my hand, a wince marring her beautiful face to let me know I was hurting her. Unraveling it slowly, I let it fall against her shoulder and leaned in to place a kiss on her cheek to ease the pain.

"I'm glad to see you came back tonight, Olivia."

She had to recognize my voice that time. I waited for her to respond, but when she did, there was no sign she knew who the man seducing her was.

Her voice quiet, she said, "I couldn't stay away if I wanted to. I don't, though."

I ran my fingertip across her cheek to her mouth and traced the outline of her lips. "I like that. What do you like, Olivia?"

She hesitated, unsure of her answer, and finally said, "You. I like you."

I liked her answer so much I wanted to feel those lips that had spoken such sweet words on my lips. Pulling her into my arms, I kissed her hard, not wanting to restrain myself. She softened in my hold, kissing me with a passion I'd only imagined lay beneath that proper businesswoman I saw each day.

Breaking our kiss, I trailed my lips over the soft skin near her collarbone, planting tiny kisses as I moved my mouth toward the front of her dress. "I like your dress. Tell me, Olivia, would you take it off for me?"

"Yes."

"What if I wanted to take it off? Would you let me?"

"Yes," she said in a breathless voice before she repeated her answer. "Yes."

Fuck, she was beautiful! So responsive to my touch, she made my cock ache with a mere word. I wanted her right there, my mouth lapping her pussy as she came over and over again, drenching my face with her juices. My cock sliding in and out of her needy cunt, filling her completely as her body gave in to the feelings I created in her.

I felt myself begin to lose control. Stepping back, I took a deep breath to calm my mind, needing to find some way to get back to that man I'd created so long ago. This was seduction, nothing more. That it would lead to sex was all the better, but that's where it would end.

Where it had to end.

Olivia reached out for me, her hands searching for the one who'd so hastily abandoned her. She had no idea why I'd needed to back away. All she knew was that I wasn't there with her anymore.

"Are you still here?" she whispered in a voice laced with sadness. "Did I do something wrong?"

I stood watching her as a frown settled into that gorgeous mouth, and I imagined her eyebrows knitting with concern that she'd made a mistake. A lick of regret seared my heart for a moment. Olivia wasn't to blame for the way I was. She shouldn't pay for my being fucked up.

Stepping forward, I answered her. "I'm here. You did nothing wrong, Olivia."

The frown disappeared, replaced by a genuine smile that lit up the room, and she tentatively ran her fingertips down the front of my shirt. "What color is this?"

"Black."

"Why don't you want me to take my dress off anymore? Is something wrong?"

I slipped my fingers under the neckline of her dress and eased it off her shoulders to reveal a pink satin bra strap. Bending down, I placed a kiss on her collarbone as I slid the strap down, noticing a red mark where it had rubbed against her tender skin. "Did you buy this bra just for tonight, Olivia?"

Her cheeks flushed a darker pink color at my question, and she bit her lip as she nodded. God, she was exquisite in her bashfulness. I couldn't remember being around a woman so shy yet so eager to shed her inhibitions. The combination was intoxicating and made me want her all the more.

Sliding my hand down her side, my thumb grazing her breast, I lifted the bottom of her dress and placed my palm on the top of her thigh just below her hip. A tiny whimper escaped her lips as I trailed a fingertip under her panties. "Tell me, Olivia. Are these pink too?"

I could have simply looked for myself, but I relished the idea of her admitting how she'd thought about this night enough to want to impress me with a new bra and panties. It had a charm unlike anything I'd experienced in so long that I wanted to make it more important than in reality it was.

"Yes," she said quietly before pressing her lips together, like she'd said some terrible word she couldn't take back.

"You're so beautiful. Do you know that?"

Olivia sat there silent with a look of sadness on her face that made me think she didn't believe me when I said she was beautiful. Was that why she was so timid? I imagined some stupid boy years before telling her redheads weren't beautiful. Some frat boy like Stefan who wouldn't know sexy if it was standing right in front of him casually declaring she wasn't pretty enough or not his type because she wasn't blonde or blue eyed.

"Do you believe me, Olivia?"

"Yes."

With the pad of my thumb, I traced the outline of her bottom lip before I leaned down to run my tongue over the seam of her perfectly full mouth. I imagined that mouth around my cock as she took every inch of me, her brown eyes staring up at me as she sucked me off.

If I didn't watch myself, I was going to enjoy this little fantasy thing of ours entirely too much.

Chapter Nine

Olivia

Swallowing hard, I tried to calm the nerves that threatened to overrun me as I sat there listening to Cash talk to me about how beautiful I was. Oh my God, I was in a fantasy room with my boss and one of the owners of Club X, Cassian March!

When Josie and Erin suggested I take advantage of the fantasy perk of my employment at the club, I never really intended to follow their advice. I mean, living out my fantasies, no matter how tame they may have seemed to others, scared me half to death. I was the type of woman whose mind routinely came up with incredible dreams, but they were just that. Dreams. Nothing more, and certainly not meant to be acted upon. It's just that after the night of the Godivas party when Cash and I sat together in a room just like the one we were in now, I realized if I ever wanted to have even the tiniest chance with a man like him, I had to shed my schoolgirl fears and begin living those dreams instead of just enjoying them alone each night.

But I'd never thought I'd be acting them out with the

very man who filled my fantasies night after night for the past three weeks!

Cassian March. Tall, dark, and stunning with blue eyes I saw every time I lay my head on my pillow. His voice slid seductively over my skin with each word he spoke, and now he was telling me he thought I was beautiful.

But why was he here in my fantasy room helping me live out my fantasy of not having control?

His tongue slowly slid into my mouth to tease mine, making my pussy run wet. The man was driving me insane with desire, and I loved every second of it. I hadn't reserved a gold or platinum level fantasy room, so there would be no sex between us. Part of me felt relief at that. If Cash and I ever made love, I didn't want it to be in a room like this one. Another part of me felt disappointed, though. I wanted him now more than ever and to know that this was just some temporary thing between the two of us that would end as soon as we left this room made me sad.

"Olivia, tell me what you want."

His words were a command I was meant to obey, but fear of rejection tore through my brain, making answering impossible. I wanted him. I wanted to feel him as he eased into me while I dug my fingernails into his back. I wanted to experience what it felt like for a man like him to satisfy me like no man had ever done before.

None of those words happened because of that fear that had always crippled me. Instead, I opened my mouth to speak and nothing came out. God, for once, couldn't I be as brave with a man as I'd always been in every other part of my life?

"Don't be afraid. Tell me. What's your fantasy?"

"I...I want to know what it's like to not always have control."

Cash ran his hands up the outside of my thighs to my waist, leaving a trail of heat where his skin touched my clothes. Even through the fabric, his touch thrilled my body. He leaned in toward me, and I felt his warm breath against my cheek. "No, I mean what do you really want?"

Even though I couldn't see him looking at me, I felt his stare as he waited to hear what my true fantasy was. Closing my eyes behind the blindfold, I prayed that once the words left my mouth that I wouldn't be left humiliated and alone in that room with only my regret and shame.

Swallowing hard, I said the truest words I'd ever spoken. "I want to experience what it's like to give myself to someone completely. No fear. No hesitation. No holding back."

They came out in a rush, like my brain had rehearsed the answer so many times and my mouth and tongue finally rejoiced in the opportunity to say the words out loud. Cash said nothing for what seemed like forever, and I couldn't help but feel utterly foolish. I sat there exposed and vulnerable, my shame growing with each moment that ticked by until I felt like it would smother me. Somehow, even the fact that I couldn't see his reaction made things worse as I was left to imagine the cold look in his eyes as he silently judged me. I was everything I'd ever feared.

Pathetic.

Then he spoke and his words made every one of my fears disappear.

"I want to give that to you. You deserve to feel all that and more, Olivia."

The way his voice dropped to a deep whisper when he said my name made an ache throb in my lower abdomen like an emptiness existed there that only he could fill. I squeezed my thighs together, but that only made the ache more acute, and an involuntary moan escaped my throat.

Never before had I been so aroused by merely being in a man's presence. He'd only kissed me a few times that night and said so little, but he could have commanded me to fulfill his wildest dreams at that moment and I would have without hesitation.

He slipped my bra strap back onto my shoulder and covered it with my dress. Gently, he brushed his lips against mine and whispered, "Our time is up, but I wanted to tell you my favorite color is black. I hope to see you again here, Olivia."

Pressing his palm to the front of my panties, he slid his finger through the dampness, making me moan as he reached my clit, lingering there far too briefly before he moved his hand away. It was all I could do to stammer out, "Yes," but he was already moving toward the door.

I heard him turn the door knob and stop as he pulled the door open. Angling my body toward the sound, I heard him say, "And Olivia, don't ever believe you aren't beautiful. There's nothing wrong with you. Don't ever forget that."

The door closed with a click, and I ripped off my blindfold to look around at the room in an effort to convince myself that it all had really happened. I'd just spent time with the man of my dreams, and he wanted to see me here again.

I needed to go shopping for a black bra and panties.

* * *

Josie stood next to me as I stared up at the wall of bras, unsure which one would be the right bra for my next Friday night fantasy date. Date. Yeah, that's how I'd begun to think of my time with Cash on the top floor of Club X. It might not have been exactly correct to call our time together dates, but that's what I was going with.

I hadn't told Josie or Erin what I'd been up to with Cash, so my sudden interest in lingerie seemed odd, at best. Josie must have been a descendent of some world class detective because we hadn't been in Victoria's Secret not five minutes before she began asking questions.

"A black bra? That's not really your style, Liv. What's going on?"

Twisting my face into a disgusted expression, I rolled my eyes. "Thanks for always reminding me that I'm your Well On My Way To Being An Old Maid friend. I can't tell you how much I appreciate it."

"That's not what I meant, and you know it. It's just that any time a person begins to act out of character, her friends should take notice."

"Thank you, Miss Marple."

Josie arched one eyebrow in her usual fashion when I said something she found odd. "Not an Old Maid? Who says Miss Marple these days? If I'm any detective, it's Beckett from Castle."

"Thanks, Detective Beckett."

"You're welcome. Now what's up with the new bra? Who's checking out these undergarments?"

"Undergarments?"

Josie's gorgeous smile spread across her lips. "I wanted to use a term you'd be familiar with. See? I'm here for you."

Turning back to face the wall of bras once again, I stared up at the assortment of black ones. Some would give me cleavage a man could get lost in, while others seemed to have tiny details to make any sex partner happy. Or so I imagined since I couldn't figure out why a teardrop shaped faux crystal would be hanging between my boobs.

"Well, here for you, which one should I pick?"

Josie looked up at the choices and pointed to one of the deep cleavage bras. "That should make your 34Bs look pretty good. What do you think?"

"I think I might never see my toes again."

Her head swiveled left and then right, and she pointed at a black lacy one. "What about that? Lace is very sexy. Just ask Miss Marple with the lace doilies."

Sighing, I shook my head. "No lace then. Next!"

Josie leaned in next to me and said in my ear, "I might be more helpful if I knew why this sudden interest in black bras."

Something inside me made me want to share my secret with someone, so very quietly I said, "I've been meeting Cassian March every Friday night in a fantasy room at Club X."

"Shut the fuck up!" she announced to everyone within earshot.

I looked around, horrified that someone might have heard her. A middle-aged mother with her young daughter checking out the table of boy shorts shot me a glaring look, and I gave her my best plaintive apology face. Pulling Josie away behind a rack of yoga pants, I worked to stifle her need to know more about my secret. "Josie! Indoor voice!" I whispered.

She looked around and said in her lowest voice, "Shut the fuck up. You're fucking Cassian March? Jesus, Liv, when did this happen and why the hell didn't you tell me before?"

"I took your advice and reserved a fantasy room. Nothing big. I just said I wanted to experience what it was like not to always be in control. It was probably the most boring fantasy request they'd ever seen."

"Then how the hell did you get that incredible piece of man meat to join you?"

I shrugged and shook my head. "I don't know. The first night the man who joined me in the room ordered me not to speak and didn't speak to me, so I didn't know who he was. Then last night I showed up expecting whoever he was not to say a word, but when the man spoke, it was Cash. I couldn't believe it."

"How was he? I have to know if I was right. Please tell me he fucks like a wild stallion. I need to know there are still men out there who know how to take care of a woman."

"I don't know. We didn't do anything like that."

"You didn't have sex with him? Why ever not?"

Sheepishly, I looked away back toward the wall of bras. "He didn't want that, I guess. He never even let on it was him."

Josie walked around me to look at me with eyes wide with surprise. "And you didn't make a move? Again I ask, why ever not?"

"I can't change who I fundamentally am, Josie. I reserved the fantasy room to try to be less inhibited, but Rome wasn't built in a day. Anyway, he seems far more interested in toying with me, now that I think about it."

"Toying with you? What do you mean?"

"He likes to touch me and talk a little, but nothing else. He hasn't even tried to have sex with me."

Josie made a face like she was mulling over everything I'd told her. It wasn't the wild sex story she wanted. "So why buy the new bra and panty set?"

Hesitating for a long moment, I finally admitted the truth. "He told me his favorite color was black."

I waited for Josie's response, expecting her to read me the feminist riot act and accuse me of being little more than a doormat for a man. Instead, she winked and smiled. "The old Livy would have been too afraid to go out and buy his favorite color bra. I think it's pretty cool that this new you is willing to make that effort, even though you aren't sure where this is going. Looks like Rome is well on its way to being built."

"Thanks, Josie."

"I just don't understand one thing. If you knew it was him, why didn't you let him know?"

"I don't know. I got the feeling he might not want me

to know, although I'd know that voice anywhere. He's got to know I know."

"Then why wouldn't he say so?"

"I don't know. Maybe he doesn't want to deal with any expectations I might have outside that room we go to."

I'd tried all last night and all morning not to obsess over that fact, not wanting to believe that our time together meant so little to him. I wanted to think he enjoyed spending those hours with me, even if he didn't want to be with me like that any other time.

"Do you plan to let him know you know it's him?"

"I don't know. There's something sexy about neither one of us admitting we're together. Like it's a secret just between us. We both know but say nothing. I guess I'll just have to play it by ear, but I'm reserving another room this Friday. That I do know."

Josie hugged me tightly and pressed her head to mine. "I'm so loving this Livy Version 2.0, you know that? I say let it ride, and if you get the chance, ride that man like there's no tomorrow."

"I think I will." Reaching up to grab a black silk bra with deep cleavage action, I dangled it in front of Josie's face. "And just in case Cash decides Friday night is the night, I'll be ready."

* * *

It was easy to be all bravado in front of Josie, but once I returned to work on Monday, I found walking the walk and talking the talk so much harder. Cash sat in his office, like he always did, and I worked in mine, sure that we'd have to speak at some point in the day. I dreaded the idea of speaking to him and craved it at the same time.

By four o'clock, I was just about ready to burst from anticipation. I'd always heard people say it's the not knowing that's the worst, and I had to agree with them. All day my mind had been busy creating a million scenarios as to how things would go when we finally spoke, most of which involved him either ignoring me for the rest of the week or worse, acting cold toward me when we finally spoke. Some of the scenarios weren't all bad, though. Every so often, my brain let a romantic idea sneak in among the doomsday ones, and it was those few sweet thoughts that let me stay optimistic.

He stopped in front of my open office door just before five, and I prepared myself to be cool. I may have been showing that on the outside, but my insides were doing the jiggly Jell-O dance. Straightening papers on my desk unnecessarily, I sat up in my chair and lifted my chin, hoping to project an air of confidence.

It was all for nothing, though. Instead of coming in to speak to me, he simply turned toward the club and walked away. Disappointed, I sagged in my chair and closed my eyes, exhausted from the not knowing. Perhaps we wouldn't speak again. That seemed normal for a boss and his assistant. Yeah, right.

"Olivia, is everything all right?"

He said my name just like he had in the fantasy room, his voice low and husky. It curled around me like a tendril of smoke. After a day of waiting, the sound of it thrilled me instantly. Slowly, I opened my eyes and straightened myself behind my desk. "I'm fine. Thank you. Did you need something?"

Cash stared at me intently for a moment and then appeared to relax. "No."

This man, who with just a word could ignite such passion inside me, stood there staring like he was looking right through me and then with a half-hearted smile, turned away and walked back into his office. Rome was burning down around me.

Worse, by Tuesday afternoon, I'd convinced myself that our time together upstairs meant nothing to him. How could it when he never even told me it was him there with me and then practically avoided me for the next two workdays? It could have been a coincidence that he was either in his office with the door closed or out of the building all Monday and Tuesday. It could be. Or it could mean that he didn't want to deal with me after our last time in the fantasy room and he was avoiding me.

I couldn't let the memory of that night go, though, so just before I left on Tuesday night, I made the decision that I'd give it one more try—one more night in the fantasy room with Cash. One more opportunity for him to let me know it was him seducing me. Rather than emailing Kane, I marched myself up the stairs to his domain and found the floor entirely empty. Peeking in room after room, I finally saw him in one at the opposite end of the hallway from the room Cash and I met in sitting behind an enormous, old wooden desk. For the first time since I'd met him, Kane looked comfortable and at home in what I assumed was his office. So different than the first floor offices, it reminded me of the kind of place a private detective worked out of in every old movie I'd ever seen. Much smaller than Cash's and mine, it was dimly lit and cluttered with books and papers. The desk sat at the back of the room away from the door, and other than that piece of furniture, there wasn't much else in there but Kane.

He looked up as I raised my hand to knock on the door, smiling for a moment before his expression turned serious again. "Olivia, what can I do for you?"

So much larger than his half-brothers, Kane always unnerved me but not in the same way Cash did. With Kane, his intimidation wasn't sexual so much as physical. Everything about him seemed hard from his short, cropped hair, to his sharply angular face and enormous frame. Where Cash was lean and cool, Kane was huge and muscular with almost an ice cold way about him. Both men shared the same stunning crystal blue color of their eyes, but Kane's never softened, at least not around me.

I stiffened briefly and then blurted out, "I'd like to reserve another room for this Friday."

"Same as the last two times?" he asked casually as he typed something on his laptop.

I began to say yes, but then I had a thought. It was now or never to be brave, so I answered, "No. I'd like to do a gold level fantasy, if that's allowed." Embarrassed, I lowered my voice and admitted, "I can't afford it if it's not included in my job benefits, though."

He stopped typing and looked up from his keyboard, his face impassive. "No, you can choose any level."

"Okay. Thanks." I turned to head back downstairs and heard him say my name. Stopping short, I turned back. "Yes?"

"Do you want the same person to join you?"

He knew. I saw it in those cold eyes of his he knew I was falling for Cash. I nodded and stood waiting for him to ask me something else, but all he did was smile, and for the first time, it reached all the way up to his eyes and they softened as he looked at me.

I quickly made my way out of the building and out to my car feeling good about my choice. Olivia Version 2.0 was back on track and making progress.

Chapter Ten
Cassian

For reasons even I couldn't defend, I'd avoided Olivia all week, even after Kane's email letting me know she'd reserved another room but at the gold level for Friday night. To be honest, she was driving me to distraction. I didn't want to think about her so much that I got little work done and laid in bed at night tossing and turning over our time together. It didn't matter, though. This was who I was, or at least who I'd been with Rachel. I'd promised myself I'd never be that preoccupied by another living soul again, and there I was nearly obsessed with Olivia after just two nights together in one of my fantasy rooms.

Obsessed. Obsession.

Since Rachel, I'd worked hard to make sure I never became that again. A long line of women I kept around solely for the purpose of sex was supposed to help me avoid becoming this man again. I didn't want to be this way. Who would? What man would want to become so focused on a woman when the ending was never in doubt?

Rachel had taught me that lesson well. Devoting yourself to one woman—trusting your heart to her even when all the signs said you shouldn't—was a mistake I never wanted to make again. Until Olivia, no woman had given me any reason to doubt I'd be able to keep that promise to myself. Each one came and went as I wished. If I enjoyed their company, they stayed around. If they became too clingy or began to act like they felt anything more than I did, I got away quickly.

Women to sleep with were plentiful, the way it should be. They gave me what I wanted, and I did the same for them. No harm, no foul. I wined and dined them, and then I fucked them. Money gave me the power to have who I wanted, and power gave me control.

And control meant I would never again feel the pain of love.

Now Olivia had invaded my thoughts, taking control of my days and nights. And me.

After staring at my bedroom ceiling for nearly an hour, I rolled over and looked at my alarm clock. 4:12. I picked up my cell phone and swiped the screen to get to my contacts. Scrolling through name after name, I finally threw the phone on the bed next to me. I didn't want to be with anyone anyway.

How the hell had Olivia weaved herself into my brain like this? The woman wasn't even my type. Well, that wasn't exactly true. I already loved her reaction to me in our fantasy room. How even my touch brought out a side in her I didn't believe existed underneath that professional woman who worked next to me. Not that I didn't like that part of her too. Olivia was smart, sexy, and gorgeous in ways no woman I'd ever met was.

I covered my eyes with my forearm and tried to push all that out of my mind. Any other night if I couldn't sleep, I'd just call someone and in a few minutes, insomnia would be a thing of the past, replaced by sex. It may not have been sleep, but at least it was better than staring at the ceiling or counting sheep.

Or thinking about some woman I shouldn't even dream of touching. Again.

In less than twenty-four hours, that was exactly what I intended to do. Olivia had upped the ante by reserving a gold fantasy room. She obviously knew it was me and planned on us sleeping together. Every fiber of my being said not to do it. *Don't shit where you eat.* But for every time that maxim repeated in my head, another chimed in to drown it out.

She could be the one.

As if that was something I needed or wanted to hear. There was no such thing as "the one." That was the kind of nonsense romantic comedies traded on to convince women to accept assholes in their lives so they didn't have to remain single. As if being single wasn't the best goddamn part of being an adult.

I could tell myself all that until I was blue in the face, but the thought that Olivia was something special, someone I should want in my life, just wouldn't go away. That didn't mean I had to act like some mopey lovesick boy. All I needed to do was sleep with her and the man I'd worked so hard to become would kick in. She'd be just another one of my conquests and within a few weeks, she'd be out of my system.

That's what had worked with every woman since Rachel, so why wouldn't it work now? Rachel. It hadn't necessarily worked with her. But she was different. It took more than just fucking to get a woman like her out of your system, even after she tore your fucking heart out.

I squeezed my eyes tightly and tried to push out the thoughts I knew were about to parade through my mind, but it was no use. They were there to stay just like they'd been for nearly five years. I'd tried to drink them away. I'd tried to fuck them away. Nothing worked. They were always right there in my brain making sure I never forgot what happened the one time I trusted another person.

My father, the quintessential player, would have a field day with me about this if he was still alive. Married to my mother for nearly twenty years, he fucked around more than any man I'd ever heard of. Fuck, even at the rate Stefan was going, he might never reach my father. Kane's mother was just one of possibly dozens of women he slept with. I remembered catching him with one of them, some cheap waitress at one of his restaurants who thought he was her dream man come to rescue her from a life of drudgery and too little pay. Little did she realize he was just a cheating bastard who believed having a cock gave him carte blanche to sleep with as many woman as he could before he died.

She'd found out like all the rest of them that they were there for his pleasure alone. What they wanted or needed was irrelevant. I'd always admired my father for his ability to have whatever he wanted. That kind of power impressed me growing up. My mother never left him for his cheating, so I thought that's what being a man meant.

Then I met Rachel and my entire world turned upside down. Nineteen and wealthier than I should have been to stay out of trouble, I fell hard for her. Drop dead gorgeous, smart, and manipulative as all fucking hell, I saw nothing but an angel sent from heaven when I looked at her. Long black hair, eyes as dark as onyx, and a desire to please me unlike any other female I'd ever met seduced me to believe she was the one for me.

And for a while she was. Against everyone's advice, I married her a month before I turned twenty-one. She was twenty-four and in love with me. Or so I thought. While I lived each day for her, she had other plans. By the time I realized her idea of love was closer to my father's than mine, it was too late.

I swore that night I found out the truth of who she really was I'd never spend another second thinking about anyone's needs and desires but mine ever again. I'd lived my life by that basic principle, fulfilling my wants and not worrying about others. My cock was happy, and I enjoyed everything life had to offer.

And then Olivia showed up and all those feelings I'd pushed down for so long were back in full force. Nothing like Rachel, she somehow had gotten under my skin and made me want to know her. I never wanted to know any woman any more than how their cunts and mouths felt around my cock. Now that had all changed.

I dreaded the thought of becoming that Cassian again. That man let himself be distracted once and paid dearly for his mistake. Who was I kidding? I was still paying for it and would for a long time coming.

Reaching across the bed, I grabbed my phone and went back to scrolling through my contacts. Cheri. Rachel. Trina. Stopping on Trina's name, I tapped on the picture of her lying naked and spread-eagled across her bed and lifted the phone to my ear. She answered seconds later without a trace of sleepiness in her sultry phone sex voice.

"Cassian March, what's new?"

Stretching my legs, I closed my eyes and let the memory of my last time with Trina run through my mind. Long black hair, perfect tits, and an ass meant to be backed up against a man, she was one hell of a lay. Perfect for what I needed to forget Olivia.

"Trina, just the woman I need tonight."

"Really? You at your place? I can be there in ten."

"Come on over. I'm up."

Moaning into the phone, she purred, "I bet you are. See you in a few."

Throwing the phone back onto the bed, I ran my hand down the front of my silk pajama pants, cupping my already hard cock. With any luck, Trina would do the trick. If not, then maybe I'd have to step up my efforts to get Olivia out of my system.

* * *

"TGIF, big brother! You doing anything interesting tonight?" Stefan asked as he barged into my office and sat down in front of my desk at seven o'clock on Friday night. He had a twinkle in his eye, which told me he thought he was being clever or he'd just gotten laid.

God above, please let it be that he's just being clever.

Crossing my arms, I stared across my desk at his grinning face. "Nothing that would concern you. Shouldn't you be out on the floor getting ready?"

"I have time. I just thought I'd stop in and see my favorite big brother."

"Favorite? You and Kane on the outs again?"

Stefan threw back his head and laughed. "No, but he's only my half big brother. Not blood like us, Cash."

I leveled my gaze on him, suspicious of his motives. Something was going on. "We all have the same father, Stef. We're all blood. So what do you want?"

He licked his lips like an animal about to feast on prey he'd just killed. "A little birdy told me something interesting and I just thought I'd see how true it is."

I hated when he was like this. It made being civil to him almost impossible. In fact, it made me want to knock the annoying fuck right on his ass. Rolling my eyes, I turned back to my laptop. "I don't have time for your games, baby brother. Whatever you heard likely isn't true, and even if it is, it's likely none of your business."

My dismissal of him didn't work. Intent on irritating me, he continued. "I hear that one of my brothers has a new woman in his life."

Attempting to remain cool, I shot him a look intended to make him think I didn't care, but my fingers stilled on my keyboard at what I knew was a reference to Olivia. "Nice to see Kane getting out. I wouldn't fuck with him and whatever woman he has in his life now. If he doesn't kick your nosy ass, she likely will."

Stefan laughed again, this time even louder. "As

much as the idea of Kane's possible girlfriend scares the hell out of me, it's not that brother I'm talking about. I can't believe you'd keep this a secret from me, Cash. I thought we were closer than that."

I stared at him in amazement. Closer than that? And fucking Kane gossiping to Stefan like some kind of schoolgirl. I thought I could trust him. "There's nothing to tell, Stefan. Drop it, and tell Kane to drop it too."

"What's Kane have to do with this?"

Turning away from my computer, I folded my arms across my chest and shot my younger brother a look of disgust. "He's the one who told you, isn't he?"

"No. Rachel told me the other day at the gym. So who is this mystery woman?"

A surge of rage coursed through my veins at the thought of my ex and my brother gossiping about my personal business. And fucking Rachel! Why I ever thought I could trust that conniving bitch was beyond me.

"Go away, Stefan, and don't spend your time believing what my ex has to say," I bit out, barely able to contain my anger at the two of them.

He stood and took a step toward the door before turning around. "I didn't mean anything bad by that, Cash. I just wondered."

"I've told you before, little brother. Don't stick your nose in my business, unless you want to endanger what you have here."

I turned away from Stefan, not wanting him to see how furious I was about him and Rachel going behind my back once again. He closed the door, and I slammed my hand down on the top of my desk. Fucking bitch! And she wondered why I'd never forgiven her.

At midnight, I left my office and scanned the club for any sight of Stefan. I didn't need him ruining Olivia's fantasy, regardless of how I felt about her. I saw him pawing up one of the bartenders behind the bar at the far end of the club, so I quickly headed up the stairs toward the room I knew Olivia would be waiting in, still angry about Stefan's visit hours before. As if our being blood meant a fucking thing to him. He'd betray me again in a heartbeat, but this time if he did, Olivia could be the one to get hurt.

Kane stood at the top of the stairs at his usual perch watching all the action in his area. I had to give it to him. The guy had every chance to fuck dozens of women every night, yet he never did anything to endanger us or the club's reputation. I could trust my half-brother more than the one I'd grown up with.

"Nice to see you again, Cash. It is Friday, though, so not a total surprise." He lowered his voice to a whisper and leaned forward toward me. "By the way, Stefan knows you've been seeing someone. He spent two hours earlier tonight pumping me for information. I didn't tell him anything."

"Thanks, Kane. What room is she in?" I asked, consciously sidestepping any discussion of Stefan and his childish antics.

"Halfway down on the right. You'll see the gold emblem on the door."

Nodding, I left him and headed toward Olivia, strangely needing to see her again like this. After hours of insomnia focused on her, I'd tried to fuck her out of my mind with Trina, but it hadn't worked. All that happened was I had sex with someone as I pretended it was her.

Maybe it was time to admit I wasn't going to get this woman out of my head until I slept with her. It had worked with every other woman after Rachel, so why wouldn't it work with this one? Once she admitted she knew it was me there with her, I'd make my move tonight. If I didn't, I was never going to shake her.

I entered the room and found Olivia there sitting silently on the chair with her blindfold on. Instead of the black skirt and beige blouse I'd seen her in all day, she wore a blue sundress and looked innocent and gentle waiting for me. She turned her head toward me as the door clicked closed but said nothing as I approached her.

"Hello, Olivia," I said quietly as stepped next to her.

"Hello," she whispered breathlessly.

"I'm sorry I'm late."

She lifted her hand to touch my shirt and traced the outline of a single button. Lowering her head, she said quietly, "I thought you might not come tonight."

I took her hand in mine and raised it to my lips. Kissing her fingertips, I watched her bite her lower lip as my tongue grazed her skin. "Tell me what you want, Olivia."

Under her blindfold, her brows knitted. As she sat silently, a frown marred her beautiful mouth. I needed to hear her tell me what she wanted and let me know she knew who was seducing her.

Finally, she sighed deeply and answered in a tentative voice that hit me deep inside in a place I thought I'd hidden away forever. "I want you."

All I had to do was fuck her and all these things that made her so appealing—so charming that I wanted to let myself be someone who could let her in—all of it would disappear. She'd become just another in the long line of women I kept at arm's length, around when I wanted them and absent when I didn't. It was all so simple.

Then why the fuck was I standing there wanting to take her in my arms and make love to her like someone who truly cared?

"I can give you what you want. All you need to do is let yourself go, Olivia. Can you let yourself go and enjoy this thing between us?"

"Yes."

"I want you, Olivia. I want to see you tremble with need as I devour you. I'm going to fuck you so good you won't be able to walk after I'm done with you."

"Yes," she said, her voice full of desire as I leaned in to brush my lips against her ear.

"If I slide my hand under that pretty dress, will my fingers get wet with your juices?"

She whimpered and squeezed her thighs together to ease an ache I knew existed between them. All I had to do was take my cock out and I could have her right there. She was primed.

Her mouth searched for mine, slanting over my lips when she found them. Eagerly, her tongue slid against mine, and I imagined how incredible it would feel moving up and down my cock, her head bobbing sweetly as she sucked me off. I held the back of her head and fisted her hair in my hand, tugging roughly even as she mewed her need into my mouth.

I wanted her. And as much as I hated to admit it, I needed her. I needed her in my bed. In my life.

Olivia's hands burrowed under my shirt, her nails dragging against my chest as she worked to remove the fabric separating the two of us. The shy girl had blossomed into a woman who knew what she wanted. Her hand slid inside my pants and palmed my cock as she sucked the tip of my tongue in a preview of what I knew those lips would feel like wrapped around me.

But still she hadn't told me she knew it was me. She needed to show me she knew. I'd give her one more chance. Breaking our kiss, I leaned back away from her and watched her beautiful face register her confusion. All she had to do was say my name.

"Olivia..."

She moved her hands to touch me, but I was just out of her reach as I waited for her to say the one word I needed to hear. Instead, she said, "Please..."

I left her sitting there, still waiting to hear my name as I closed the door behind me.

CHAPTER ELEVEN

Olivia

The pain of rejection still stung the next morning as I lay in bed going over every moment of my time with Cash, inside and outside that fantasy room. What had I done wrong? Why did he leave me sitting there just as we were about to finally get together?

That man was going to drive me mad.

I heard a pounding on my front door, so I dragged myself from the bed to find Josie and Erin standing in the hallway staring at me with expectant faces. "Where's the fire?"

The two of them pushed past me into my living room and took their places on my sofa. I trudged back in, knowing why they were there. Erin stared at me, obviously waiting for me to say something. I looked around, unsure of what to say, until Josie finally spoke up. "We're here to find out what happened last night. We want the details, and we're not leaving until we get them."

Just as I'd thought. I slunk over to the chair and plopped down onto it. "Nothing. Not a damn thing happened, unless you're a fan of some sexy talk and being left hanging."

"What the fuck? I'm beginning not to like Cassian March much," Josie said with a sneer.

Erin reached over to squeeze my arm. "Are you okay, honey?"

"I'm fine. He didn't hurt me or anything like that. I guess I just was hoping he'd want me like I want him."

"Sweetie, you sound horrible. I hate hearing you like this. I feel a little guilty too since we egged you on to do this," Josie added.

"It's not a big deal, guys."

Their silence as they looked at me with sad eyes made me feel even worse. The new Olivia was just as lame as the old Olivia. Olivia 2.0 had failed miserably in beta testing.

"Liv, it is a big deal, not because of him but because of you," Josie said as she stood and began to pace.

I'd seen her do this before when she was trying to unravel a problem in her mind. Part of me wished she would be able to figure this out so I wouldn't feel so awful about being left high and dry. At least if I could blame it all on something other than being a woman he just didn't want I could feel better.

"You shouldn't feel like this is about you, honey," Josie continued.

"How is it not about me? I took a chance and put myself out there only to be handed a big fat rejection. Sounds like it's all about me."

"He's probably got some baggage you don't know about," Erin said in her usual sweet way. "You know, like he can only be with women who don't intimidate him. That's probably it."

That didn't make me feel any better. I'd spent my entire dating life dealing with the fragile male ego, unsure if I should let boyfriends win at everything from poker to friendly games of softball, so to find out that a man like Cash only wanted some weak thing to hang on his arm would make me feel like there was no chance at any happiness for someone like me.

"I've seen the women he takes out in public, Liv. They're gorgeous, like you, but other than that, they're nobody big in business or law or any other career."

Josie's description of Cash's other women as gorgeous didn't help either. I knew, like everyone else, that there were different types of gorgeous. There was gorgeous your friends said you were, and then there was real gorgeous—the kind that made men fall at a woman's feet.

My feet had never had any attention paid to them.

"So what are you guys saying? I should only put myself out there with men who have no problem with smart women? You might have wanted to mention that before you got me all gung ho on the idea of a fantasy room."

Erin hung her head and quietly said, "In my defense, I never realized you were going for your boss. I just thought you'd have a good time and shed some of your inhibitions. I never would have told you to risk your job."

And there it was, the real problem. I hadn't even thought of that before. I'd been spending all my time nursing my bruised ego when I should have been concerned about losing my job. Fanfuckingtastic.

Josie stopped her pacing across the room and pointed at Erin and me. "Oh, don't even go there. I will get you the finest sexual harassment attorney on the East coast and when he's done with the March brothers, you'll be the owner of Club X. I hear one peep about you losing your job, I'll be on this like white on rice."

I lifted my hand to calm her down. "Relax. Nobody's losing anything. The only harm here is to my ego. I never even let on that I knew it was him."

Erin narrowed her eyes. "Are you saying you never let him know you knew, Liv?"

"Yeah."

"Why?"

"What does it matter?" Josie interjected impatiently as she made her pass by us.

Turning to face Josie as she walked toward the window, Erin said, "It matters because the male ego is fragile. What man wants to think a woman can't even recognize his voice as he's standing there seducing her?"

"He must have known she knew, Erin. The man's not an idiot."

"But Josie, can't you see? He shows up week after week and she never even lets on that she knows the man there with her is the very man she works with every day. That's got to bug him."

"It doesn't matter anyway, guys. He proved he wasn't interested, and that's that."

"I disagree, Liv. I don't think that proves anything."

I looked in amazement at Erin. "Are you suggesting this is my fault?"

"No, not really. What I'm saying is that you may not be seeing the real picture. What if all the guy was looking for was some recognition that he was the one getting you all hot and bothered and all you made it look like was you were into some stranger whose voice you didn't even recognize? I'm just thinking we should try to put ourselves in his place."

Josie began arguing the case against Cash in her usual dogged fashion and pacing even more determinedly, but as Erin's words sunk in, I began to think I'd played this thing with Cash all wrong.

"I never considered that. At first, I didn't show him I knew who he was because I was so surprised, but then as it kept going, I didn't know how to bring it up. My fear of rejection mixed with my insecurity over the whole thing added up to me just never saying anything."

"Liv, I say give him one more chance and let him know you know. Reserve another room and see what happens. If after you show him you know it's him he's still not into you, then fine. His loss. But I think you have to give him a chance."

Erin's suggestion sounded like the scariest thing I'd ever heard. Give him another chance to reject me? Was I a masochist now?

"I don't know. I don't think I can handle him knowing I know and still not wanting me," I said quietly as her idea settled into my brain.

"I agree," Josie chimed in as she took her seat on the couch. "Why give him another opportunity to be a dick? I say walk away."

"But you were the one who told me to take the

chance with him. Now I'm just supposed to give up?"

Neither of my friends said anything for a long time, but finally Josie answered, "I just don't want to see you get hurt, Liv. What if he's playing some kind of game?"

I looked over at Erin, hoping for some counterbalance to Josie's natural suspicious nature. "Nothing to add?"

She shook her head. "I still stand by my hopeful suggestion. Give him one more chance and let him know, but I will add this. If you like him, I think you have to take the chance. The question is, do you like him?"

Looking away, I avoided their gazes as I admitted the truth. "I do like him. It's been a long time since anyone has made me want them as much as Cash. I liked how I felt when we were in the fantasy room. I'd like to see if we can be that outside Club X."

"Then there's your answer. I think even our resident cynic here would agree. Go for it!"

Josie scowled at being called a cynic, but Erin was right about her and my situation. "Okay, I'll give him one more chance, but I'm not waiting until next Friday. I'm sure Kane tells him when I reserve a room, so I'm going to get one for Monday night. Olivia Version 2.0 might be braver, but she's impatient."

"Now that makes me happy," Josie said as she elbowed Erin. "At least if she's going to do it, she's going to do it on her timetable."

I reached over to grab my laptop and logged into my work email. Typing an email to Kane, I let him know I wanted to reserve a gold level fantasy room with the same man at midnight on Monday. Then I clicked Send, and that was that. Now the ball was in Cash's court or soon would be.

Looking up at my friends, I pressed a smile onto my lips even as my insides began to shake from the real fear that Cash really wasn't that into me. "There. It's done."

Josie steepled her fingers and cocked one perfect eyebrow. "Now we wait."

"Thanks for the evil villain thing there," I joked.

"How long does it usually take for Kane to confirm a reservation?" Erin asked.

I looked down at my work email and clicked refresh, sure that he wasn't even awake at that time on a Saturday. "Not long, but he keeps much later hours than I do. He probably just got to bed a couple hours ago."

"Sounds sexy. I need to find a man like that instead of the workaholics I keep dating," Josie said. "He's the scary brother, right? I could handle scary, don't you think?"

"I'd be more worried about him," I said with a chuckle. "All joking aside, now that he doesn't scare the hell out of me every time I see him, I sort of can see what someone would find attractive about Kane. He's got a dark thing about him."

As Erin began asking for more details on Kane, my email dinged and I looked to see his reply. "I was wrong. He's already emailed back. Here's what he has to say. 'Monday night is confirmed for a gold room with all the same components. Reserved for midnight in Room 12. Please follow the same instructions as always.'"

"He's as personal as my credit card company when they explain why they're raising my interest rate, Liv. Does it always sound like that?"

I nodded at Josie's question. "Yeah. Nothing new there. I'm just surprised he replied so soon."

"It's a sign. I say it's a good sign," Erin said in her chipper voice.

"Let's hope so." I steepled my fingers and grinned. "Now we wait."

* * *

I'd never worked late on a Monday night, so I was surprised at how many people actually partied at Club X on the first working day of the week. I'd obviously been missing out on a lot of life. Cash and Stefan had been out of the club all day, only showing up in time for the crowds to appear. I tried to get a sense of Cash, but other than being professional and friendly, I couldn't get a vibe from him.

Just before midnight, I poked my head into his office and found him sitting behind his desk wearing a serious expression. He looked up at me and smiled. "Decided to work the late shift tonight?"

"I did. I have plans tonight, so it worked out."

I watched for any change in his expression, but I saw none. That didn't mean anything, though. It's not like he was anything but cool in the office on most days, so I tried not to read anything into it.

"Have a nice night, Olivia."

"Thanks! See you later."

As I made my way upstairs through the crowds dancing to the techno music, I worked to still my jitters about what I was about to do. It was a big step, but Erin was right. I had to take this chance. I flashed a smile at Kane as I passed him at the top of the stairs and headed to my assigned fantasy room. I'd chosen a very informal sundress for work that day, so all I had to do was tie the blindfold around my head and wait.

Like every other night, my other senses kicked into overdrive once my vision was taken away. Each creak of the floor outside in the hallway put me on edge as I wondered if the noise signaled Cash's arrival. Wiping my sweaty hands on my thighs, I tried to remain calm even as the reality that it was all going to be laid on the line in just minutes hung over my head.

I took a deep breath and let it out. I could do this.

The sound of the door opening made my heart pound, and I sat up straight on the chair, ready for him. He closed the door, and I quickly licked my dry lips, hoping my nervousness didn't leave me with cottonmouth.

I sensed him standing in front of me and took the initiative. It was now or never, but I wanted him to see my eyes when I spoke to him. Sliding the blindfold off my face, I stared in amazement at the man looking down at me.

"Where is Cash?"

"He's not coming."

Leaping off the chair, I angrily threw the blindfold on the couch. "Kane, what the hell is going on? I said I wanted the same person, so why isn't he here?"

Kane simply stared at me, his blue eyes hard. "I don't know, Olivia. I just know he said he wasn't coming."

I couldn't decide if I was hurt, humiliated, or angry. They all mixed together inside me like some emotional stew. Whatever I was feeling, I wanted some damn answers. I deserved better than having his half-brother give me some vague bullshit answer. If Cash didn't want to do this anymore, he damn well better be prepared to tell me himself.

As I stormed down to the first floor, my brain filled with what I wanted to say to him. Who the fuck did he think he was? I wasn't some bimbo plaything he could just throw aside when things got too real. If he didn't want me, he was going to have to be a man about it and tell me to my face.

The crowd nearly parted as I walked through the nightclub. I imagined my expression told people to get the fuck out of my way, but I didn't care. Hell hath no fury like a woman who wanted answers!

I knocked on his office door and didn't even wait for him to invite me in. Throwing the door open, I saw him sitting in front of his laptop as he had been earlier, like leaving me waiting up there in that fantasy room was perfectly okay. I marched up to the front of his desk, placed my palms on the glass top, and when he turned to look at me, stared straight into his eyes. "What the fuck is your problem?"

His eyes flashed emotion for the briefest moment—anger or maybe confusion—and then he was calm again. "Excuse me?"

Leaning toward him, I said even louder, "Excuse me nothing. There's no excuse for what you did."

"Oh, so now you admit you knew it was me all along."

His statement surprised me, and I stood up to my

full height, folding my arms across my chest. "So that's what this is about? Is this a punishment because I didn't show you I knew?"

Cash calmly closed his laptop and pushed his chair back away from his desk. "I don't want to have this conversation, Olivia."

My blood pressure soared, and I felt my heartbeat hammering in my ears. "So that's it? You decide you don't want to tell me what the fuck tonight was about and I'm supposed to be okay with that?"

"You wanted to feel what it was like to not be in control all the time, so no, you don't get to demand any answers from me."

I stood staring at him, stunned at how cold he seemed compared to the man I'd grown to respect at work and the one who'd driven me half out of my mind with desire in our private room. "Are you kidding?"

He stood from his chair and straightened the knot in his black silk tie. "I simply decided I didn't want to continue our time together."

"And that's it? Don't fucking pretend that you didn't enjoy our time together, as you call it."

Cash appeared to consider my words for a moment before he returned to fiddling with his damn tie. Brushing a piece of lint off it, he said, "I don't deny that I enjoyed it. I simply decided I didn't want to continue it."

"You're an asshole, you know that? You knew I liked you, and still you left me sitting there tonight and had your brother tell me you weren't showing up."

I felt tears building up inside me from the anger I couldn't seem to express well enough. His icy answers stopped me dead in my tracks, leaving me unable to tell him exactly how shitty he'd treated me. I watched for any reaction to my words, but all he did was brush off his fucking tie.

"Look at me! Stop fiddling around with your goddamned tie! Is this how you are to people you care about? I know you were into me. I know you liked spending time with me. I'm not stupid, Cash. I may be shy, but I know when someone likes me. Why are you acting like this?"

He looked up from his tie and those stunning blue eyes of his stared directly into mine. "You seem to know my name well enough now, Olivia."

"Don't do this. If I did something to offend you, I didn't mean to. That doesn't mean I deserved to be humiliated upstairs."

Cash ran his hand through his short hair and took a deep breath, as if he was working to keep himself calm. I didn't want him calm. I wanted to know how a man who could be so bothered by me not admitting it was him there with me in that fantasy room could be so cold to me now.

"Good night, Olivia."

Chapter Twelve

Olivia

I wasn't going to let it drop like that. As he stood there behind his desk, I marched around it to stand right in front of him. I wasn't sure what to do next, but I wasn't going to let this go.

"No! I want an answer from you. I know you wanted me like I wanted you, so why are you acting like this?"

He stared down at me with a look that was ice cold and searing hot at the same time. I felt the heat coming off him and knew whatever he was saying wasn't how he truly felt. Moving closer to him, I lowered my voice. "Cash, I just want to understand what's going on."

"I don't think that's what you really want, Olivia." He stepped forward, his chest brushing against my breasts making my nipples squeeze into hardened peaks. Lifting his arm, he pressed his palm against the wall, trapping me, and looked down. "So what do you really want, Olivia?"

"I'm not doing this little show for you. You want me to tell you I want you so you can throw it back in my face because I didn't let you know I knew it was you there with me."

My hands shook at my side as he continued to stare down at me so intently. A tiny lick of fear flickered in the back of my brain at the chance that I didn't know Cassian March as well as I thought I did. I'd always seen him as a calm, almost cool person, not easily ruffled, but maybe that controlled façade was just that—a façade meant to hide something far more violent that lived inside him.

The problem was that even as I shook in fear at what might happen next, part of me had never been more turned on by any other man. I waited for him to react to my refusal to play along like we were still in the fantasy room, unsure what to do but knowing I wanted him more than ever.

"So instead of just going after what you want, you're going to stand there like a little girl angry that you don't get what you want. Is that it, Olivia?"

"Fuck you! Fuck you and your games. I should have just trusted my instincts about you."

He stepped closer, his body pressing full against mine, but never broke his stare into my eyes. Low and deep, he asked, "And what did those instincts tell you?"

My defensiveness kicked into high gear and before I could stop them, the words I knew would hurt him most tumbled out of my mouth. "That the only March who could ever show me a good time is Stefan."

I turned to look away, but I was too slow. His expression morphed into one so full of anger that I instinctively moved to run. He grabbed my arms and pushed me back against the wall as his leg pressed into my thighs just above my knee. In a voice so low I barely heard it, he said, "Then you should have played your game with him, little girl."

Every way I turned, I saw his face. It was the face of betrayal, and I'd done that. I didn't mean to. I'd just lashed out without thinking and before I knew it, those horrible words had come out. Instantly feeling awful, I quietly stammered, "I'm...I'm sorry. I didn't mean..."

"I know what you meant," he bit out. "And you were wrong."

He released his hold on my arms and backed away like I disgusted him. All at once, my fear turned to disappointment at myself and the entire situation. I hadn't wanted this to turn out this way. Suddenly feeling alone even as he stood there in front of me, I reached out and grazed his shirt sleeve with my fingertips, hoping to stop him from leaving.

My touch surprised him, and he looked up at me with eyes so full of intensity I had to believe he cared and there was a chance I could make up for what I'd said. If I didn't do something now, he'd leave and we might never know if there could have been something between us. So I stepped toward him and before I could chicken out, I kissed him full on the lips. It was crazy and stupid and I'd never felt more vulnerable. If this was never going to be anything real between us, at least I'd be able to say I'd conquered my fears and done everything I could to make this happen.

His lips hardened against mine as he fought kissing me, but gradually they softened and he kissed me with a passion he'd never shown me in our fantasy room. I felt like I was burning up as his mouth devoured mine, like at any moment the two of us would be consumed by our desires if we kept this up.

But I didn't want to stop, and if the way his tongue slid over mine was any indication, he didn't want to stop either. My hand clung to the back of his neck, desperate to have him closer. His cologne filled my nose, a powerful male scent that added another layer of need to my desire. He was sensory overload, taking my mind and body to a level I wasn't sure I knew how to handle.

He pushed his hips forward, thrusting so his cock pressed long and hard against the front of my dress. I wanted to feel him—feel his skin against mine instead of through the barrier of our clothing. I knew it might look eager, but I angled my hips upward like he was fucking me, needy for some release after everything I'd felt that night.

"Olivia..." His voice was thick with passion and the promise of more. I wanted more. I wanted it all.

My core clenched at the thought of actually having more from Cash. Just kissing, he overwhelmed me, nearly taking my breath away. He intimidated me and enthralled me, all at the same time. Outside his office door, the rhythm of the music pounded like the beat of my heart, each moment faster and faster as we shared this moment together.

He directed me toward the conference room behind his office, never once breaking his kiss. As the realization of what was about to happen settled into my brain, I opened my eyes to see the man I was about to sleep with. I needed to see he wasn't that cold fuck anymore but the sensual man who'd thrilled me every Friday for the past month.

Cash stopped moving as we entered the other room, and for a moment I worried whatever magical something I'd thought we shared was all in my mind. Crestfallen and confused at the change in momentum, I saw instead that he hadn't stopped to reconsider but to begin undressing. He looked at me seductively with those gorgeous blue eyes as he loosened his tie, sliding it from around his neck before he threw it over one of the high backed chairs that ringed the long, mahogany conference table. My eyes followed it and watched as the black silk tie slid like it was in slow motion down the back of the black leather chair.

He spoke, drawing my attention back to him as he stood there unbuttoning his sapphire blue dress shirt. "Are we still playing the game we started upstairs, Olivia?"

I didn't know how to answer him. This had never been a game to me. At first, it had just been to prove to myself and the girls that I wasn't as boring as they thought—that I could be that sexy woman I'd always wanted to be. Then once I knew it was Cash, our time together began to truly fulfill my fantasy about him. He was sexy and irresistible, the gorgeous public face of the most exclusive club in town, and in that fantasy room, he wanted me, shy and inexperienced Olivia.

Now, I didn't know what this was to either of us. To him, it was likely just another night of sex which he likely had more often than I changed my underwear. To me...to me it was more. I was probably the world's biggest fool, but I wanted it to be the beginning of something bigger than just great sex.

He shrugged out of his shirt, revealing a muscular body filled with tattoos. For a moment, I stood there in shock, amazed that the straight-laced and serious businessman who sat behind that glass desk in his minimalist office hid a totally different person under those tailored dress shirts and thousand dollar suits he wore. His left arm was covered from his shoulder down to his elbow with an intricate dragon in hues of dark and light green with gold eyes, and it looked like another design had been outlined on his right bicep. Visually stunning, those tattoos were nothing compared to the one that stretched in an arc across his broad chest. Black and red letters spelled out the words LUCK HAS NOTHING TO DO WITH IT. I wasn't sure I'd ever seen a more perfectly chosen tattoo on anyone.

I couldn't help but stare, not only at the tattoos and his pierced right nipple but also at how stunning his body was. I'd only ever seen him fully dressed in a suit and tie, and even upstairs as I ran my hands over him in the darkness of that blindfold, I never could have imagined him being so well-built. My eyes traveled down from his toned pecs to a set of abs honed washboard perfect and cut hipbones angling down toward the bulge that still remained hidden beneath his pants.

By the time I realized I hadn't answered his question, he wore nothing from the waist up and was slowly sliding his belt from around his waist. My mind reeling, I mumbled, "No game," as I stood on wobbly legs not sure what to do next. He'd upended all my bravado the moment he'd taken off his shirt and showed me he wasn't that stern March brother, gorgeous but all business. That man had seemed somewhere close to my league. Now as I stared in adulation at the man who stood in front of me, I knew Cassian March was so far out of my league I wasn't even sure we played by the same rules.

Hell, I wasn't even sure we played the same game.

"I like the way you're looking at me, Olivia."

"Why do you say my name all the time?" I asked, immediately feeling awkward as he stepped close to me, running his fingertips over my shoulders.

"Because there's no sweeter sound to the human ear than the sound of one's name."

Jesus, why did everything he said seem so effortlessly sexy? As I stared up at him, unsure of what to say to that, he dipped his head and placed a soft kiss just below my ear. Closing my eyes, I tried to let myself enjoy this moment, but the reality that I didn't know what to do with someone like Cash wouldn't leave my mind.

Sensing my fear, he trailed his tongue up to the shell of my ear and whispered, "Relax."

"I don't...I think..." I wanted to stop, to say that I wasn't the type of woman for him, but all I could do was stammer those few words out.

He lifted his head and cradled my face in his hands. Looking down into my eyes with a gaze so sure, he smiled. "We both need this, maybe even more than we want it."

"But what about work and...and...everything else?" I asked in meek protest, my insecurities raging.

"Don't worry. I promise I won't fire you. Everything

else means nothing. Unless I'm not the man you want?"

"No! That's not what I meant at all." Was it possible he wasn't as confident as I thought?

He slowly ran his tongue along the seam of his lips and smiled. "Then relax, Olivia, because you're the woman I want."

Something in the way he said those words eased whatever doubts lingered inside my brain, and I let a feeling of genuine anticipation take me over. I wanted to know what it felt to sleep with this man. I wanted to believe whatever else I was, I could be that sexy woman with him.

His mouth covered mine in a kiss so sensual it felt like a jolt traveled straight from his tongue to between my legs. From that moment, I was lost. Whatever he wanted, I'd give him. I felt his fingers gently tug my dress off my shoulders and then his strong hands were cupping my breasts. He gently rolled my nipple between his thumb and forefinger, sending waves of pleasure through me. Pushing the dress down my body, I stepped out of it as it hit the floor, barely conscious of the fact that I stood there in just panties and pumps.

Everywhere his fingers touched excited me. I wanted to feel them on the most sensitive parts of my body, bringing me to that sweet edge and over it as I came.

I reached out to touch him, dying to feel what hung between his legs. I'd fantasized about that part of him since the first day I walked into his club, never truly believing I'd find out what he felt like inside me. Tugging his zipper down, I brazenly reached my hand in to gently squeeze his cock in my hand, amazed by its size as I began to stroke him from root to tip. Thick and hot against my palm, he was harder and bigger than any man I'd ever slept with.

"Mmmmm...don't stop," he whispered as the thought of his size began to make me slow my strokes just as my hand touched the swollen tip. "Right there, baby."

Cash buried his hands in my hair, pulling me to him, and I heard him groan again as my thumb grazed the spot just below the head of his cock. He was rock hard yet so silky in my hand, and with each ragged moan I grew more and more confident. There he was standing in front of me loving what *I* was making him feel.

His mouth crushed against mine, and he thrust his tongue into my mouth like it was his to do with as he pleased. Whatever control I thought I had evaporated in a fleeting moment as he transformed from a man receiving pleasure to one taking what he desired. He was intoxicating, and I couldn't get enough of him.

Pushing a chair out of the way, Cash backed me up until I felt the edge of the conference table against the back of my thighs. He wrapped his hands around my waist and picked me up, easing me back onto the cool surface of the polished wood table. My legs hung off the end, rather indelicately leaving me wide open as he remained standing. I looked up at him, hoping he'd soon save me from this embarrassing position.

He unbuttoned his pants and let them drop, revealing no boxers or briefs underneath. Feeling awkward, I instinctively joked, "Commando? I would've never guessed."

I received a smile and moan in return for my moment of humor. "Come here," he groaned as he tugged me toward him. I slid down the table until I felt the crown of his cock press full against my opening. A tiny whimper escaped from my throat at the feel of its thickness. Cash simply smiled and slowly ran his hand up my thigh to stroke my needy clit.

"Relax. You look so beautiful lying there. Let yourself go, Olivia. You're ready."

To prove that to me, he slid his finger inside me with long, slow strokes that sent waves of pleasure tearing through me. I hadn't been touched there is so long I wasn't sure I wouldn't come just from his delicious finger fucking me.

"So fucking tight. God, I want to be inside you."

I gave him a meek smile, but my heart slammed against my chest at the thought of him fitting inside me. Closing my eyes, I heard him tear a condom package open. He planted his hands on both sides of my head and kissed me full on the lips. Then I opened my eyes and saw him staring at me with those blue eyes so intense as he slowly eased into me, each inch filling me so completely that I couldn't imagine being able to take any more.

He sensed how unsure I was and stopped for a moment to lightly massage my sensitive clit, sending more waves of exquisite pleasure through me and allowing me to take more of him. The combination of his finger drawing those tiny circles on my clit and his cock deep inside me filling me like I'd never been filled before thrilled me. I wrapped my legs around his waist to accommodate all of him, feeling deliciously stretched by the time he was fully seated in me.

"You feel so good, Olivia. I promise I'll go slow."

He inched out of me, leaving me empty and missing the feel of him. As he promised, he slid back into my body slowly, ratcheting up my desire and filling me once again. Kissing me hard, Cash grunted into my mouth as the base of his cock stretched my opening. My body ached, a sweet pang forming in the pit of my stomach, making me want more.

He eased out of me again, but I slid my feet down his back and pushed my heels against the base of his spine. "Cash…faster…please…"

Raising himself up above me, he flashed me a look of concern. "You sure? I don't want to hurt you."

Cupping the back of his neck, I pulled him back down to kiss him, my body begging for more. "Yes. Faster. Fuck me faster."

Cash narrowed his eyes in a sexy smoldering look. "Mmmm…such words coming from that pretty mouth of yours. Faster it is."

Rearing back, he slammed his long, thick cock in until he was balls deep inside me and then retreated from my body only to crash into me again. He was power personified, and with every plunge into my willing body, I wanted more.

I wanted to finally live my fantasy of having no control.

Deep inside, a tiny kernel of release began to form, weaving its way through my body as Cash continued to fuck me. His deep grunts filled my ears with every thrust of his cock into my body. He was animalistic and primal, unlike any man I'd ever slept with. I felt small and vulnerable. And out of control. I loved it!

My orgasm curled through my core, a tiny exquisite sensation that grew with each moment. Sliding my hands down over his shoulders, I dug my nails into Cash's back and moaned, "Don't stop. Please don't stop."

His abs and chest, hard and unyielding, slid over my breasts and nearly crushed me under his weight. I lay there helpless underneath him and clutching him like I couldn't get enough of this man. I was already sore, but I never wanted the feeling of him inside me to end.

My body clenched around his thick cock to signal the beginning of my orgasm. Crying out, I struggled to hold on to him as he pistoned into me, grunting his pleasure deep in my ear. "Let yourself go, baby. Let me see you come."

"Ah, God, Cash! Don't stop!"

He watched as I came, his blue eyes focused on me as I bit my lip and scratched down his back like a wild animal. Never before had I come so hard, my thighs shaking violently against his hips as the last of my release wound through me.

But his was yet to come. I felt every muscle in his back tighten and tense. He buried his face in my hair and let out a long deep groan as he buried his cock completely inside me. "Fuck..."

We lay there silently for a long time, still joined together on that conference table as the sounds of the nightclub outside his office began to once again drift in to where we'd just had sex for the first time. It felt secret and sexy. When Cash raised his head, he licked his lips and kissed me, making me feel sexy too.

"Olivia, that was incredible."

I couldn't put my finger on it, but something in the way he said that made me feel open and self-conscious. Forcing a smile, I nodded, hoping he couldn't see my insecurities rearing their ugly heads. Nothing was unsexier than looking needy after sex. Letting my hands drop from their hold on his back, I forced myself to sound confident. "It was."

He slid out of me, and a feeling of emptiness joined my insecurities. I knew it was foolish. What had I expected—the two of us lying there for hours in each other's arms as we drifted off to sleep? We'd just fucked on the table in the Club X conference room. Cuddling wasn't on the menu.

I stood to put my dress back on as he slipped back into his clothes. Watching him, I took in the last sight of his beautiful body, sad to see it covered up with his dress shirt and pants. Unsure of what to say as we finished dressing, I fidgeted with my shoes to avoid feeling any more awkward.

Cash seemed entirely at home with this part of the night, though. Adjusting the knot in his tie, he once again did that brushing off movement he'd done earlier and then looked up at me. "You were incredible, Olivia."

Two mentions of that word made me certain I'd been anything but that, but he pulled me into him and kissed me full on the lips and my insecurities disappeared, at least for the moment.

"I promise I won't act strange tomorrow. I'll be the same stiff Cassian March I've always been."

"Well, you have a reputation to keep."

He laughed at my joke, but I'd subconsciously been referring to his other reputation that now seemed to take up so much of my mind. Cash dated the most beautiful women in town, and undoubtedly, he slept with them too. As he escorted me out to his office, that's all I could think about. Yes, I'd gone into this whole thing with him with my eyes wide open, but now I didn't want to go back to being simply his assistant.

I tried to read his expression to see if he felt anything for me, but there was nothing but that cool man who was all business in front of me now. He kissed me again, soft but without all that passion that had been in his kiss before, and told me he'd see me the next day. We parted ways, boss and assistant once again, no matter how much I wished that wasn't all we were.

Chapter Thirteen

Cassian

I watched Olivia walk out into the nightclub looking sexier than any woman should without a man on her arm. I should have stopped her or taken her home, but I was already regretting having sex with her. Whatever was happening between us couldn't happen, no matter how much I wished it could. I'd thought I'd avoided going any further with her when I left Kane to deal with her. It was a shitty thing to do, but my ego was making the decisions then.

Too fucking bad my ego hadn't stayed in control. Instead, my heart thought it should weigh in on the issue of Olivia and what had just happened proved there would be no fucking her out of my system.

This couldn't happen.

I ran my hand through my hair before I headed out into the club for a drink. Tonight definitely called for a stiff one. Stopping at the end of the bar, I raised my hand to call one of the bartenders over. A tiny blonde, she leaned over to hear my order over the music and give me a full view of her tits. I had to assume Stefan's workers thought this was some way to ensure job security since they acted like this every time I came out into the club for a drink.

"Give me a Makers, neat."

The blonde answered with something I couldn't hear and a smile, and I was thankful the music was so loud. I wasn't in the mood for her thing tonight.

From behind me I heard, "Hey, Cash! I didn't realize you were still here." Stefan. I thought about not answering him, but there was no point in ignoring him. He'd just keep talking. Turning around, I saw him wearing a shit-eating grin and instantly the thought ran through my mind that he'd seen Olivia and me together.

"What's up, Stefan?"

"What are you doing here? I thought you were going home early tonight. Kane mentioned something about it, so I figured you were gone already."

The blonde returned with my drink, and grabbing it, I took a gulp and pressed a smile onto my face. "Just leaving."

"Hey, I thought I saw Olivia leaving a few minutes ago. Maybe you should take it easy on her. Don't want to ride her too hard."

"I have no idea. I didn't see her since this afternoon."

I watched Stefan's expression for any evidence that he knew I was lying, but the blond bartender had caught his eye and he set off to likely cost us more money in legal fees. It was time for me to leave. The club had nothing to offer me other than work, and I wouldn't be able to concentrate much anyway.

By Wednesday, I'd avoided the club for two days and worked from home, even blowing off a charity function for the new bayside park because I just didn't have any interest in seeing the same people as always who traveled the circuit. They'd gotten my check, so it wasn't like the important part of me hadn't shown up.

Standing in front of my window overlooking the bay, I looked out at the action taking place at the end of the day I never saw from my office at the club. As much as I didn't want to admit it, I was avoiding Olivia. The sex had been great. No, great was the wrong word for it. I hadn't enjoyed fucking a woman like that in a long time. Something in the way she'd shed her inhibitions so willingly charmed me. The physical feeling had been off the charts incredible, but even more the emotional connection had made it one of the best nights I'd ever had with a woman.

That was the problem. If all we were was good sex, I'd have been back at work bright and early Tuesday morning at eleven and planning for the next time she and I could revisit that conference room table. I'd be planning on how to wine and dine her around town to get her back to my bed whenever I wanted her. That routine I knew well. Fuck, I'd mastered that routine. Sex meant a connection between my cock and a woman's cunt. No more, no less. Emotions had nothing to do with it. I'd made sure of that since Rachel.

This thing with Olivia smashed all my nonchalant ideas about sex to pieces and left me with no way to know what to do with her. I'd promised myself never to let another woman get close to me again after what happened with Rachel, and now some part of me whispered quietly in my brain that this woman was worth a chance.

My mind went back to the moment I became the man who wanted nothing to do with truly being with a woman again. I remembered it like it happened yesterday. Even now, years later, the events of that night were as vivid and real to me as if I was experiencing them today.

Rachel stood beside me as the line of people filing into the club moved past us, thrilled to be a part of the biggest night all year at Club X—the Halloween Ball, known throughout west Florida as the wildest party around. Nobody did Halloween raunchier or more debauched than my club. I turned to slide my arm around her, the woman I adored as my wife and who tonight was dressed as the sexiest cat I'd ever seen.

But everything about her was the sexiest I'd ever seen. Just a few years older, Rachel had schooled me in so many things about women, and I'd fallen hard and fast for her. I woke every morning more in love than the day before, and as I ended each day deep inside her, I would have given up everything I owned with just a word from her gorgeous mouth.

I was as lost as any man had ever been for a woman he loved.

"Cash, let's go join your brothers at the bar. You don't have to be at the door to greet your customers and the party's about to get started."

Her wish was my command, so we walked over to stand next to Stefan and Kane, my arm instinctively wrapping around her waist as we stopped in front of them. My younger brother was all compliments for her cat costume, and Rachel lapped them up like a kitten with a saucer of milk. Twirling out of my hold, she showed him her tail, shaking her gorgeous ass for him so he could see it move.

"Isn't this costume adorable?" she cooed.

Kane looked away, interested more in the crowd and his job upstairs than my wife. Never his type, they tolerated each other more than anything else. Kane preferred a far more submissive female, something Rachel definitely wasn't. Stefan, on the other hand, enjoyed all women, without exception. To say he didn't discriminate would be an understatement.

Rachel backed up toward Stefan and said, "Feel it! It's fake fur, but it feels so real."

Shooting me a look, Kane raised his eyebrows as Stefan stroked her long, black tail, pulling it up to tickle her neck. "It does feel real."

I pulled her back next to me and leaned close to her to whisper, "I can't wait to use that tail when we get home."

She turned her back on my brothers and ran her hands over my chest. Smiling up at me, she winked. "That's not all I want you to use when we get home."

When she said things like that, I had to fight the urge to steal her away to my office and make love to her right there on my desk. Looking down into her almost black eyes, I smiled. "Do you know how much I love you?"

I closed my eyes to push the memory of that night from my mind. Fixating on it did no good, so there was no point. I couldn't change what happened.

A knock on the front door tore me from my misery, and I opened it to see Olivia standing there still in her work clothes and staring up at me with big eyes. So much for avoiding her. "What are you doing here?"

"It's nice to see you too, Cash. Can I come in?"

Moving off to the side, I nodded. "Sure. Come in."

She walked past me and began looking around my condo as I closed the door. By the time I'd joined her, she was at the window admiring the view. "This is stunning, Cash! I love this view!"

"It's pretty nice. Definitely one of the selling points when I bought the place."

Turning to face me, she rolled her eyes. "Always so understated. If you saw the view I have, you'd say this was stunning."

I forced a smile and nodded, but there was no denying the tension between us. Olivia was an intelligent woman. She knew I'd been avoiding her. How she'd approach that fact remained to be seen.

A sheepish look crossed her face. "I hope you haven't been sick. I noticed you haven't been in work for the last two days."

"No, I'm fine."

A long lull followed my denial and then she said, "That's good. I'd hate to hear you were under the weather."

She stood there with that sweet look on her face, but I knew we couldn't continue this for much longer. "Would you like to sit down?"

"Sure."

We sat down on the very couch where I'd told Rachel I didn't want to see her anymore. Then I'd been unsure how I felt about Olivia but wanted to explore whatever there was between us. Now I knew how I felt, but I couldn't act on it.

She looked around like she needed to memorize my every inch of my home. "You have a really nice place."

This was even worse than I'd imagined our first conversation after the other night would be. We'd spent some incredible time together, and now we sat there exchanging pleasantries like two people waiting for a bus or stuck in a waiting room at a doctor's office.

"Olivia, what are you doing here?"

Taking a deep breath, she let it out slowly and hung her head. "I guess I'm not too slick, am I? I want you to know it took every ounce of courage I possess to come here, so if you're going to tell me you don't even like me enough to talk to me other than at work, I'm not sure I can promise I'm going to handle it well."

I touched my fingertip to her chin to force her to look at me. "I do like you, Olivia, and more than just to talk to you at work."

That smile she so rarely gave me lit up her face. "That's good. I mean, I'm not a fool. I know that the other night probably didn't mean much to you. I know I'm not your usual type of woman you spend time with."

She wasn't wrong. My usual type didn't look like her or act like her, but most of all, they didn't make me feel much of anything. Not that caring about her was any good for either of us. I knew how this would end.

"You're smart and fun, but it's true. You aren't my usual type."

No sooner were the words out of my mouth had I realized I should have said something more romantic. What kind of woman wants to hear she's smart when she's comparing herself physically to other women?

My answer registered on her face in a frown, and she leapt to her feet. "I'm going to leave. This was a mistake. I'm sorry."

I reached out to grab hold of her, but she slid out of my grasp and nearly ran away from me. Chasing after her, I caught her just as she opened the door. Pushing it closed, I tried to find the right words to say. "Don't leave. It's okay."

Still facing the door, she said quietly, "No, it's not okay. I thought that maybe if I came over here you wouldn't want to avoid me anymore. I thought that maybe you liked me like I like you, but the only person doing the liking is me. It's better if I go."

Her voice was so full of sadness that I already regretted every mistake I'd made that had brought me to that point. I didn't want to hurt her. I just couldn't give her what she wanted.

"Olivia, turn around. I want to talk to you."

She sighed and slowly turned around to face me. Staring up at me with big brown eyes so full of fear, she bit her lip nervously. "Okay."

"I liked what happened the other night. I don't want you to think I didn't. But I'm not able to give you what you deserve."

"And what's that?" she asked, her tone defensive.

I struggled to find the right words but then just said the painful truth. "You deserve to be with a man who can at least promise you the future might include something long-term. I can't do that. Not now, anyway."

A look of relief came over her. "That's what you thought? That I wanted you to profess your undying love and commit your life to me? I guess I really do have that good girl thing going on. Cash, I don't expect anything exclusive."

"You don't?"

"No," she said with a smile. "I just hoped we wouldn't have just that one night. I'm not going to deny that I'm definitely attracted to you, and I think you're attracted to me."

She was trying to be brave, but I felt her body tremble. I saw it in her eyes too. She was afraid. Not of me, but at what I might say at any moment to crush all her bravado. I wouldn't do that to her, though. Other women? Yeah. But not Olivia.

I leaned forward to trap her inside my arms. Sliding my thumb over her cheek, I smiled, liking how close we were. "I am definitely attracted to you. I have been since the first day you walked into the club."

"Really?"

Nodding, I tucked her hair behind her ear and dipped my head. "Yeah. Then when Kane told me you'd reserved a room, I decided I'd be the one to be in there with you."

Olivia looked up at me and grinned a sexy smile. "Oh. Was there someone else who was supposed to do that since you're one of the owners, or do you often drop in on female members' fantasies?"

I liked this woman. She was smart and sweet at the same time, and in my experience, those were hard to come by in someone. "Kane wanted to send in one of his guys. I didn't think he was right for the job, though."

"I see." She arched one eyebrow and gave me a

skeptical look. "I have to know something. Were you planning to ever sleep with me in that room?"

Shaking my head, I said, "No."

"Oh. Even when I reserved a gold fantasy?"

I pressed my mouth to hers and kissed her. "No. You're too good to fuck in some generic fantasy room."

"So you did plan to sleep with me then?"

I couldn't stop the smile that spread across my lips. "No."

The hurt was evident all over her face. Her dark eyes narrowed, as if she was in pain, and she said, "Then what the fuck am I doing here? Is this the icy cold Cash from the other night because if it is, he can go fuck..."

Before she said something we might both regret, I stopped her with a hard kiss, my tongue sliding into her mouth as I pushed my hips forward to let her know how excited she'd already gotten me. Her body melted into mine as all her anger and defensiveness faded away. Trailing my lips across her cheek, I gently sunk my teeth into her earlobe before I said, "As for what he can fuck, he's already made his choice."

There was nothing else to say. I wanted her, and I wasn't going to wait or try to fight what I felt for her. I didn't exactly know what I planned to do about all those reasons I shouldn't continue this with Olivia, but I liked how she made me feel. As long as I kept her at arm's length, we'd be fine.

Sliding my hands down her back, I cupped her gorgeous ass and picked her up to carry her over to the couch. I laid her down and eased my fingers under her dress and panties to find her pussy wet and waiting for me. She arched her back to give me a better angle, and I slipped one finger inside her. She was burning up, but I saw her wince as a second finger joined the first. "Is something wrong?"

"No. Just still a little sore," she answered shyly, like she was embarrassed.

I lifted her dress and peeled off her panties. Bared to me, her pussy was perfect but a little too pink. I'd been a little too rough our first time. Looking up, I ran my tongue over her wet slit and gently sucked her clit between my lips. "I don't want to hurt you, so we're going to have to figure out a Plan B."

"I'm fine. I'm sure once we get started, things will ease up a bit."

"I've got a better idea."

I spread her open with my fingers and lightly licked straight up the middle of her pussy. Olivia squirmed, but I knew it wasn't because I was hurting her. Lifting my head, I asked, "What's wrong?"

That gentle pink blush that told me when she was feeling bashful spread across her face. "I feel...just really exposed here in the middle of your living room in front of that big window..." Her voice trailed off as the blush deepened, but I knew it wasn't my neighbors that concerned her.

Placing a tiny kiss on her clit, I said, "Your pussy is beautiful—pink and perfect and evidence that you're a natural redhead. There's no reason to be embarrassed."

"I know, but I..." She stopped talking and bit her lip as I ran my finger down to her opening.

"Shhh. No more talking. The next sound I want to

hear from your lips is you crying out in complete pleasure when I make you come all over my face. Understand?"

With a sly smile, she bit her lower lip and moaned, "Uh-huh."

I lashed my tongue over her tender skin, first slowly and then faster as the tension built in her body, my fingers gently fucking her tight pussy. The sound of her tiny coos each time the tip of my tongue slid over her swollen clit made my cock harden until it stood like steel in my pants. I wanted to be inside her, but I could wait.

Her cunt tightened around my fingers, and she cried out my name, scratching my shoulders as her orgasm tore through her. I hadn't gone down on a woman in years. That wasn't part of my routine. I'd missed looking up and seeing pure pleasure wash over a woman's face as my mouth took her over the edge into that place of oblivion, the feel of her hands urging me to stay between her legs as she screamed for more.

I slowed my tongue to suck her clit gently between my lips while her thighs trembled against the sides of my head, coaxing a second orgasm from her even more powerful than the first. So responsive to my mouth's manipulations, she pulled the back of my head into her as she whimpered her pleas for me not to stop. Barely able to breathe except to take in her delicious scent, I stayed there as much for myself as for her.

When I finally sat back on my heels, she still had her eyes closed and that perfect orgasm expression all over her face. Of all the looks a woman could give, that was one of the best. Looking down at me, she gave me a tiny smile. "I don't think I have any bones left. That was incredible, Cash."

Running my hands up her legs, I licked my lips to taste her once again. "My pleasure."

Her gaze traveled to my still rock hard cock, and she slid off the couch to join me on the floor. "Turnabout's fair play, though. Don't you think?"

I shrugged out of my shirt and pants and sat back down. "Definitely."

She wrapped her hand around the base of my cock and slid her mouth over the tip, sending waves of pleasure rippling up and down my shaft. I closed my eyes and leaned back against the cushions as she worked to suck all of me into her mouth, her hands stroking the last few inches as she slid back up to the top to begin all over again.

My cock slid from her mouth, and I opened my eyes to see her looking up at me. "God, I want you inside me."

"You sure?"

"Yeah."

She didn't have to say it twice. I watched as she slipped out of her dress, and pointing to the bedroom, I told her where to find a condom and watched her jog into my room to get one. Fuck, she had a great body!

Returning with a pack of six, she dangled them in front of me as she sat down next to me. With a grin, she ripped one off and handed it to me. "Just in case one's not enough."

I slipped it on and pulled her onto my lap. "Planning on making sure I'm sore this time?"

"As I said, turnabout's fair play."

"Come here," I said as I pulled her mouth toward mine. Sexy and sweet, I wanted to be inside her feeling her body clinging to me as I fucked her until both of us came harder than ever before. I positioned my cock at her opening, sliding the pad of my thumb over her eager pussy to her clit. Still wet from when my mouth had fucked her, she was ready for my cock.

She moved slowly, timid and fearful now that the full length of me began to slide into her. I fought the urge to lift my hips to thrust in balls deep knowing that I needed her to set the pace so I didn't hurt her already sore body. Each inch more into her cunt felt better than the last until I was fully seated in her, and a soft whimper escaped her lips as we joined completely.

My thumb rubbed tiny circles on her clit while my hand on her waist kept her still, and she looked down at where my cock spread her wide open. "I was worried it might hurt, but it feels so fucking good. I can't stand it. Please let me move."

"Tell me what you want, Olivia."

She tried to move, but my hand pressed hard against her hip stopped her. "I want to ride your cock. Please…"

"Your cunt's so tight. I'm afraid I might hurt you."

Olivia leaned toward me, capturing my lower lip in between her teeth. Biting gently, she moaned, "I don't care. Fuck me. Fuck me hard."

Lifting my hand from her hip, I cradled the back of her head and tugged her hair. "Ride my cock, baby. Let yourself go."

She raised herself up on her knees slowly and lowered herself back down onto me, rolling her hips and arching her back. I watched her cunt swallow my cock, her lips spreading wide every time she took all of me inside her. Up and down, her body sent strings of sensation over my shaft, making me wish she'd move faster. I grabbed her hips hard and directed her fucking me, guiding the pace of our pleasure. She liked the feel of me controlling her, even as I pushed her faster and faster and risked the danger of hurting her. The feeling of my cock fucking her hard made me forget how easily she might bruise.

Her mouth pressed hard against mine, devouring my kiss as she begged me to give her what she so desperately wanted. My thighs ached from her slamming down on them, but I didn't care. Each of us raced toward that one sublime point where our bodies would explode in release. We both panted and tugged at one another's hair, forgetting anything else but the need to come.

"Oh, God...Cash..." she cried as her nails dragged across the back of my neck. "I'm so close..."

My mouth pressed to her face as her cheek skidded over my lips with every time she bucked up and down on my lap, I groaned, "Come for me. I want to feel that pretty cunt squeeze my cock when you come hard all over me."

My voice rasped from panting, and Olivia moaned in my ear, "Harder...faster...it's right there..."

I lifted my hips from the floor and rammed into her one last time and then she came, her body falling hard against mine as every inch of her shook from her orgasm. She didn't stop riding me, though, and all it took was the feel of her cunt contracting around me again and again to take me over the edge.

We sat there still joined together for a long time recovering from the sweet torture we'd inflicted on one another. My fingers slowly moved up and down on her back feeling the light film of perspiration that covered her skin, and Olivia still clutched the back of my neck now less forcefully than just a few minutes before.

"I'm not going to be able to walk out of here," she whispered in my ear. "I don't think my legs work anymore."

"You'll just have to stay then."

After the words came out of my mouth, I couldn't believe I'd said that. I hadn't offered to let a woman stay at my place for years, and there I was telling Olivia she'd have to.

She leaned back and gave me a skeptical look. "That's the post fuck haze talking, Cash. I don't expect you to set me up here. Just give me a few minutes to regain my ability to walk."

I wanted to say even though I hadn't meant she should move in I didn't want her to go. I didn't say it, though, preferring to stay silent instead of risking offering something I couldn't give her.

Chapter Fourteen

Olivia

By the time I got home, it was nearly ten and Josie and Erin were waiting for me. Gossip knows no time limits, and sex gossip trumped even a good night's sleep. Camped out on my doorstep, they sprang into action when they saw me hit the top of the stairs outside my apartment. As much as my legs were killing me and all I wanted to do was crawl into bed to hopefully have sexy dreams of Cash, I knew that would have to wait a little longer.

"Where have you been? We've been waiting here for nearly an hour. Remember we were supposed to all go out for drinks?" Josie asked as she scanned my frame looking for any clue as to my recent whereabouts.

"I'm sorry. I didn't forget. The time just got away me, I guess."

Erin narrowed her eyes to slits and stared directly into my eyes. "Olivia Lucas, you're lying to us. What's going on?"

I took my keys out and unlocked my door, readying myself for my friends' inquisition since I hadn't told them

I'd even had sex with Cash yet. Stepping into my apartment, I made my way to the living room to sit down and rest my legs.

Josie and Erin followed silently and took their seats on my couch to hear my answer. I took a deep breath and just said it. "I had sex with Cash."

"When?" Josie asked.

"Tonight?" Erin added.

"Yes, but the first time was Monday night."

Josie crossed her arms. "You told us the fantasy thing didn't pan out because he was out of work sick."

"I lied. It didn't work out like I planned. He didn't show up so I marched myself downstairs to his office and demanded to know why he'd stood me up. One thing led to another, and before I knew it, we were on the conference room table having sex."

"Shut the fuck up! And you kept this to yourself since Monday night?" Josie asked in amazement.

She knew me all too well. Normally, I would have told them everything, but something about how Cash and I got together that night made me hold back. I didn't know if it was shame or fear that they'd ask about us ever getting together again when I knew full well he was avoiding me, but part of me couldn't tell them if it had been just a one night thing.

"It's no big deal. Two consenting adults having sex happens all the time," I answered, trying to sound nonchalant.

"Don't give me that bullshit, Liv. You like him. It is a big deal," Josie said to show me she saw right through my lies.

Erin waved Josie's developing interrogation aside. "Don't give her a hard time. Liv, if you don't want to give us the details, it's okay. I mean, we never asked Josie about how it was with Sebastian."

Josie's expression twisted into one of disbelief that made me chuckle. "Are you kidding me? Was there any point at which you didn't know how it was with him and me? It was the only time in my life that public displays of affection were the norm. We almost fucked a dozen times right in front of you two, so don't give her any reason to keep hush hush about this thing with Cassian March." Turning back to face me, she leveled her stare at me like the investigator she was. "Spill it or we'll get it out of you one way or another."

"It's not a big deal, Josie. We had sex. It was pretty incredible. Tonight I went over to his house and we had sex again."

"So are you two dating?" Erin asked, her eyes wide with curiosity.

I didn't know how to answer that. So far, all we'd done was have the most phenomenal sex of my life. He had been avoiding me after our first time together, which wasn't a good thing, but that had been because he thought I expected him to court me like I was some maiden who expected a man to marry her once he slept with her. The truth was I liked the idea of taking it slow with Cash, but for an entirely different reason than he did. His was fear of commitment. Mine was fear of him, or more accurately, my fear of falling too hard for him.

"I'm not sure what we're doing. I know I like him and find him unbelievably attractive. I think he feels something similar for me. Other than that, I can't say."

Erin appeared satisfied with that answer. Josie, on the other hand, had already moved on to the juicier details of my time with Cash. "So, what's he like? Was I right? Is he incredible in bed?"

I tried not to smile at her description of him, but I couldn't stop myself. The man was a sex god. Not that I wanted to tell them that, though. For the first time ever, I wanted to keep that part all to myself. So instead, I rolled my eyes and said, "I'll say this. The guy isn't all just good looks and money, okay?"

"I knew it! I knew beneath those expensive suits was a guy who knew how to take care of a woman. This is so great! You need this, honey. This is exactly what you've been missing in life. I knew that job was going to be good for you."

Erin reached over and squeezed my forearm. "I think as long as you're having a good time, that's good. You know this is going to kill Jake, though, don't you?"

"He doesn't feel that way about me, Erin. We're just friends."

"And anyway, he knows he's always been out of his league with Liv," Josie added. "Money isn't everything, Erin."

"I know. I'm just saying I think he's always liked Liv more than just friends. The last time I saw him the first thing he asked about was her and how she was faring at her new job at Club X."

"Well, for someone who's supposed to like me, he sure has an odd way of showing it. I called him after I got the job to say thanks for paving the way, and he barely had a minute to talk," I said, remembering how abrupt he'd been with me that day on the phone.

"He's been a dick ever since his stepmother began telling his father he needs to be doing something more with his life than spending their money. From what I hear, stepmama has been pressing pretty hard to make Jakey get a job and stop mooching off his family," Josie said with a grin, displaying the dislike she had for him.

"Oh, Josie. You always want to find the negative in Jake. He's had it tough since his father remarried," Erin said in his defense, as she always did.

"I think somewhere between the hate you have for him because you used to date him a million years ago, Josie, and the sympathy you have for him because you remember the boy he was in high school, Erin, is where I stand on Jake. He's a good friend, and we all had a good time back in the day. Those days are long gone, though. It might be time for him to grow up."

"Maybe, but I still think he's going to be heartbroken over this, Liv," Erin said with a slight frown.

Josie rolled her eyes. "Forget him. I want to know more about Cassian March. You've obviously decided to go military silence on us regarding the sex, which makes me think he must be off the charts fucking good, but you need to be giving me something before I leave here tonight. I'm a single woman who works way too much. I'm living vicariously through you these days. Don't let me down."

Erin's mouth hung open in shock. "Josie!"

"It's okay. How about this? I'll tell you one of my favorite things about him. Sound good?"

They both nodded, and I tried to decide what I liked best about Cash. There was no denying he was gorgeous. Those blue eyes made me want to melt when he looked at me. And that body. Oh, that body! And those tattoos. And the piercing. The list was never ending. I'd never been with a man so incredibly sexy. I had to choose something, but telling them about those things didn't feel right. They weren't going to let me get away with saying his business acumen made me hot, though.

"He's got this way of talking dirty that makes my toes curl."

Josie's eyes lit up. "That's the first time I've ever heard you say something like that about a man, you know that? I expected you to say you liked his clothes or something about his eyes. That you went with something so sexy tells me he's good for you, Liv."

Erin agreed. "I think so too. Just remember as long as you're happy, we're happy."

"I am. It's nothing serious, and I'm okay with that, guys." Standing from my chair, I hugged the two of them as I led them to the door. "Now let me get some sleep because I have work tomorrow like you two. I'll call you."

"Night, honey," Erin said as she hugged me again. "Call me before the weekend, okay?"

"Got it."

Josie waited for Erin to begin walking down the stairs and whispered, "By the way, you're walking like you just got off a horse. He must be one hell of a man in that department too."

Heat rushed to my cheeks in an embarrassed blush and I rolled my eyes, but the evidence was there. Josie grinned like a Cheshire cat. "I love it! Call me. I won't promise not to want details, but call me anyway."

"You bet. Be careful. I'll talk to you later this week."

Minutes later, I climbed into bed and stretched my aching legs. Even now, hours later, it still felt like he was inside me, stretching me as we fucked. Sometimes even pain was a good thing.

* * *

Dressed in black pants and a light green shirt that only served to make his dark hair look almost black, Cash stood in the doorway to my office just after six on Friday afternoon looking like he had a secret he couldn't wait to tell someone.

In that sexy voice that made an ache form in the pit of my stomach, he asked, "What are you doing around eight tonight?"

In truth, I'd been at my desk since eleven that morning working hard on the end of the quarter numbers and felt pretty tired. However, the sparkle in his eyes told me if I could just push past that, I might find something great on the other side. "I don't know. I've been here since before noon, so I was probably just going to go home at seven. Do you need me for something?"

He walked in and closed the door before coming around my desk to stand behind me. Bending down, he rested his hands on my shoulders, making my body instantly come alive, and whispered, "I feel like taking a drive. Want to come with me?"

I closed my eyes and leaned back against him, loving the feel of his muscular chest. "Sure. Where are we going?"

"Just down the coast. I'll meet you outside the club at eight sharp."

His refusal to walk out with me past Stefan and the rest of the employees who'd be in the club at that time stung, but I quickly reminded myself that we weren't officially a couple. We'd gotten together once more after that night at his condo, and I had a feeling he wanted more, but so far we were just two people having mind-blowing sex and I wasn't interested in spoiling that by putting restrictions on it.

I tilted my head back to look up at him. "How will I know where you are?" I joked.

Flashing me a stunning smile, he kissed me and said, "I'll be the man in the black car waiting for the gorgeous redhead."

"Okay, then. I'll be the woman looking for the hot guy in a black car. See you at eight."

"Good. By the way, I've been hard since I decided on this, so you've been warned. If we don't make it all the way to our destination, I'm more than prepared to fuck you in the car."

He walked away before I could answer, but it wouldn't have mattered. I had no words when he said things like that. The man had the ability to make me wet just with a few really hot words. I could definitely get used to that.

The next hour and a half flew by in a blur as I spent the time fantasizing about where Cash might be taking me. Needless to say, my reports didn't get done, but for one of the first times in my adult life, I didn't care that I hadn't taken care of business. It felt good to venture off the straight and narrow.

Pushing my chair out from my desk, I looked down at my outfit and shook my head. My black pencil skirt and pink silk blouse weren't exactly the look I would have chosen for a night out with Cash, but I didn't have other clothes with me and something told me that the man who'd practically promised me he wouldn't want to wait until we got to wherever we were going to have sex wasn't going to want to stop so I could slip into something more comfortable.

I straightened my look and closing the door to my office glanced over at Cash's and saw his door already closed. The club was still quiet, so I headed toward the front door and whatever he had planned for me. Just before I hit the exit, I heard someone call my name and turned to see Stefan standing there with a questioning look on his face.

"Taking off early tonight? Don't you usually stay late on Fridays?"

He'd obviously noticed my Friday night schedule for the past month. Struggling to keep my expression as emotionless as possible, I shook my head. "No, I have plans tonight. Have a good one, Stefan."

"You too! Hey, by the way, is Cash still back in his office?"

"I don't know. I didn't notice before I left. I guess I was preoccupied. Gotta go. Have a good night."

Hurrying out of the door, I hoped I hadn't been as obvious as I felt in front of Stefan. He definitely seemed suspicious, but maybe it was all in my head. Whether it was or not, I'd deal with that on Monday.

I looked up and down the street outside the club but saw no black car. Was I early? I stood there for a moment and then my phone rang. I didn't recognize the number but answered it anyway. "Hello?"

A voice like silk moaned into the phone and said, "You look so fucking hot. Look down the block to your right."

I turned my head and there was Cash leaning against a black sports car looking sexier than I thought a man could. Gone were the dress pants and shirt, replaced by jeans and a black T-shirt. From a distance, he sort of looked like Stefan, strangely enough.

"I see a black car, but I don't know that man. The Cash I know is always in a suit. This guy looks pretty relaxed and casual."

"Smart ass. I see a very hot redhead. Know her? She's supposed to come with me."

I chuckled and pretended to look around. "I don't see her. Looks like you're stuck with me."

"I'll be waiting."

I started down the block to where he was parked. "You're making me walk to you?"

"Mmmm...I like watching you walk. See you in a minute."

He was still leaning against the side of his car when I finally reached him, and I saw by the smile he wore that he was enjoying himself. "Enjoy the show?"

Sliding his arms around me, he cupped my ass through my skirt and pressed a kiss just below my ear. "Immensely. Let's go."

"Where are we going?"

Tapping me lightly on the ass, he winked. "It's a surprise. Now get in the car and we can get out of here."

"What kind of car is this? It's gorgeous!" I asked as he opened the passenger door for me.

"A Maserati GranTurismo. Wait until you see how it rides."

We drove for about two hours in the most luxurious car I'd ever been in, and for the first time, we talked—really talked. Always guarded, Cash played his cards close to the vest, but I learned more about how Kane fit into the March brothers' business and became an equal partner in Club X. I sensed Cash liked his half-brother more than his own brother and stayed away from any questions about Stefan, sure from my time working at the club that there was some bad blood between them. To be honest, I really didn't want to ask because I didn't want to find out the man I was falling for had done something terrible to his own flesh and blood. For at least the time being, I wanted to believe Cash was the great guy I'd built him up to be.

I also learned that Cash could be really funny when he let himself be. Not that I didn't really like the man he was at work, but to see him smile and laugh instead of trying to be professional all the time made me even crazier about him.

We were so busy talking and having a good time that I didn't realize where we'd driven to. When he finally stopped the car in front of a beachside house, I stared out in confusion. A whitewashed cottage didn't seem like his style.

"Is this yours?"

A slow smile spread across his lips. "Yeah."

"It doesn't seem like you. I guess I just associate you with the only other places I've seen you in. You know, your office and condo are clean, minimalist. This seems very…quaint."

"It is. It was my father's and it transferred to me when he died."

"Oh. I didn't mean to…" Leave it to me to make a comment on something that brought up a dead relative. Smooth.

He gave me a gentle smile to let me know my comment hadn't ruined anything. "It's okay. Let's go in."

The inside of the cottage looked nothing like I'd expected it to. I'd assumed the beachy exterior would lead to a place with lots of white wood, seashells, and wicker, but I couldn't have been more mistaken. While the house may have been that quaint cottage at one time, Cash's style had very much been imprinted on the design and instead of feeling like I stood mere feet away from the beach, it felt like I was back in his condo.

"It's not much, but I like to use it to get away sometimes," he explained as he headed toward the kitchen.

I heard his keys land on the granite countertop as I looked around at yet another place Cassian March owned. Sleek lines, expensive furnishings, and what I suspected were fine pieces of art filled out the cream and black rooms. Turning toward the kitchen, I saw him pouring us drinks. "Again with the understatement. I think this place is a lot more than not much."

"Come. Have a drink. That was a long ride."

Even now, dressed so casually and standing there in this beach cottage, Cash took up all the space in the room and made me feel slightly out of place in my work clothes that made me seem more like his secretary than his lover or girlfriend, whichever I was. I took the glass he offered and watched him lift his in a toast.

"To always being surprised, Olivia."

He downed a healthy gulp of whiskey while I inhaled the strong smell, afraid if I drank even a little without eating that I'd lose my head. "I'm not a big fan of surprises, to be honest."

Lifting his glass again, he smiled in a way that made my core clench in need. "Then to me changing your mind."

Something about him had changed. It may have been almost imperceptible, but he wasn't the person who'd smiled and laughed with me as we drove there. Had I done something? I didn't know. All I knew was Cash had reverted back to that man he'd usually been around me—cool and sexy, but closed off just enough to keep me at arm's length.

CHAPTER FIFTEEN
Cassian

I slowly opened my eyes, vaguely aware that someone lay next to me. But that was impossible. I never spent the entire night with anyone. Not for a long time anyway. My eyes fully open, I looked over to my right and saw a flash of red hair against the white pillowcase next to mine.

Olivia.

What the fuck was I doing? Instead of keeping my distance like I'd planned, I'd ended up sleeping with her not once but twice. Then instead of keeping her at arm's length, I'd been foolish enough to bring her here on some kind of mini-vacation, like we were goddamned dating. This couldn't happen, so why was I being so stupid?

It's not that I didn't want to be with her. I just couldn't. Period. Everything I was, everything I'd done in my life made it so. Why my cock and his brand new best friend my heart were having a hard time dealing with that fact escaped me. So now those two had entirely disregarded what my brain had been saying since the day she walked into my life and we'd all ended up at the beach house on Gasparilla Island like she and I were some couple in love who wanted to get away from it all.

Just one problem. There was no getting away from who I was or all the shittiness I brought into this thing between us, whatever it was.

She was so close, though. I wanted to reach out and run my fingertips over her skin to remember how she'd felt in my arms just hours before. I wanted to be the man who'd thought it was such a grand idea to bring her here instead of the man I really was.

Closing my eyes, I worked to push all that from my mind. I couldn't change the past or what that past had made me, no matter how much I wanted to. I didn't want to let her go, though. It was selfish and thoughtless, but I wanted the kind of sweetness she gave my life. That I didn't deserve an ounce of it didn't change the fact that I didn't want to let her go.

She rolled over and looked at me with a cute, sleepy look. "What time is it?"

"I don't know. Sun's up, but I don't think it's too late."

Pushing the hair out of her eyes, she smiled shyly. "I'd have thought you'd be an eye on your watch kind of guy."

Smiling, I wondered why I wasn't at that moment. My watch sat on the nightstand, but I didn't want to know what time it was. I didn't want to think about anything but lying there with her, no matter how wrong that was.

"I usually am. I guess this place just has that kind of effect on me," I lied.

Propping her head up on one hand, she asked, "Do you come here a lot?"

I shook my head, trying to remember when I'd last slept in this bed with a woman. Suddenly, the memory of that last time flooded my mind. Exactly one week before Rachel and I separated. "No, not really," I lied again.

Olivia sensed something was wrong and sat up quickly, her feet hitting the floor before I could say another word. Looking around for her clothes, she muttered, "I think we should probably get back. I have things to do today."

While she picked her things up from the where they'd been thrown hours before in the heat of passion, I reached out to run my hand down her back, loving the feel of her silky skin under my hand. "Grab a shower while I run out to get some breakfast. We have some time."

She stopped moving and turned to look at me with an expression filled with confusion. I couldn't blame her. One minute I was Prince Charming and the next I was as cold as a fucking iceberg.

"Try the shower. It's got like ten showerheads. I don't think you'll find a better shower anywhere."

Raising her eyebrows, she smirked. "That's one hell of a shower. I guess I can't possibly leave without trying it."

I sat up and slipped my pants on. "Good. I'll get some breakfast and be back in a few."

As Olivia walked toward the bathroom, I grabbed my phone to call the local store that thankfully delivered whenever I visited this place. Or at least it did the last time I was here. Five minutes and two teenage boys with squeaky voices later, I came to find out that the store's owner had retired and no, they didn't deliver anymore.

What the fuck was I doing? I had a gorgeous woman naked in my shower, and there I was spending time talking to pimply-faced kids about fucking bagels. I slid out of my pants and headed into the bathroom as my conscience scolded me for once again making the wrong choice with Olivia.

It only took a few seconds of looking at her wet, naked body before my cock was ready to go. Between the guilt and the knowledge that what I was doing was wrong, I thought it might have let me down, but like my heart, it stood ready to go.

She turned around, surprised at first, but then she smiled. "I thought you were handling breakfast."

Closing the shower door behind me, I stepped close to her as the water poured down over me. "Didn't work out. This is a far better way to wake up anyway."

I slid my arm around her waist and pulled her close to me, but she pressed her hands to my chest to push me away. "What the fuck is with you, Cash? We have a great time all the way here, and then you run ice cold on me as soon as we arrive. Then we have sex and you're all about me, but we wake up and you're the ice man again. Now you're all about me again?"

I'd brought this upon myself. No intelligent woman would let me get away with what amounted to running hot and cold in some crazy ass bipolar fashion for long, and Olivia had every right to demand an answer. I couldn't give her one, but she had every right to demand one.

She stood staring at me waiting for me to say something, but I just leaned back against the wall, unable to explain that as much as I wanted us to be that couple we were when I was all into her, we couldn't be more than what we were when I was cold. If she wanted to be with me, she'd have to accept this was how I was.

That wasn't who she was, though. Stepping toward me, she pressed her body against mine and slowly pushed her hips forward to run her wet pussy over my cock. "No answer? You're just planning on standing there with a raging hard-on and giving me the silent treatment?"

"Olivia..." I stopped myself and shook my head.

Frustrated, she knitted her brows and frowned. "Fuck, Cash! What do you want from me? What? Just say it!"

I lunged at her, slamming her against the tile wall and covered her mouth with mine in a kiss that contained all the pent up shit my fucked up mind was dealing with. I wanted her. That's it. I wanted to not be the man I was so I could be the one Olivia deserved. I wanted to forget the mess of my past and believe something good could happen with her.

She matched my need with her own, clutching at my neck as her mouth pressed hard against mine. The heat between us threatened to burn me up, but I wanted more. Olivia's moans echoed off the walls, ratcheting up my desire for her. Sliding my hand between her legs, I pushed two fingers into her hot cunt, thrusting in and out fast and hard to feel her come from my touch.

"I want to see you come so fucking hard you can't stand."

She climbed up my body desperate for the release only my fingers could give her. I slammed them into her as her teeth sunk into my shoulder. Everything between us now was raw and primal with no reason or thought to hold us back. Her nails scratched over my shoulders, and she cried out against my skin at the first sign of her orgasm ripping through her.

I pressed my forehead against the tile and heard Olivia groan, "Yes, Cash! God…yes!"

"Come for me, baby. Let me feel you come apart."

As the water rained down over us, she came until her legs shook and she couldn't stand anymore. Before her body stopped trembling, I lifted her and she wrapped herself around me, giving me the perfect angle to enter her.

"God, Olivia, you're killing me."

She pressed her heels hard against the base of my spine as she bucked against me. I drove hard into her, and with each thrust the wall I'd built around me began to crumble. If we could be this real together physically, maybe I could let go of the past and this could be something. And maybe who I was could be with someone like Olivia.

Her voice weak, she whimpered, "Cash, what are you doing to me? You're driving me crazy."

I stared into her dark eyes and let myself feel all those things I'd pushed away for so long. In those eyes I saw a chance for more than just fucking and leaving all the time. All the things that stood in our way could be overcome. I just had to give her a chance.

Her cunt contracted around my cock, and she came a

second time, her body mine if I wanted to claim it. The feeling of her giving in to me sent my body into overdrive, and I came until there was nothing left inside me. Pushing wet strands of hair off her face, I kissed her long and deep and answered her question. "I want you. That's what I want."

She looked at me like she was searching for some answer in my eyes. "You can have me, but I can't do this with you if all I am is someone you sleep with. I know that sounds old-fashioned, but as much as I love doing this with you, it's just not enough."

How the hell she could be so brave to put herself all out like that baffled me. I'd never showed her I could be trusted with a sentiment like that, yet she'd laid it all on the line knowing there was every chance I'd run ice cold and walk away without looking back.

She gave me my out. I should have taken it. I knew that. I also knew I hadn't met a woman like her before, and I liked how she made me feel when I let her in.

"I can't promise forever, Olivia. I will promise to only be with you as long as we're together."

Pursing her lips, she considered what I'd said and finally nodded her head. "I guess for someone like you that's pretty big. It's a deal."

I lowered her to the floor and cradled her face in my hands. "Not really. I haven't been with anyone else for a while. There's something about you I can't seem to shake, Olivia. Makes being with other women hard."

She flashed me one of her stunning smiles and traced her finger across the tattoo on my chest. "Then I guess it's my job to make that impossible."

* * *

I stood in Olivia's office doorway waiting for her as the club behind me began to fill up. A typical Friday night at Club X, it was anything but a typical night for me. Tonight would be the first time Olivia and I appeared in public as a couple after our breakthrough just six days before. As I ran through every reason why this was another in a long line of my bad ideas concerning her, she emerged from the conference room dressed in a short black dress that hugged every beautiful curve and four inch heels that made her legs look like they went on for miles.

"Wow…you look stunning."

She walked toward me on shaky legs and looked down at her feet as she stopped in front of me. "They're a little higher than I usually go for. I don't think I'll be dancing tonight."

Wrapping my arm around her waist, I pulled her toward me and kissed her on the lips. "I hadn't planned on us dancing anyway. I had something else in mind."

"Something else? Like what?"

"Another visit to the top floor."

Her expression turned skeptical. "Really? I thought I was too good for that."

I gently gripped her chin between my thumb and forefinger and lifted it to look into her eyes. "You're too good to simply fuck in a fantasy room. You're perfect to spend some time alone with there, though. I thought it might be fun. Maybe see some more of the dancers."

Flashing me another of her gorgeous smiles, she ran her hands over my shoulders. "By the way, you look incredible. I don't know how you do it, but you have a way of making a black dress shirt look so hot."

Pressing my lips to hers, I slid my tongue inside her mouth, loving the feel of her in my arms. That conference room just a few feet away looked like a much better idea than spending time out in the bar, but Olivia pulled away just as I'd decided to go for another round on the mahogany table.

"Time to go. Our first public appearance awaits."

Even though we'd talked about this for days, suddenly the idea of dealing with Stefan and his questions or worse, his comments about my personal life, seemed like the worst idea I'd had in a long time. I'd worked hard to keep my personal life private, but now I was about to upend all that work to show Olivia how much I wanted to be with her.

The rhythm of the music pounded through the club, matching our steps as Olivia and I walked toward the bar, my hand pressed lightly on the small of her back to guide her. The room teemed with people, but the crowd fell away to make room for us to pass. I spied Stefan do a double-take when he saw us, and instinctively I tightened my arm around Olivia's waist.

She looked more stunning than every other woman in the place when she turned to look at me confused about my sudden possessiveness, her big brown eyes staring up at me as if to ask, "Is something wrong?"

Stefan beat a path to us, pushing past people on his way to where we stood. Pulling me toward the end of the bar, he said in my ear, "How long have you been with Olivia?"

I simply stared at him, amazed he thought he should ask anything about my personal life even now. He saw he wasn't going to get any information from me, so he turned on the charm and leaned down to say in Olivia's ear, "I see you let yourself get comfortable here. Good for you!"

Unaware of my past with my brother, she beamed a smile up at him. "Thanks!"

"So what are you two planning tonight?" he asked over the music. Before we could escape, his buddy Jake sidled up next to him with a look that screamed he couldn't believe his eyes. For a friend of Olivia's, he didn't look too friendly.

"What's up, Liv? I didn't think this was your type of scene."

"Hi Jake! Long time, no see," Olivia chirped sweetly at the jackass.

He hadn't said twenty words and already I hated Jake Richfield. His gelled dirty blond hair and cheap ass watch and clothes made me want to knock him flat on his ass. My hold on Olivia tightened even further until she was pressed right to my body. Prying his stare off my date, he looked me dead in the eyes as if we were close friends and asked, "What's up, Cassian?"

Olivia looked up at me, and I gave her a tiny smile. "See you later, Stefan. Have a good night. Looks like the crowd is great tonight."

I didn't give him or his asshole friend a chance to answer or continue the conversation. Taking Olivia's hand in mine, I led her to the stairs and we made our way up to the fantasy rooms. Kane stood guard at his usual place at the end of the hall with one of his rare smiles on his face.

Leaning down, I whispered low in Olivia's ear, "Wait for me in room ten. I'll be there in a minute."

As I watched her walk down the hallway, I heard Kane say behind me, "So that's why you reserved a room. I wondered what was up."

Olivia entered room ten and closed the door. I turned to face Kane, hoping he'd be a little more mature than Stefan. I needed a brother who could act like an adult now. "Thanks for not saying anything to Stefan. I appreciate it."

"No problem. Olivia's a sweet girl. She's good for you, and since she's obviously okay with the whole Rachel thing, I have to give her credit."

I looked away to avoid Kane's stare. "She doesn't know about Rachel."

And in just those few words was the very problem that haunted every minute I spent with Olivia. Until that moment, I hadn't said them out loud, only allowing them to exist in my mind and torment me. I knew it was wrong not to tell her, and yet I couldn't bring myself to explain that part of my past.

"That's not good, Cash. Women don't like finding out the man they're falling for still has a wife."

"She's not my wife. We separated years ago. All that remains are legal formalities."

Kane wasn't buying my excuses. Leaning forward, he leveled his gaze on me. "You're either married or divorced. Separated means nothing to a woman like Olivia."

"I can't divorce Rachel. I never had her sign a pre-nup. We divorce and this club is one of the first things she'll go after. I know her."

Kane's eyebrows shot up in disbelief. "No pre-nup? What were you thinking, Cash?"

"I wasn't thinking. I was a kid in love."

"And now you're a grown man who if he doesn't tell Olivia the truth is going to lose her."

I looked down the hall at the room where Olivia waited. "I'd planned on telling her tonight. I just don't know how to."

"You know me, Cash. I'm all about leaving the past in the past. Nobody should have to deal with what I was. But Olivia's going to find out, and if she doesn't find out from you, you're done. You can't come back from that kind of lie, even if it is just a sin of omission."

I nodded, knowing every word he said was right. I needed to tell Olivia everything, and all I could hope for was that she'd understand. There was nothing between Rachel and me anymore. There hadn't been for a long time. I just needed to make sure Olivia knew that too.

Chapter Sixteen

Olivia

I sat on the couch in the fantasy room waiting for Cash, anxious for us to finally spend time together here as a couple. No, I didn't plan to sleep with him in this place where God only knew what had gone on before us, but it felt sort of naughty to be here again. I liked how sexy being with him made me feel, and hanging out in a fantasy room in Club X fulfilled at least one of my fantasies of Cash.

The door opened, and he stepped in looking just as stunning as always, but for the first time in one of these rooms, I got to see the man before he seduced me. Taking a seat next to me, he leaned back against the couch cushions and took my hand in his. "A little different this time, isn't it?"

"Sort of like the first time you and I came to one of these rooms that night you gave me the grand tour of the club."

Bringing my hand to his lips, he placed a tiny kiss in the center of my palm. "That's right. I didn't think you liked this world of mine then."

I shrugged, remembering that night a little differently. I'd been crazy about him even then. I just didn't have the nerve to let him know like I did now. Climbing onto his lap, I hiked up my dress and straddled his hips. "I liked you then. I wasn't sure what to think of your world, though."

He slid his hands over my ass and around to rest on my legs, making my pussy run wet when his thumbs began gently stroking the insides of my thighs. Looking up at me with those ice blue eyes, he asked, "And now?"

I tilted my hips and inched up against his already hard cock. A slow sexy grin told me he liked what I was doing. "I like the way I get to be with you and your world."

Cash closed his eyes and moaned as I rubbed against him. "Things aren't always what they seem, Olivia. Sometimes there's a lot more going on beneath the surface."

I sensed he wanted to tell me something but was hesitating. I waited, slowing my hips, and hoped he knew he could say anything to me. He grimaced for just a moment and then his expression stilled before he opened his eyes and gave me a forced smile. I leaned in to kiss him and whispered, "I like the surface already, but I'd love to see what's going on beneath."

Cash seemed to consider what I said, and I wondered if he was trying to tell me those three incredibly scary words. Was he planning to say "I love you"? I didn't know if I was ready for him to go there, but I knew how terrifying it was to say those words when the other person might not feel the same. Things had moved pretty fast between us, but even though I might not say I love you yet, that didn't mean in many ways I wasn't already crazy about him.

"Olivia, I never thought I'd meet someone I could really be myself around like I am with you."

"I like that, Cash. You don't have to pretend to be anything but what you really are with me. I hope you know that."

I waited for him to say something, but instead he pulled me down and kissed me like I'd never been kissed before. His mouth captured mine and possessed it like he was claiming me. Every inch of my body came alive, and I wanted him right there in that room. My hips bucked against him as my clit throbbed with need and my fingers raced to get his shirt open. I wanted him naked under me as I rode his cock until there was nothing left in either of us.

"Olivia…not here."

Even as his words said no, he stroked the pad of his thumb over my clit, nearly sending me over the edge with just one touch. "Yes…" I moaned as I slid his tie from around his neck and opened the last button on his shirt. "Right here."

He stopped my hands as they skimmed down from the black and red words tattooed on his chest over the chiseled cuts of his abs just above his belt. "You need to know…"

I stared down at him as I waited for him to continue. He didn't have to explain that this room wasn't private or that he didn't want me to think he saw me as some cheap thing if we did this. I knew that, and still I wanted him inside me right there in that room just like I'd fantasized about all those weeks.

Whatever he wanted to say never came from his lips, and slowly, he loosened his hold on my hands until they were free. He stared up at me with hooded eyes that told me he wanted this as much as I did. I reached into his pants and palmed his hard cock. "I want you right here. Right now."

Cash lifted me off him and with both hands gripped my hips tightly. Hesitating for a moment, he opened his mouth to speak but said nothing again and lowered me down onto him. Already sopping wet, I gasped at how full I felt as he slid into me. Finally, our bodies completed joined, and he held me still there on him.

"You feel so fucking good. Ride me. I want to see you ride my cock, baby."

With his hands guiding my pace, I slid up and down on him slowly, loving how sensual this thing between us was. Pressing my lips to his neck, I inhaled the scent of him as he slid in and out of my slick pussy, loving the masculinity that filled me. Cash grunted low in my ear, and it registered deep inside me in a place only he'd ever reached.

In a husky voice, he commanded, "Lean back. I want to watch you, Olivia."

I sat up tall on him and lifted myself off his cock, only leaving the head inside me to tease him. His thighs tensed against my calves and his fingers dug into my hips, and then he lifted his hips and pushed his cock hard into me. I watched his face twist in a mixture of power and need, loving the control he possessed over me.

This was my fantasy come true.

With every thrust into me, Cash overwhelmed my senses. The sound of our fucking echoed around us, moans and whimpers that grew louder with each moment as we raced toward that sweet oblivion I'd only ever experienced with him. The sight of those blue eyes so intent as they stared down at the spot on our bodies where his cock stretched my opening to take all of him. The musky scent of his cologne tinged with the smell of sex filled my nose. The sensation of him filling me more completely than I thought possible made me want to give him all of me.

Our lovemaking pushed every thought of anything but Cash out of my mind. I rode him with abandon, desperate to give him what he gave me. My body exploded into a million pieces, and I clung to him even though I barely had the strength to hold on. In my ear, I heard him moan my name, and then he came with one last thrust into me, flooding my insides with heat.

I stilled in his arms and buried my face into his neck, the subtle saltiness of his skin making me lick my lips to taste him. His hands gently stroked up and down my back as if to comfort me, but I didn't need comforting. Being with him was all I needed.

Pressing a tiny kiss on the shell of his ear, I whispered, "You okay?"

He inhaled, expanding his chest against me, and let the air out of his lungs slowly. "That was incredible." Gently pushing me back away from him, he smiled that sexy smile that never failed to thrill me. "Was this your fantasy?"

I bit my lip. "Part of it," I said coyly, unable to contain my smile.

"Just part?"

"Yeah. I'll save the rest of it for another time."

Cash leaned up to kiss me and then lightly ran his tongue over the seam of my lips. "I'll have to keep that in mind."

* * *

"Livy, you sound utterly exhausted."

I smiled at Josie's entirely correct description of me. My time with Cash in our fantasy room had exhausted me physically and emotionally. In just a short time, he'd become such a huge part of my life, and our first time out in public had shown me how much he was into me too. "I got to bed late last night, so I'm a little beat."

"I hear that you and Cassian made an appearance at Club X last night. Seems you two are the new hot couple there."

"I wouldn't go that far, Josie. We just took our dating public last night. That's all."

"Erin said Jake couldn't talk about anything else last night. I'd expect a call from him anytime now, Liv. Can you say jealous?"

The way she said jealous in a sing-song voice told me she was enjoying herself. "Jake and I are friends. Period. He knows that. I'm going to grab a shower and a bite to eat. I'll give you a call later."

"Call me the second you get off the phone with Jake. I'm dying to hear his tale of woe."

"Talk to you later, Josie."

I ended the call and shook my head at her not-so-secret desire to see Jake miserable. Hell hath no fury like a woman scorned indeed. Checking the time on my phone, I mentally chastised myself for spending the entire morning in bed. It may have been Saturday, but sleeping in until noon wasn't my style. Another side effect of dating Cassian March.

That sounded so strange as I repeated those words in my mind. Dating Cassian March, the owner of the hottest club in town and one of Tampa's most eligible bachelors. Stretching my arms and legs, I enjoyed the sweet ache between my legs from our lovemaking. A girl could definitely get used to a man like Cash.

A knock on my door put an end to my memories of our time together, and I shuffled my tired self out to the living room to see who it was. I saw Jake's face through the peephole and opened the door to find him standing there with flowers in his hand.

He stuck the bouquet out toward me. "Hey, Livy, I thought I'd come over and see how you're doing. It's been a long time."

"Thanks! Come in. I just got up, so don't mind the fact that I look like a bus hit me. Late night, you know?"

Jake followed me into the kitchen as I found a vase for the wildflowers he'd brought. From behind me as I stood at the sink to fill it with water, he said, "It was great seeing you last night. I didn't think I'd ever see you at Club X."

Arranging the flowers, I chuckled. "I didn't think so either, but I guess everyone ends up there." Turning around, I showed him his gift. "These are beautiful, Jake. Thank you."

"So now you're with Cassian March? I wouldn't have thought he was your type, Livy."

Jake's pale blue eyes flashed anger. I'd never seen him as anything but a good time, but now he was frightening me. "I don't know if I have a type, Jake."

"He's quite a player. Not exactly the type of guy you usually go for. Or was that just an excuse why you never wanted to be with me?"

Suddenly, my galley kitchen seemed entirely too small for our discussion. I moved to walk out into the living room, but he stuck his arm out in front of me and stopped me cold with a hard forearm to my midsection. "Jake, let me out. Now."

He pulled me fast against his body. "Stop being such a cock tease, Liv. You like players now, so why shouldn't we have a good time finally? You know I've wanted to get inside those yoga pants for years."

I looked up and saw him smiling down at me, like this was fun for him. "Jake, let me go. You know I only like you as a friend. It has nothing to do with Cash and me. You and I have always been friends. You, me, Josie, and Erin are the four musketeers."

Jake slid his hands down to grab my ass and pulled me against him so I could feel his erection. His fingers pressed hard into my skin, hurting me. "Jake, let me go NOW! You're hurting me!"

He pulled my hair hard and jammed his knee between my thighs. "What is it you like? The money? I've got as much or more. The fact that he's fucked more women than he can remember? Me too. So no more fucking teasing me, sweetheart. I've waited long enough."

Tears burned my eyes, and I cried out, "Don't do this!" He looked down at me and gave me a sinister smile, so I begged, "Please, Jake, you don't want to do this."

"Oh, yes I do. All these years you've been sweet little Livy, too good for me. Your friends weren't, but you were always out of my reach. I've been patient and stuck in the friend zone for way too fucking long, but no more."

I twisted out of his hold and ran to get my phone, hoping that if I could call 911 the cops might get there before Jake really hurt me. He grabbed me just as I reached it, yanking me back by my hair so I fell back against him. His hands clawed at my breasts, squeezing them painfully. I screamed, but he stifled my call for help by covering my mouth with his palm.

The phone was too far from me, and there was no way anyone had heard my screams. Fear tore through me that Jake was going to rape me right there in my apartment and nobody would be there to stop him. He jammed his hand down the front of my panties, bruising my skin, and I knew I had to do something. Opening wide, I bit down on the fingers covering my mouth until I tasted the metallic tinge of blood on my tongue. Jake howled in anger and sent me flying with a backhand to my cheek. I fell hard to the floor but instantly scrambled for my phone as he stood looking at his bloody hand, stunned at what I'd done.

My hands trembled so badly I could barely hold the phone. "Get the fuck out of here before I call 911 and have your fucking ass arrested. Get out!"

He sneered and snapped, "Fuck you, Liv! You're not

worth it. I didn't want Cassian March's sloppy seconds anyway."

Jake flung the door open, slamming it into the wall, and stormed out. My hands still trembling, I dialed the only number I could think of, praying to God I didn't get a voicemail.

"Olivia, I'm glad you called."

I tried to stop the tears, but the reality of what just happened washed over me and I couldn't hold back. Sobbing, I said, "Cash, I need you to come get me at my apartment. I can't stay here."

"What's wrong? What happened?" he asked over and over as my sobs nearly drowned out the sound of his voice.

"Please just come. I can't stay here. Please."

"I'll be right there. Don't cry. Whatever it is, it'll be okay."

The phone went silent, and I let it drop to the floor. Hugging my knees to my chest, I sat there in that spot where Jake had thrown me, in shock at what he'd done. I had no idea how much time passed between me calling Cash and him getting to my apartment. All I knew was that I couldn't stay there but I couldn't move on my own either. All I wanted to do was bury my head and cry.

"Olivia?"

I looked up and saw Cash standing in my doorway with a stunned look on his face. How could I tell him what happened? I didn't know what to say.

"What happened? Who did this?"

"Jake," I answered quietly, still not believing it myself.

Cash crouched down beside me and pushed my tangled hair away from my face to examine my cheek. Looking down, I saw it already had begun to swell. His blue eyes filled with rage, and when he spoke, his voice came out in a low growl. "He did this to you? I'm going to kill him."

"I don't know what happened. He was so angry. I'd never seen him like that. I don't know why."

As he helped me to my feet, he pulled the two pieces of my torn T-shirt together at my neck and leaned down to kiss me. "Let's get you out of here. Tell me what you need to take and we'll go to my place."

I held my shirt together and looked down at what I was wearing. "I don't have pants on, Cash. I need pants."

"Okay, we'll find you pants and some shoes. Bring whatever you need for as long as you need to. You can stay at my place where I'll make sure you're safe."

Clutching my collar, I staggered into my room and threw a shirt over my head. I slipped on my yoga pants and flip flops and headed back out to where Cash stood talking on the phone.

"Stefan, if I ever see him anywhere near my fucking club, I'll hold you responsible. You don't need to know why I don't want him there. Just make fucking sure his membership is voided and I don't see him there again."

Quietly, I let him know I was behind him. "Cash?"

He turned around and stuffed his phone into his pocket. Wrapping his arm around me, he pulled me close. "Let's go. I'll get you something to eat and we'll spend the day at my condo."

My body melted into his protective hold, and I

looked up at him to see his expression so serious. "I don't want you to feel like you have to do anything to him. This isn't your fight, Cash."

"Olivia, he hurt you."

"I just want to lay down and relax. Everything hurts."

Cash pressed his lips to my forehead and whispered, "Okay. Let's get you back to my place and you can relax there."

"Thank you. I didn't know who else to call. I hope I didn't interrupt you doing…anything."

He shook his head and smiled. "You didn't interrupt anything more important than you. I'm glad you thought of me first."

Chapter Seventeen

Olivia

The hot water eased the pain that seemed to be everywhere in my body. I closed my eyes and soaked in Cash's tub for nearly an hour as I listened to him exact his revenge on Jake in the March way. Anywhere he tried to go, he'd find he was suddenly unwanted, from Club X to virtually every one of the best restaurants in town. Cash left nothing of his social life to enjoy, and I knew this would devastate Jake most. Other men might have been hurt by another man beating the hell out of them, but not Jake. More than anything else, he lived to be that player he'd always been and Cash took that away from him with an hour's worth of carefully placed phone calls. From this point on, Jake Richfield would be persona non grata everywhere he turned.

Opening my eyes, I looked down my body at the evidence of Jake's rage. Purple bruises dotted my breasts where he'd grabbed me, and all down my stomach scratches marked me. Marked. Bruised. How could Jake had done this to me?

I struggled to fight back the tears, hating the idea

that I was so weak that he could get to me again. No. I wouldn't let that happen. I wasn't some helpless girl. I'd trusted him, and that was a mistake, but he wouldn't get any more than that from me. At least I could control that.

After an hour, I knew I couldn't hide out in Cash's bathroom anymore. I had to face him. I'd called him because I needed someone to save me, but now I felt embarrassed and unsure I'd made the right choice. We weren't at that point in our relationship. What if he felt obligated to help me? I didn't want a man who felt obligated to be with me because I was some broken bird.

Slipping back into my shirt and yoga pants, I walked out through his bedroom to find him sitting on the couch. Something between us felt awkward now, and I hated that. It was nothing he meant to do, but I saw the look on his face. He pitied me.

"Come here. Sit down with me."

I didn't even want to face him, so I looked away. "I think maybe I'll go stay at Josie's. I don't want to impose."

Cash walked over to me and took my hand. Raising it to his lips, he kissed it and led me to the couch. "Olivia, you're staying here. I want to make sure you're safe. Now sit."

I did as he commanded and sat down next to him. "You're pretty bossy, aren't you?"

"I am your boss, remember?"

"I think we're past just being boss and assistant, aren't we?" I didn't know why I asked that. I sounded needy, and I hated sounding that way. Looking down so I didn't have to see his face, I said, "Forget I said that, okay? I'm not thinking clearly."

Cash lifted my chin with his finger and stared into my eyes with a look that made me forget everything else in the world but him. "We are past just being that. I hadn't realized until last week just how much past that we were. Then when you called me today and I heard the fear in your voice, I couldn't think of anything but racing over to your apartment and protecting you. I'm not sure where this will end up, but we're way past you just being my assistant."

"So what happens now? You make Jake Richfield's life a living hell?"

"He'll be lucky if I stop there."

The threat in Cash's voice was real, and for a moment I felt bad for Jake. Cash was about to make his life an empty shell. "Just don't do anything you can be hurt from."

He gently tucked my hair behind my ear so my bruise was visible. "I'm not worried about me. You're the one he attacked."

"I'm fine, Cash. I'm not some piece of precious China that breaks easily."

I had no reason to get defensive. He was just showing me he cared. I knew this, but my gut was sending all sorts of red flags up, even though I had no idea why. Something in the way he'd become so affectionate made me think it was just a matter of time before this all fell apart.

"Olivia, I'm not saying you can't take of yourself. All I'm saying is I can take care of you too."

"Well, it's not necessary. I'm sure you have other things to do on a Saturday afternoon."

Cash frowned, like what I'd said hurt him, and shook his head. "Nothing more important than you."

I moved toward the end of the couch, putting some distance between us, even though part of me wanted him to hold me in his arms and never let me go. "I'll probably head out in a little while. Josie has a spare bedroom."

"What's this about, Olivia?"

"Nothing. I just don't want to be in the way if you have something planned."

"What would I have planned that wouldn't involve you tonight?"

"I have no idea. Maybe work. Maybe some other plans you might not want to tell me about. I don't know."

"What are you talking about? Did Jake say something?"

I turned and stared at him, seeing him as Jake had described. A player who'd slept with more women than he could remember. Lying, I said, "No. Why?"

"Because you're acting like I did something wrong. What did he say?"

I quickly stood to move away, not wanting to have this conversation. "Nothing. He said nothing."

"You're lying. I can see it in your eyes. Tell me so at least I can explain."

Something exploded inside me, and I screamed, "Explain what? That you're just like him? That you've slept with more women than you can remember and I likely don't mean anything to you?"

The look on his face crushed me. I hadn't meant to say any of that, but somehow it all came flowing out of my mouth from somewhere deep in my mind. I couldn't do this with him. Even if he was who Jake claimed he was, he didn't deserve this.

Quietly, I said, "I'm going to lie down for a bit."

And with that, I went to hide in his bedroom and hate myself for what I'd done. Somehow what Jake said had triggered that fear I'd had about Cash since the moment I realized I liked him. There were leagues, and he was out of mine. He came with a past that intimidated me and made me feel insignificant. I'd hoped my insecurities wouldn't ruin this thing with him, but Jake's words had brought them all front and center.

I didn't know how long I lay there alone in Cash's bed, but the moment he opened the door my stomach twisted into knots. I'd dropped all that emotional shit in his lap and there was no way we were ever going to move forward if we didn't talk about it.

Talking about it was the last thing I wanted to do, though. Masochism wasn't my thing, and hearing about all the women he'd been with before me sounded like the purest form of emotional torture.

My back turned to him, he slid in under the covers and pulled me close. I'd expected to feel him hard against my ass, but nothing pressed against me. This wasn't about sex. If it had been, maybe I could have kept it together. No, this was about him being there for me and me being the kind of emotional wreck who'd actually brought up his past because I felt inadequate.

Fucking Jake! I'd been so happy with Cash. Maybe my insecurities would have reared their ugly heads at some point, but they hadn't yet. Now that happiness was gone, replaced by the ugliness Jake had forced on me. The physical attack I could get past. Bruises faded and scratches healed. Words never went away, though. They replayed in the mind haunting until they became truth.

"Olivia, you up?" he asked in a voice that flowed over me like silk.

I pretended to be asleep, but it was no use. I had to face him. "Yeah, I'm up."

"Let's talk."

His soft tone unsuccessfully disguised what I knew to be a command. Weaker men might have let me explode like I had and then wait for me to calm down. Not Cash. Used to having control, he'd given me time only because he wanted it, not because I demanded it. Dominant men were like that. It's one of the reasons I'd fallen so hard for him. Now, though, it made for an inconvenient conversation I wasn't really ready for.

Rolling over, I avoided his gaze. He wasn't going to let me get away with that either. Gently but firmly, he turned my face so I had no choice but to look at him. "I want us to talk, Olivia. The least you can do is look at me. After what you said out there, I think I deserve some answers."

"I don't know what to say."

"Then I'll talk. Jake Richfield wasn't wrong when he told you I'd been with a lot of women. I've never denied that. I won't apologize for my past. I don't expect you to apologize for yours. But that has nothing to do with you and me and what we have together."

"I know. I don't know why I said that before. I know

what your past is, and even though it scared me a little, I hadn't given it much thought until…" I let my sentence trail off, not wanting to say Jake's name.

"I've never pretended to be anyone but who I am, Olivia. If the fact that I've been with a lot of women before you is a problem, then there's nothing I can do to change that. I can only say that since I began to care about you there hasn't been anyone else."

His words sounded so final they scared me. "Are you saying you don't want to see me anymore?"

Leaning in, he kissed me softly on the lips. "No. I'm saying there hasn't been anyone for a while and I don't want anyone else."

"Oh." I couldn't look at him staring at me with those gorgeous blue eyes so close that I worried he could see inside me. "I'm sorry, Cash. I don't know why what he said got under my skin, but it did. I hate that. I'm not some pathetic girl who can't handle the man she's with having a past. That's teenage girl nonsense. That's not me."

"I do want to tell you something about my past, though."

I shook my head and stopped his talking with a kiss. "No. No more about your past tonight. Tomorrow you can tell me anything, but tonight I just want it to be you and me."

He hesitated, and I kissed him again, not wanting to hear any more about other women. He was here with me. That's all that counted. Reaching down, I stroked his quickly hardening cock, needing the closeness that sex with Cash would give me.

I climbed on top of him and tilted my hips to feel the full length of him against my wet pussy. His hands slid down my sides and cupped my ass, even as his eyes showed me his concern remained. "I don't want to hurt you if you're still sore."

Sitting up on him, I pulled on his boxer briefs to reveal his thick, stiff cock. I wanted to feel that stretch me as he made love to me. "I want to feel sexy—the way I always feel when we're together. Please don't let him take that from me. I've never had that before. I love that feeling."

Cash eased me onto my back and slowly slipped my T-shirt and panties off, his mouth following wherever his hands touched with kisses that made me feel adored. For the first time between us, our bodies joined not in lust so much as something more meaningful. Gentler than usual, he cradled my face in his hands as he entered me, staring down into my eyes with a look full of sweetness.

Slowly thrusting in and out of me, he filled my body with his, stretching me to fit him. I wrapped my legs around his waist to bring him closer. I wanted his skin on mine, to feel each movement of his muscles as he made love to me. My hands slid over his back, and I reveled in his body's power even as he could be so tender and attentive.

We said nothing as we gave one another everything we were. I was bruised and hurt, but he soothed me by showing me I could still be that sexy woman he wanted when we were at the club. More than anything else, he made me feel safe and adored.

My release rushed through me, and I clung to him as

it made my legs quiver in ecstasy. He came soon after, filling me once again, and we remained there in each other's arms, silent and sated. I could have stayed there in his hold forever, protected and worshipped and for the first time in my life wanting that.

He rolled off me and pulled me close so my head rested on his shoulder. In the dim light of his bedroom, I traced my fingertip over the tattoo that stretched across his chest. LUCK HAS NOTHING TO DO WITH IT. Curious, I asked, "Why did you get this tattoo?"

Cash smiled one of those thoroughly sexy grins I loved. "I wanted to get one that meant something to me. As the oldest brother, I often seem to be luckier than Stefan and especially Kane. People think because my father left me so much that it's luck. It's not luck. I was the son I was expected to be, unlike Stefan, who was the son who gave my father nothing but trouble. Kane was just the son my father never publicly recognized until right before his death."

"What about the ones on your arms?"

He extended his right arm above me and looked up at it. "Each one was important when I got it. Now they just remind me of times past."

"I like the dragon with the green and black. Do you plan to get more?"

"Probably."

I ran my finger over his chest to the right nipple pierced with a silver hoop. "And this? Planning on getting anything else pierced?"

He laughed. "No. Got anything in mind?"

"I once dated a guy who had his tongue pierced.

That was pretty cool," I said with a giggle.

Squeezing me tightly to him, he growled in my ear. "A tongue piercing? I don't think I could stand all that metal against the back of my teeth. Stefan's damn near drives me out of my mind sometimes when he talks."

"I had no idea he had his tongue pierced. How did I miss that?"

Cash growled again. "Enough about Stef." Then he kissed me and I heard him sigh as he pulled me close to him again. Finally, we'd reached that sweet place I'd never believed could happen with Cassian March.

I woke hours later with Cash still next to me. He lay there silently, his muscular chest moving up and down with each breath he took. Even sleeping, he was stunning. Fighting the urge to touch him, I watched him admiring the man who had awakened feelings in me I'd never known existed before. I considered waking him up, but he looked so peaceful there sleeping so soundly that I grabbed his shirt and my panties to head out to his kitchen for a bite to eat. Famished after everything I'd been through that day, I found a box of angel hair pasta and a jar of marinara sauce in a cabinet next to the stove and some shrimp in his refrigerator. It wasn't five star cuisine, but with a little culinary love, it could be a nice surprise for him when he woke up.

As the water for the pasta came to a boil, I prepared the shrimp the way my mother taught me by steaming them and then quickly coating them with parmesan cheese I'd found on the fridge door. It wasn't freshly grated cheese, but since Cash was a bachelor living alone, I considered myself lucky I'd found any of the ingredients for my surprise meal at all.

With the shrimp done and the water boiling, I tossed the pasta into the pot and began looking through his cabinets for some thyme and rosemary, the secrets to my own special spaghetti sauce. Rifling through shelves full of boxes of expired crackers and cereal, I saw a few bottles of what looked like spices all the way in the back of the cabinet. I stretched to reach them and heard a voice say behind me, "I doubt you'll find anything there."

Startled, I spun around and saw a woman standing in front of me across the center island. Tall with long jet black hair that shined like hair in shampoo commercials, she looked like a model, complete with bought and paid for boobs that even without a bra seemed to sit up perfectly near her collarbone. Her full lips shined with deep red lip gloss that I imagined never faded or feathered, and as I scanned her face for some flaw or imperfection, I saw nothing but perfectly applied makeup to skin I could only dream of having.

"You must be the girl in Cassian's life now. I'm Rachel. Nice to meet you."

She stuck her perfectly manicured hand out to shake mine and I shook hers, meekly apologizing for the shrimp remains that hung from my stubby nails. "I'm sorry. Who are you and what are you doing here?"

"Cassian didn't tell you about me? Bad boy." She practically purred when she spoke, but even her smoothness couldn't make what she said easy for me to hear.

"I don't understand. Who are you?" I asked a second time as I wiped my hands clean of shrimp guts.

"Rachel, his wife. Well, his estranged wife, but wife nonetheless. I can't believe he didn't mention me," she said with a smile that I was sure was anything but friendly.

"His...his wife?" I stammered out, sick to my stomach after hearing the word wife four times in just seconds.

She flashed me an even broader smile as I listened to her repeat her explanation about her being his estranged wife, but it didn't matter. He'd never even given me a hint he was married, separated or not. He wore no wedding band, and there was no indication on his ring finger that he hid a ring when he was around me.

Was it possible Cash had been married this whole time? How? No, I couldn't believe it. A long line of women in his past? Yeah, I believed that. But married? The man I'd grown to love couldn't be the kind of man who'd cheat on his wife and lead a double life.

Rachel's description of how close she and Cash were floated in and out of my brain as I tried to understand what was going on. She mentioned something about them marrying young, but after that all her words started to run into one another. My hands began to tremble as the truth of what this woman was saying settled into my brain. Cash was married and he'd been married the entire time. Everything we were was based on a lie.

"Is that food I smell? I hope so because if this is a dream, I'm going to be really disappointed."

I turned to see Cash standing in the doorway to his

bedroom in just his boxer briefs and instantly knew everything Rachel had said was the truth. She looked at him like he was a possession of hers, her eyes sliding over his muscular torso like it was something she owned and appreciated.

She said something to him, but my heart pounding in my ears made it impossible for me to hear anything. I needed to get the hell out of there and away from him. As the water boiled over onto the stove behind me, I stumbled toward his bedroom, pushing past Cash to quickly get into my pants and leave. He tried to explain and held my arm to stop me, but I yanked it away from him and ran as fast as I could with my arms full of my things and still dressed in his shirt. I didn't know where I was going or how I'd get there, but it didn't matter. I couldn't stay and listen to his lies when the evidence of the truth stood right in front of me with perfect looks and a purring voice coming from that smiling mouth of hers.

What I'd always feared had come true. Cassian March and I were in different leagues, and even though for a short time it seemed like I could be the kind of woman he'd want, the reality was the kind of woman he should be with was standing in his kitchen in designer clothes and looking like a supermodel, likely eating the meal I'd prepared for him and me. Rachel belonged in that gorgeous condo with him, not me.

I heard him call my name as I ran down the hall, his voice tinged with fear. I pressed the down arrow like a madwoman, somehow convincing the elevator to come quickly enough that I could escape this place before I had to hear him try to explain again. The last I saw of him he was trying to stop the doors from closing and apologizing again, his blue eyes pleading along with his words, but it was no use.

Whatever we were had all been a lie.

CHAPTER EIGHTEEN

Cassian

I raced down through the stairwell to catch up with Olivia, but she was gone by the time I made it to the main floor of my building. I'd run out of my condo without my phone, so I couldn't even call her. Disgusted at how I'd fucked up, I rode the elevator back up to my place cursing my stupidity and found Rachel standing in the kitchen just where she'd been when she'd succeeded in ruining everything.

Pushing past her to turn off the stove before pasta and water boiled completely over, I looked at her and felt sick. "Why are you still here?"

"I hope I didn't do something wrong there. I just came by to see how you were doing."

I had no idea how she knew I was there with someone, but she knew. "Rachel, I work every Saturday night. There's no reason for you to believe I'd be home, so why are you here?"

Her expression turned sheepish, and she pressed a smile onto her lips. "I just heard you were out with someone at the club last night and I wanted to know who she was. I never expected to find her here."

"You're lying. Get the fuck out, Rachel. I don't want you here."

I leaned against the counter and shook my head at how much I'd fucked everything up. Olivia had just told me she was worried about my past, and not twenty-four hours later, my past showed up acting like the possessive bitch she truly was.

"Cash, she seems nice. A little wholesome for your taste, but she certainly is a change of pace from your usual. You didn't give her that bruise, did you? I don't remember you being that kind of man."

Turning to look at Rachel, I stared at the woman I'd once would have given my life for I adored her so much. Perfect with flawless makeup that made her look like the finest airbrushed picture, she was still beautiful in a way that most men would give their left arm for. To me, though, she looked fake. Maybe it was because I knew what ugliness lived under the designer clothes and plastic surgery.

"I'm not interested in your opinion on my private life. You're not a part of that anymore, so don't let the door hit you on the way out."

I saw my words stung, but she wasn't about to give up easily. Coming around the island, she stepped in front of me and reached out to touch my face, as if she wanted to console me after ruining everything between me and Olivia. Catching her by the wrist, I held her arm away from me and shook my head.

"You can't be mad at me, Cassian March. You know that. And I've known you long enough to know this girl will pass. They always do."

Fighting the urge to squeeze my hand even tighter around her bony wrist, I pushed her back away from me. "You don't get it, do you, Rachel? We're done. As for Olivia, you don't understand that I could care for her because you don't understand me. I'm convinced you never understood me."

"Don't say that. We loved each other. We always will."

"I loved you. Fuck, I adored you, Rachel. You were everything to me. And what did I get in return? You cheated on me with the one person I have to see every fucking day! Don't tell me you loved me. Don't."

She stood there staring at me with that sexy look in her dark eyes she used so expertly on me and every other man she manipulated, and all I could think was I hated her. I hated how naïve I'd been to think she'd ever loved me. I hated how hurt I'd been when she tore my fucking heart out. I hated how empty my life had been since her. And now I hated that the one good thing in my life had been ruined because of her.

"Cash, baby, don't be mad. If you really wanted me gone, you would have taken my key a long time ago. Admit it. We're right for each other. Whatever this girl means now, it'll pass and we can go back to the way we've been all these years. Nothing has to change."

"Get the fuck away from me! How can you stand there and act like you know anything about me? All I ever fucking wanted was to share my life with someone so I could leave behind the world of that club every night—someone who knows the kind of man I have to be there and still loves me. That's all I ever wanted, and now that I found someone I might finally be able to have that life with, you come here to make sure I won't have it."

Suddenly, the femme fatale my estranged wife had been for so long disappeared and the woman I'd loved stood in front of me. "Cash, you really care about this one, don't you?" she asked in a soft voice I hadn't heard her use in years.

Turning away from her attempt at kindness, I walked past her toward my bedroom. "Leave your key on the counter when you go, Rachel."

I listened as my front door closed behind her, my mind scrambling for the answer to how I'd ever explain her to Olivia. I couldn't lose the one person who'd made me believe I could have something more than just temporary happiness. Sex wasn't enough anymore. For the first time in years, I had to figure out a way to win back a woman's heart.

* * *

After spending hours sitting in my car and staring up at Olivia's apartment windows for any sign she'd returned, I had to admit winning her back was going to be harder than I'd thought. I had no idea where she was, and she wouldn't answer my phone calls. She'd mentioned some friend name Josie, but I didn't even know her friend's last name.

Thinking I'd get my chance to speak to her at work, I waited each day, my heart leaping in my chest whenever I heard footsteps coming toward my office, but she never showed. I couldn't concentrate on work and I hadn't slept since she left my place. By the time I left the club on Tuesday night, I'd nearly gone out of my mind thinking about her, so as I had every night since Saturday, I drove to her house and hoped to find her.

Parked on the street across from her place like some kind of stalker, I waited and finally saw a light flicker on around three in the morning. Probably too late to be knocking on someone's door, I did it anyway, unable to wait any more.

I stood outside in her hallway until she finally gave in and answered the door. Her brown eyes still had the same look of hurt in them that I'd seen as she left my place days earlier, but the bruise on her cheek had faded slightly.

"Cassian, it's late. I need to go to bed."

She began to close the door, but I stuck my foot in to stop her. "I need to talk to you. Let me just explain."

"This isn't about you or what you need. Go home to your wife, Cassian."

She leaned hard against the door, squeezing my foot between it and the doorjamb, but I couldn't let her give up on us yet. "Olivia, let me in. At least let me explain so you know my side. Then I'll go if you want."

The door stopped crushing my foot, and she finally released it and walked into her living room. Following her, I reached out to touch her, missing how she felt in my arms, but she pushed me away. "Say what you have to say and then go."

"I'm sorry I didn't tell you about Rachel. I wanted to. I tried at the club Friday night, and then I tried again Saturday. It just never happened."

Her expression twisted into an angry grimace. "Is that the best you can do? You're a grown man, Cassian.

Just admit you lied to me the entire time we were together. At least respect me enough to tell me the truth."

"It's not the truth. Rachel and I haven't been together as husband and wife for years. I never wanted to lie to you, Olivia. I just never found the right time to admit that I wasn't divorced yet, but I swear to you we aren't together."

"What's the difference? You aren't divorced, but you aren't with her? Why should I believe you? She obviously has a key to your condo, and she looked right at home there. She's perfect for you. Just the type of woman you probably always go after."

I stepped toward her, but she backed away with a look of disgust that made my heart feel like it was being squeezed in a vice. "Olivia, listen to me. I know I should have told you, but I swear, there's nothing between me and Rachel. You and I have something great between us. Don't let my stupid screw up ruin it."

Tears welled in her eyes, and she shook her head. "No. It was bad enough to think that I was just one in a long line of women. I can't be the other woman for you. I won't be."

I grabbed hold of her shoulders and made her look at me. The pain in her beautiful brown eyes nearly made me look away, but I forced myself to say what was in my heart. "Don't do this. Please. I know I screwed up, but don't let that ruin what we have. You're the only woman for me. She's nothing. Please don't give up on us. Don't give up on me."

Olivia fought back the tears, but it was no use. They flowed down onto her cheeks as she sobbed, "There's no us, Cassian. There's you and her together and stupid me over here who was dumb enough to believe someone like you. How could I have been so blind?"

"You weren't blind. She means nothing to me. Olivia, I don't want to lose you. For the first time in a long time, I want more and that's because of you."

She hung her head and quietly said, "I don't ever want to see you again. I won't be coming back to work either."

Her words hit me like a fist to the face. Scrambling to find some way to change her mind, I held her close. "You can't afford that. Come back to work, at least. I don't want to lose you there." She shook her head again and I knew I wasn't getting through. Feeling her slip away, I begged, "Jesus, Olivia. Don't do this."

She yanked her arm from my hold and pounded her fists on my chest as the tears rolled down her face. "Don't do what, Cash? Make you fucking pay for lying to someone who foolishly cared about you? Do you feel bad, Cassian March? Do you?"

God, the way she looked up at me with all that pain in her eyes killed me. "Olivia, I'm sorry. Please, I—"

Burying her face in her hands, she sobbed, "Just go. Go back to your life and all the women you can fuck and just leave me alone."

I wanted to take her into my arms and make it all better, but I couldn't. I'd fucked this up. What I'd always feared would happen had, and I had nobody to blame but myself.

"I'm sorry, Olivia. I'm sorry."

I didn't want to walk away and leave her there. If I

did, I might never see her again, but she wouldn't listen to me now. All I could do was give her some time and hope if I didn't give up, she wouldn't either.

My phone vibrated in my pocket as I walked back to my car. Checking it, I saw Stefan's name flash across the screen. He was the last person I wanted to talk to. I silenced it and turned my phone off. The only person I wanted to hear from refused to talk to me, so there was no point in keeping it on.

Heading back to my condo, I thought of hundreds of ways to show Olivia I was sorry, but the reality was as long as I stayed married to Rachel, Olivia and I would never have a chance at anything. Even if I convinced her of how much I cared, I wasn't able to offer her anything more than the present.

She deserved more than that.

I crawled into bed and smelled her perfume all over my sheets. Soft and flowery, it was warm and gentle and so her. Closing my eyes, I replayed our time together there as an ache settled into my chest. This was all I had left of her now.

Someone banging on my front door roused me from my misery, and I answered it hoping that the impossible had happened and Olivia had decided to give us another chance. Instead, I saw Stefan and Kane standing in the hallway looking like they had bad news to deliver.

"What? Whatever it is, I'm sure it could have waited until I get to the office tomorrow."

Stefan forced his way into my home and Kane

followed, leaving me to close the door and deal with them. Taking a seat on the couch, Kane opened up the laptop he carried and turned it around for me to see.

"This can't wait."

"That gorgeous piece of ass from that website who came to interview you published an expose about the club. Ciara whatever the fuck her name is has all sorts of details in this article of hers," Stefan ranted. "You said you had Olivia talk to her and she took care of it."

I thought back to that day and nodded as I replayed what I'd heard the two of them talk about. "I did. She got nothing from Olivia."

"Then where the fuck did this Ciara person get all this info about the fantasy rooms, Cash?"

"I don't know, Stefan."

"Where has Olivia been anyway? I didn't see her in her office Monday or Tuesday."

I didn't want to explain to my brother the whole mess I'd made of my relationship with her, so I simply shrugged as if I didn't know what was going on with Olivia. Kane sat silently watching me, and I was sure he already had a sense that something had happened between us.

"I thought you two were together now, Cash. What's going on?" Stefan pushed further. "You don't think she'd ever do anything to hurt us or the club, do you?"

There was no way I could believe that. Olivia may have hated me now, but she wasn't vindictive. No way.

Kane finally spoke and everything I believed was thrown into doubt. "This is what that Ciara girl wrote. 'A playground for Tampa's big spenders, Club X is secretly an illegal sex club frequented by wealthy playboys and some of the most powerful men in our area.'"

I avoided my brothers' stares, but Kane knew what I'd been up to with Olivia in the fantasy rooms. Was it possible she'd told Ciara that? But members of the club would know those things too.

"For what it's worth, Cash, I don't think Olivia would ever do that. She's not that type of person."

I looked at Kane and wanted to believe he was right. The problem was after what had happened between Olivia and me, maybe she felt I deserved something like this. What was the old saying? Hell hath no fury like a woman scorned?

Inhaling, I let the air out of my lungs slowly and sat back against the couch. "Olivia found out about Rachel before I could tell her. We're finished, at least for now."

My brothers looked at me like I'd just admitted to committing murder. Their expressions were a mix of shock and confusion. I guessed since neither one of them had seen me with any woman for more than a few hours since Rachel, they'd gotten used to me being a man whore.

"I thought you were going to tell her Friday night when you were in the fantasy room," Kane said.

"I tried, but somehow I just never found the right words."

Stefan looked confused. "Then how did she find out?"

"Rachel came by Saturday night when Olivia and I were here. She told her she was my wife, and Olivia ran out of here before I could explain exactly what Rachel was."

"Then that's it. She's pissed at you and took it out on all of us."

Kane shook his head, still not believing Olivia would do it. "I don't think so, Stefan. Olivia isn't vicious or mean. She's been around all of us for a while now, and even if things didn't work out with Cash, I still don't think she'd betray us. There's got to be another answer."

"Have you talked to her since Saturday?" Stefan asked.

I nodded, not wanting to tell them that she'd quit already. With each minute, I began to believe that it had been Olivia who'd been the source for Ciara Danson's article.

"What did she say? How do you two plan to work together now that you're not together? And by the way, I hope you see that even though I routinely hook up with my bartenders, they don't talk to the press."

I looked at Stefan and shook my head in disgust. "Your hook ups usually end up in lawsuits that cost us millions, Stefan, so don't start with that shit. As for us working together, Olivia quit, but she can't afford to leave so I don't know where we stand."

"She quit? Then she definitely is the one who spoke to that website. We need to decide what we're going to do. I say we sue that rag."

Kane sat back against the couch and looked like he was thinking things through. "I don't think it was Olivia, but I agree with Stefan that we need to do something. You may have been successful in getting the cops and the politicians to become members of the club, but if they think their jobs are in jeopardy because of this website, we'll be on our own. Without them, we can't stay open. Even that fuck Shank won't be around to help."

Stefan spun the laptop around to face me and pointed at the screen. "Read this."

My eyes scanned the words just beneath his fingertip. "Club X may appear like your average, run-of-the-mill nightclub, but the upstairs floors hide a dirty little secret. Set up like their own personal brothel, the fantasy rooms at the March brothers' club are little more than a whorehouse for the owners."

Those words did just what they were intended to do, and I pushed the laptop away. There was no denying it now. Olivia had sold us out to Ciara Danson after what had happened between us, and now the future of my club was in doubt. Fuck!

I stood and walked over to the window to hide the pain I knew was written all over my face. "I'll call Ben Jessup in the morning and see what our options are. Until we find out, it's business as usual. I'll deal with Shank too, so don't worry. We're not shut down yet."

"What about Olivia?" Kane asked with a hint of concern in his voice.

"What about her? She fucking betrayed me—betrayed us—so there's nothing more about Olivia. Let me get some sleep, and I'll let you know what Ben and Shank say after I speak to them."

As Stefan headed out the door, I heard him say, "Women. Now you see why I only play, Cash. Take your little brother's advice. Fuck 'em and forget 'em."

How ironic that he, of all people, thought he should give me relationship advice. If I didn't feel like I'd just been gutted, I would have taken a shot at his long deserving face.

Kane tapped me on the shoulder. "Cash, I think you got it wrong about Olivia."

Turning to face him, I looked into his blue eyes so similar to mine and saw he was serious. "You heard what that story said. Tell me that doesn't sound like Olivia, Kane."

"My gut says you're wrong. Don't make any decisions about her just yet, okay? Let me check some things out first before you decide to end it for good."

I chucked him on the shoulder and pretended like this all wasn't tearing me up inside. "Check all you need to, but she and I are done."

"Okay, Cash. I'll see you tomorrow. Try to get some sleep."

He left me standing there looking out at the gorgeous view that had been the reason I bought this place. Fresh off my breakup with Rachel, I'd been looking for somewhere I could have a good time, but what had clinched the sale was this view. All those women I brought here, and never once had I taken the time to just stand there to look out at the world with anyone until Olivia. I'd been so sure she was different from all of them.

How fucking wrong I'd been.

Chapter Nineteen

Olivia

I watched as the door closed and Cash walked out of my life, and all I could think of was how stupid I'd been. *There are leagues, Olivia. Who did you think you were kidding thinking you could be with someone like Cassian March?*

Whatever we'd had together had been all in my mind. He'd never cared. He was just another player who cared only about getting laid. I'd been such a fool!

Curling up on the couch, I couldn't stop the tears from coming again. I'd missed Cash so much the past few days. Each night I'd lay in bed as my mind replayed memories of us, unable to stop myself from wishing he was right there next to me even as I told myself it all had been a lie. I thought I'd cried him out of my system, but just seeing him again tonight had brought all the sadness back like a tidal wave.

I missed him so much. Not having him next to me made my chest ache. But it didn't matter. Whatever I'd thought we had was nothing but a lie. I had to accept that.

A knock on my front door shook me from my

misery, and I opened it sure I couldn't handle any more of Cash's excuses. I wanted to lash out, and when I saw the person standing in my building's hallway, that rage only intensified. There right in front of me stood Cash's wife in all her model-perfect glory wearing a stunning white and black Calvin Klein sheath dress and sky high black Louboutin pumps with their trademark red soles.

"Go away. I'm not seeing him anymore, so he's all yours. I hope you two enjoy your life together."

"Let me in, please. I'd like to talk to you."

I couldn't believe my ears! She wanted to talk to me? "No. Go away. I have nothing to say to you other than I didn't know he was married. I am sorry about that."

"Olivia? That's it, right? Olivia? Let me in. I want to explain."

What on earth could she have to explain? Why would the wronged wife want to explain anything to me? I was the mistress, albeit an unwitting one. Wives didn't explain things to mistresses. "I don't think so, Rachel. Whatever's going on, I don't want to be a part of it."

She stepped toward the door and placed her hand over mine. "Give me five minutes. I think you'll want to hear what I have to say."

I looked down at her long fingers tipped with their perfectly manicured red nails and worried if I didn't agree she might gouge my eyes out with those talons. I didn't want to hear what she had to say, but if listening meant the end of this whole ugly mess, then I could spare five minutes. It wasn't like I was going to be sleeping any time soon.

Standing back, I held the door and watched as she

sauntered past me into my apartment. Instantly, I felt out of place in my own home. "What do you want to say, Rachel?"

She sat down on the couch and waved me over. "Come. I want to tell you the story of Cassian March."

I plopped down in my favorite chair and crossed my arms. "I already know that story. It's an oldie and not a goodie. He's a player and I got played. What I can't figure out is why you're here to say anything to me about him. I already told you I won't be bothering with him anymore. He's all yours."

Rachel shook her head. "No, he hasn't been mine for a long time. And just in case you're wondering who left who, he left me."

I couldn't hide my surprise at that bit of news. "Really?"

She flashed me a million dollar smile. "I bet you didn't think any man would ever leave someone like me. Not true. Cassian left me and he had good reason to."

Nothing like being humble. "I can't imagine what that could be."

"I cheated on him with his brother Stefan."

Suddenly, all the nasty looks and comments Cash had made about his brother made sense. No wonder he hadn't wanted me to spend any time around Stefan. "He obviously forgave you. You're still in his life."

"I don't think he's ever forgiven either of us, but Stefan is blood. I don't know why he kept me around for so long."

"I think it's a bit disingenuous to sit here and tell me you don't know why your husband kept you in his life,

Rachel. He still loves you. It's that simple."

She shook her head and frowned. "No, he doesn't. I wanted to think he still loved me all this time, but it was too easy for him to tell me he didn't want me in his life anymore when he met you. I never had a chance once you showed up on the scene."

A sudden laugh escaped from my throat, and I quickly covered my mouth. "I'm sorry. I didn't mean to laugh at what seems to really bother you, but you never had a chance once he met me? You've got to be kidding me. I have eyes, you know. No man would choose me over you."

"He did. He told me a while ago that he wasn't interested in having me in his life anymore. I think he might have kept me around all this time just to punish me, or maybe it was to punish himself. I'm not sure. All I know is that he told me he didn't want to see me anymore, and I knew by that look in his eyes that he was crazy about someone. He told me you were different from anyone he'd ever been with, and I knew I'd lost him for good this time."

"When did you two separate?"

"Right after he caught me with Stefan five years ago. You should have seen him before I did that. The Cassian you know who's so cold and controlled all the time didn't exist back then. God, he was so incredible. I fell in love with him the day I met him. He was so sweet. That's the only way I can describe him then. He fell hard for me, and I felt like the luckiest woman in the world."

"And then you cheated on him with his brother." I

couldn't stop myself from showing her my disgust. She'd had an incredible man, and she'd thrown him away, just like I imagined she threw away whatever else she didn't give a damn about. Women like her saw everything as disposable, including people.

For a moment, Rachel's perfect face twisted in what looked like pain but then the façade returned along with that fabulous smile. "Not exactly. We fell in love and married. He was young and wealthy and I'd snagged one of the hottest guys in town. Then everything changed. He wanted a family, but I liked our life like it was. You see, our Cassian isn't by his nature the man whore he's been for so long. He wants a wife who'll give him children so he can escape the life he has to live at work, but I wasn't that woman. I wanted the man he'd been when I met him—wild and sexy and devoted to me."

"Why Stefan then? Because he's a player who wouldn't get serious?"

"I don't know. We were thrown together so often and it just happened. Before I knew it, I'd cheated on my husband and he found out."

"Then why didn't he divorce you if he didn't want you back?"

"One word. Pre-nup. He never had me sign one. He was so in love that he never even asked. I think he believes if he divorces me I'll make damn sure I get as much of that club as I can."

"Wouldn't you? It looks like you can afford the best lawyers in town, so you'd probably keep him and his brothers in court with that for ages, all the while making his life and theirs a living hell."

"I don't want that club of his. All I wanted was him, but that's not going to happen."

"So you still love him?" I asked, needing to know, even though it didn't matter anymore.

"I do. I'd take him back in a heartbeat. I've always loved him, but I ruined what we had. I know that. I'd just always hoped he wouldn't find anyone else and we'd get back together eventually. I thought that was going to happen since all he's dated since me were women he just wanted to sleep with. Until you. Once you came along, I knew any hope of us getting back together was gone."

"Why are you telling me all of this, Rachel? Nothing's changed. You're still his wife, and he still lied about you."

"Because for the first time in years, he was happy. That was because of you. Those beautiful blue eyes that for so long seemed so cold finally had that look back in them that he used to have with me. That was you. You did that for him."

I cut her off because I just couldn't hear any more. "I'm sorry, Rachel. I'm just not—"

"Maybe I'm hoping that by telling you this he'll finally be happy and I'll have some good karma. I never wanted to hurt him, and I certainly don't want to see him miss out on the happiness he deserves. I'd hoped it could be with me, even after what I did, but I know that's not possible."

I'd heard enough. Standing to show her to the door, I shook my head. "He's still married to you, Rachel. As long as that doesn't change, he and I can never be anything."

She walked toward me and stopped to open her purse. Reaching in, she took out a stack of papers and held them up to show me. "I'm giving him these tomorrow. As long as he signs them, we won't be married for much longer. I want nothing from him, so I won't be dragging this out to hurt him or his brothers. The way is cleared for you. I won't cause you any problems from now on."

I leaned forward to read the words on the paper and saw she was telling the truth. Looking up at her, I asked, "Why are you doing this, Rachel?"

"It's just time. I figure if Cassian can find happiness, maybe I can too, but that can't happen if we stay stuck in the past together. Give him a chance, Olivia. You might just get to see that man he was before I hurt him."

I closed the door behind her and remembered how open and gentle Cash had been the last time we were together. I'd already seen that man, and I missed him.

But could I go back to him?

* * *

Josie sipped on her morning coffee and listened as I told her everything, from Jake's attacking me to Cash having a wife who looked like one of the Real Housewives of Beverly Hills, stopping me every so often just to make sure she understood my story. When I finished, I sat back in my chair and let out a sigh. "So that's the whole story. Now what do I do?"

"I have no idea. All I know is that for someone who's supposed to be so fucking boring, you live one hell of a life. I guess you have to take things one at a time. What are you going to do about Jake?"

"There's nothing to do about Jake. I'm done with him. He hated being stuck in the friend zone? Well, now he can fuck himself because I don't even want to be friends with him. And with what I heard Cash do when I was at his place, Jake's going to need friends now more than ever."

"Did you tell Erin yet? You know she's had it bad for him forever."

"No. How can I tell her the guy she obviously idolizes attacked me? But he said something about being with both of you. Do you know anything about that?"

Josie sneered at my mention of her with Jake. "No. If she's been with him, it's news to me and not good news. I knew he was a shit way back when. His problem has always been the same. He's spoiled rich and thinks he can have whatever he wants because of it. I hope Cash ruined him for what he did to you."

"I think at some point I'm going to have to tell Erin what happened, Josie. What if he tried to do something like that to her too?"

"Jake's an ass, but I never thought he'd do something so awful, Liv. Erin just can't see how much he's not that boy from high school anymore. I can't tell her. She won't listen to a word from me about him."

"I don't know how I'm going to handle that. I don't give a shit about his feelings, but Erin is a good friend."

"I'd say dealing with her is going to be easy compared to deciding what to do about you and Cash."

"I know you aren't his number one fan. You

probably think I should leave him in the rearview mirror, right?"

She shook her head and rolled her eyes at me. "You always think I dislike your guys, Liv. That's not true. I just want to be sure he deserves you. He is still married. That fact is inescapable."

Looking down at my hands in my lap, I mumbled at her succinct statement of the hardest part of the whole thing with him. "I know."

"But unlike other married men who say they're not with their wives, he actually told the truth. Add to that the bizarre visit and confession from the barracuda, and I have to wonder if the marriage thing is as big a deal as you first thought." Chuckling, she added, "I mean, it's not every mistress who gets a visit from the wife pleading with her to go with the husband."

"Thank you, but if we can never call me that again, that would be good."

Josie reached over and slapped my knee. "Oh, come on. It's got a sexy, reality TV show vibe to it, don't you think? Olivia, the mistress, is visited late one night by the wife, Rachel Barracuda, hell bent on convincing the other woman to take her man, no matter what."

"Really? No, thank you, and if it had been reality TV, there would have been hair pulling and screaming. Sorry to disappoint, but all we did was talk."

Josie's eyes lit up with excitement. "And one of you would have ended up naked just in time for him to walk in and join you both."

I nearly choked on my coffee. "Uh, that's porn, not reality TV, Josie!"

"Sorry. I told you I'm living vicariously through you these days. I guess I need to get out and get my own life, huh?"

"Could we get back to my mess and deal with your lack of a life later? What would you do if you were in my shoes?"

She took a deep breath and blew it out until there was no more air left to expel. "I'd go back to him, especially since you know Rachel is filing for divorce. I'm never a fan of lying, but it's not like he had a little wife at home with some kids he was stepping out on. That relationship has been dead for a while. Plus, you need that job, Liv, and you like it there."

"I can get another job."

"Okay. Then it's all about Cassian."

That had been the truth since the first moment I laid eyes on him. "I can't get another Cash."

She smiled sweetly. "Then there's your answer, Liv."

"Now I just have to find the courage to go back to my job in a few hours wearing my heart on my sleeve. No sweat, right?"

Standing, Josie took her mug out to the kitchen and returned to where I sat to grab her purse. "The course of true love never did run smooth."

"Shakespeare before nine a.m.?"

She flung her purse over her shoulder and shrugged. "I know. I'm a wild woman today. Call me with all the details, but remember, you got this. The guy's crazy about you, Liv. Now you just have to show him you're crazy about him. You two can work this out."

"Yeah, I know. I'll call you later."

I finished my coffee and with caffeine coursing through my veins, I summoned the courage to go back to my job and Cassian March. At least I could believe it wasn't as if his brothers knew everything that had happened between us. This was between Cash and me.

Why didn't that make me feel any better?

CHAPTER TWENTY

Olivia

I parked my car in my usual spot outside of the Club X building and closed my eyes to calm my nerves. My stomach had been doing somersaults from the moment I left my apartment, and now that I sat just yards away from where Cash was, I thought I might throw up from fear. What if he'd changed his mind after I sent him away? I'd tried to call him three times that morning, and each time my call had been sent to voicemail.

Checking out my look in the mirror, I tried to reassure myself that Josie was right. Cash was crazy about me. Now I had to show him I was crazy about him.

You can do this.

I hoped that Beck's Loser playing on the radio at that moment wasn't a sign or bad omen. Pushing that silly thought out of my mind, I took one last deep breath and headed toward the front door. I could do this. This was the new Olivia, Version 2.0, and she could handle this, no problem.

The bar area looked empty as it always did when the club was closed, and as I walked through I looked for

Stefan or Kane, but they didn't seem to be anywhere nearby. All the better. I wasn't in the mood to make small talk. I'd practiced what I would say to Cash half a dozen times on the drive there, and I didn't want to forget it all by getting stuck in some distracting conversation, particularly with Stefan.

As I approached my office, I saw a box sitting next to my door. I got closer and realized it contained everything from my office. He'd taken me seriously when I said I quit. My bravado sank to its lowest point. This was not going according to plan already.

Cash's door was slightly ajar, so I knocked lightly and peeked my head in hoping to be greeted by his typical workday smile. He looked up from his laptop and instead of seeing a smile, all I saw were his eyes ice cold staring back at me.

"Do you have a minute? I'd like to talk to you, if you're free."

"Olivia, your things are in the box outside of your office. Your last paycheck will be direct deposited in your account, as usual."

And with that he returned to typing away on his laptop, effectively dismissing me. I stood there with my cheek pressed up to the side of his door in shock. Why was he acting so cold toward me? What had changed?

I pushed the door open and stepped into his office, closing it behind me so we could have this discussion in private. He looked up as the door clicked closed, but again returned his attention to his work, leaving me standing there feeling awkward and unwanted.

"Cash, about my resignation. I've thought about it and I'd really like it if we could sit down and talk about things," I said quietly, my plans barely holding up under his frigid reception.

Without even looking up, he said, "I'm not interested in talking about anything. Your things are outside in the box."

His tone was so cold, so distant, that I stepped back feeling like I'd been slapped across the face. This man who'd been so wonderful now refused to even acknowledge my request to speak to him. What had happened?

"Why are you being like this? I thought we could…that you…What's changed between us, Cash?"

He spun his laptop around to face me. "This changed between us, Olivia."

I sat down in front of his desk and began reading an article on the club written by Ciara Danson. Somehow, she'd found a way to get information only available to members, and she'd gone to town ripping Cash and his brothers as "owners of a modern day whorehouse" and "overgrown boys who used their business as a front to satisfy their own depraved desires." The entire article smacked of ignorance and petty jealousy, and by the time I finished reading what Ciara had written, I understood what had changed.

He thought I'd betrayed him and everything we'd had together.

I looked up and saw his expression full of hatred for me. "I didn't do this, Cash. You can't believe I'd ever do something like this to you and your brothers."

"Tell me that doesn't sound exactly like something you'd say. That it doesn't sound like what you wanted to say to me when you left my place the other night."

"No, I was hurt. I'll admit that, but I wouldn't do that to you. I care about you. You have to know that."

He turned his laptop around toward him and stared over it at me. "I don't know anything like that. All I know is that reporter wrote things only a member could know, and of all the members, you're the only one I see with a reason to want this place closed."

"No! That's not true. I came here today to tell you I wanted to keep working here…" I stopped and tried to collect my thoughts as my mind reeled from his hurtful words. "I came here because I wanted to tell you that I miss you. I'd hoped we could try again."

"There's nothing more to try."

I fought back the tears as his words felt like they were cutting into my heart. This time he didn't turn away but just stared at me with a look full of hate. My emotions began to spin out of control, and I scrambled for anything that would convince him I wasn't the one who'd betrayed him.

"Don't do this, Cash. I swear I never spoke to her, except that day right here in your office. I wouldn't do that, no matter how hurt I was about what happened the other day. You have to believe me. I didn't do that."

He sat there saying nothing, his expression emotionless like everything he'd felt for me had hardened over. I'd never felt so alone just inches away from another person in my entire life.

"Cash, please listen to me. I thought about what you

said last night and you were right. I don't want to throw away what we have. Please..."

My words weren't getting through. He sat there just staring at me, his blue eyes so icy I wanted to look away. All the sexiness and tenderness they'd held in the past were gone. When he finally spoke again, his words crushed me.

"Go home, Olivia. There's nothing here for you anymore."

I stood to leave, stunned at how distant and uncaring he'd been and unsure what to do next. I couldn't leave things like this, but he wasn't even listening to me. I walked out to collect my things from the cardboard box and couldn't hold back the tears any longer when I saw the nameplate he'd had made for me right after I began working for him. Running my fingers over the gold outline of my name, I cried as I remembered how wonderful things had been then.

A voice behind me quietly said my name, and I looked up to see Kane standing over me. I lifted the box and struggled to wipe my tears away so he didn't see me falling apart right there outside my former office.

"Hey, I was just getting my stuff. I guess you know all about what happened and you think I told that Ciara woman everything too."

Kane reached out and took the box from my arms. "Here, let me take this. Let's go into the club and talk for a minute."

I followed him, still a wreck emotionally from Cash's coldness but happy at least one of them didn't think I'd betrayed their trust. He set the box down on the bar and waved someone over. I turned to see Stefan smiling at me.

"Hey, Olivia. I see Cash is still not feeling in a forgiving mood. Not that I think you were part of that Ciara's story."

"He thinks I told her things, but I swear to you both I didn't do that. I have no idea how she found out details about the fantasy rooms, but it wasn't me," I sobbed, unable to stop the tears from streaming down my cheeks again. Drying my eyes, I added, "I told Cash all that too, but he won't listen."

"My brother's stubborn," Stefan said with a smile. "Don't worry. Once we figure out who was behind this, he'll warm up again."

I hung my head, embarrassed I couldn't keep it together in front of these two men. "I don't think so. He was so distant toward me you'd swear we'd never been anything but strangers to one another."

"That's how you can tell you got to him. When Cash is hurt, he goes into himself. It's like he presses a button and the walls just go up around him."

It didn't help to think I'd gotten to him as the memory of his iciness replayed in my mind. Never before had anyone shut me out so completely and so effortlessly, or at least it seemed that way.

"You can deal with Cash later, but for now, who do you think could have been Ciara's source?" Kane asked.

I shook my head. "I have no idea. I've never seen her since that day in his office."

"Well, I saw her Monday night outside with some guy. Tall, dirty blond hair, acted like a jackass when he couldn't get in. They seemed very interested in one another, but he couldn't be her source since he couldn't even get in the door."

Kane's words rang in my ears. "Tall with dirty blond hair? Was he wearing a black watch with a huge face?"

"Yeah. You know him?"

Before I could answer, Stefan slammed his hand down on the bar. "Jake! After Cash made me void his membership the other day, I knew Richfield was pissed. I told him to just let Cash calm down, that it likely wasn't anything that had to be permanent, but he threatened to make him pay for what he'd done. I figured he was just blowing off steam."

I raised my hand to my face to cover the last of the bruise that hadn't completely faded from my cheek. "Jake's all about blowing off steam these days, it seems."

Stefan leaned down and narrowed his eyes to look at me. "Did something happen with Jake and you? Is that what made Cash go all scorched earth on him?"

Nodding, I looked away, embarrassed. "Yeah. It's no big deal."

"Fuck it isn't. Jake hit you? If I'd have known, I'd have kicked Richfield's ass the minute I got off the phone with Cash. Are you okay?"

"I'm fine. I'm more worried about what Ciara Danson's article is going to do to the club than a bruise or two from some jackass. Isn't there anything that can be done about it?"

"I think it's time for me to pay Miss Danson a visit," Kane said with a smile. "You know, to convince her and her boss that the article needs to go."

I could only imagine what Kane would do to the flirty Ciara Danson. She'd likely try to use her feminine charms on him, but I didn't see that ploy working on someone like Kane. But if it was Jake who talked to her, I wanted to hear the truth from her firsthand.

"I want to go with you," I said, forgetting how scary this brother could be. He looked over at me and raised his eyebrows, like I'd just made the most bizarre suggestion, but merely shrugged after a moment. "Since Jake likely did this because of me, I'd like to know for sure if he's her source."

"That's fine with me. We might even stop over at his place if I'm in the mood after talking to her. Just so you know."

Stefan moved to join us, but Kane held his hand up to stop him. "You stay here with Cash. I'll let you know what happens."

"I'm not exactly the person he wants to be around when his love life is crashing down around him, you know?"

I shot him a knowing glance as Kane answered, "And you think he'd be happier with you and Olivia going somewhere together?"

A sly smile spread across Stefan's lips. "Point taken. Give Jake a shot for me. Better yet, I'll handle that myself." He turned toward me and put his hand on my shoulder. "Don't worry about Cash, Olivia. It'll all work out."

As I turned to follow Kane, I mumbled, "I hope so. Right now, I can't see it."

* * *

Spending time with Kane turned out to be far different than what I'd expected. The largest and scariest Club X brother said almost nothing to me the entire time we rode to the offices of All The Rage in his black 69 Mustang, but strangely enough, the silence didn't make me uncomfortable. Unlike with Cash, Kane not talking felt right.

We walked into the building where Ciara Danson worked and found her sitting in a cubicle on the second floor. The look on her smarmy face showed she recognized me immediately, but I noticed unlike when she'd come to interview Cash, she wasn't dressed so her coworkers could see all the blessings that God had given her. She'd have to use something else if she intended to charm this brother.

"I guess you saw the article, Miss Lucas. Your boss is probably very unhappy, but I'd have thought he'd come here himself instead of sending his secretary and one of the club's bouncers."

Amused by her ignorance, I smiled and said, "Ciara, this is Kane. He's one of the owners of Club X."

She looked him up and down, obviously liking what she saw, and smacked her lips. "Nice to meet you, Kane. I'm sorry, but I didn't realize there was a third brother involved in the club. All my source told me about was Cassian and Stefan. If they had told me about you…"

Kane stared down at her with his usual steely look, unfazed by her attempt at flirting with him. "Let me tell you what's going to happen, Miss Danson. I'm going to turn around and go speak to your boss. When he asks me why I think you should get rid of that article, I'm going to explain to him just who Ciara Danson is. Seems you've had a few run-ins with the law, and from what I hear, that degree of yours isn't all you claim it to be. Florida State is a big school, but with the right man searching, it's easy to find out the truth."

The tone in his deep, raspy voice should have told her to stop while she was ahead, but Ciara wasn't going to give up so easily. Looking up at him with her big blue eyes, she said syrupy sweet, "I don't know what you're talking about, but perhaps we could meet over a few drinks and discuss this."

Kane let her speak and then continued, "Now you can delete that article and everything associated with it and keep your job snooping into exciting events like pie eating contests and other nonsense worthy of your time, or you can claim some kind of journalistic ethics and I can go in there and get you fired. Your choice."

I'd never heard Kane say so much at one time. Ciara stared up at him with a stunned look, like she'd just been slapped across the face. Everything seemed to stop for a moment, and then she turned in her seat to face her laptop. "Fine. You win."

She typed a few words and before our eyes the article disappeared from the site. When she claimed it was all gone, Kane walked behind her and leaned over her to type his own words onto a screen I'd never seen on my computer. A few keystrokes later, he stood up to his full height and returned to my side.

"And now you're going to tell us who your source was," Kane said in a flat voice.

"It's not enough that I deleted everything?" Ciara

whined, all her charm and flirtatiousness gone now.

"No. Tell Olivia who your source was, or I'm heading into your boss's office."

Ciara hesitated, and Kane turned to walk away. "Okay! His name was Jake. I met him outside the club the other night when he was denied entrance, even though he's a member. I heard him bitching about the owners, and I figured he was ripe for the picking. He told me everything."

Hearing her confirm what I already suspected didn't make the betrayal any easier. Kane threatened Ciara with revealing her past one more time before we left, and then we headed back to his car. Closing the car door, I turned to face him, dying to know what she'd done to get arrested.

"You have to tell me. What did the lovely Ciara do to get in trouble?"

Kane started the engine and shifted the car into gear. With a slight smile, he said, "Our little Ciara has a penchant for the five-finger discount. And her real name isn't Ciara Danson. It's Cheryl."

"Shoplifting? And a new, sexy name? How did you find out?"

"That's my job, Olivia. I handle all the dirty work for Club X—the sex, the fantasies, and finding out things about the people who want to come to the club." He turned his head and smiled at me. "And yes, I know all about you. That's why I was pretty sure you didn't do this."

"There's not much to know, I guess. Investigating me must have taken all of five minutes."

His smile grew bigger, and he chuckled. "You're one of the rare people I've met in this business. You have no real vices, no problems with the law, and from all reports, you're honest."

"Pretty boring, huh?"

"Not so much. Seems to me those are the perfect qualities for an executive assistant."

Kane's allusion to my working for Cash again buoyed my spirits. We pulled up to the front of the club, but it was obvious that Kane had other places to go rather than return to work. I would have felt better if he was with me when I walked back into the club, but I had a feeling I knew where he was going.

"You aren't coming in?"

Shaking his head, he narrowed his eyes to slits. "No. I'm going to pay Jake Richfield a visit."

"Oh. Okay. I'd say be careful, but I think he's the one who needs to worry about that."

Kane chuckled low and looked over at Club X. "I think you have a box to take care of. Tell Stefan I'll be back later."

"Okay." I got out of the car and leaned back in through the window. "And thanks for believing in me, Kane. I appreciate it."

"Any time, Olivia. Don't worry about Cash. Things have a way of working out."

"Yeah. But hey, if this is the last time I see you because I don't have a job anymore, it was nice meeting you. You turned out to be way different than I thought you were. Even if what you do isn't exactly legal."

That rare, genuine Kane smile brightened up his face

and went all the way to his blue eyes. "The club is the club. I let Cash worry about the legality of it. As for me, don't tell anyone how I really am. I won't be able to do my job if people think I'm a nice guy. Let that be our little secret."

"Got it."

As he drove away, I looked at the front door of Club X with a lump in my throat. Whatever lay behind that door, I had to face it, even if it meant the end of my time there.

CHAPTER TWENTY-ONE

Cassian

Staring down at the papers in front of me, I breathed a sigh of relief. All I had to do was sign on the bottom line and my marriage to Rachel would be over. No muss. No fuss. No dragging my brothers and me through hell so she could peel off a piece of the club for herself. She'd given me everything I'd hoped for.

Before she'd left, I asked her the natural question, knowing I shouldn't look a gift horse in the mouth but needing to ask anyway. I had to know. Why now? Why, after years apart, was she willing to walk away amicably now?

Her answer? Uncharacteristically philosophical for a woman who cared more about the outside of people than the inside. "This is a chance for us to be happy, Cassian. Take it and don't look back."

Looking back was what I'd done for so long I wasn't sure I knew how to look ahead anymore. My life since that night I caught her and my brother together had been one long look back wishing what I'd believed was real. Every woman I'd slept with since then had been an effort to avoid looking forward to a future I didn't want to admit.

In some way, never divorcing Rachel meant never having to move on. As wrong as that was, it was also comforting. A meaningless marriage, it still gave me an excuse not to get serious about anyone. Somewhere deep inside I'd always known it was a cop out, but it was safe.

Then Olivia came along and safe went out the window.

I had a choice to make. I could either spend my life alone, sleeping with women for what they gave me physically, or I could listen to that voice inside me that had been whispering that same refrain since nearly the minute I'd met her.

She could be the one.

Kane sat in his office doing whatever the hell he did during the day. I tapped on the door, unable to contain my curiosity anymore. He looked up from his laptop and shot me a casual glance as he closed it.

"Stefan told me what Ciara Danson said."

"Yeah, it turned out pretty much how I thought it would. I think the only reason she didn't offer to fuck me right there in her cubicle was because Olivia was with me, though. That woman's got desperate written all over her."

"So you took care of it?"

"Fucking Ciara?"

I stood silently staring at him, not in the mood for brotherly ass busting. "The article."

"All taken care of, Cash. Club X is safe again."

"Good."

Stretching his arms above his head, Kane laced his fingers together and cracked his knuckles. "And I took care of Jake Richfield too, but that was more for fun than anything else. Men who hit women are fucking scumbags. They need to be taught a lesson."

"Good."

"What about Shank? What does he have to say about all of this?"

"He's coming by later, so we'll have to see."

He waited for me to speak again, but I simply nodded and turned to leave. As much as I wanted to know what, if anything, Olivia had said to him, I couldn't bring myself to ask.

"Do you still have an assistant? I didn't see her when I got back."

"I don't know."

"You should have known she wouldn't do that to you or us, Cash. Not all women are like Rachel. For what it's worth, I like Olivia. She's genuine. That can't be said about many people anymore."

"Yeah."

"Maybe it's time to let go of the past."

I looked at him, surprised at his words. "You're going to tell me to let go of the past?"

"This isn't about me, Cash. I fight to escape my past every day. It seems like you're happy to be stuck there."

"Thanks, Kane. I'll see you later."

"My pleasure. Advice is always free."

John Sheridan strolled into my office about an hour later with a look on his ugly face that told me he thought our recent misstep with Ciara Danson gave him the upper hand. Taking a seat in front of my desk, he leaned back and shook his head. "Fucking female reporter. You know she's got a record? Petty theft or some kind of bullshit like that."

"Give me a minute, John. I want my brothers here for this." I picked up the phone and told Kane to come down to my office. Stefan's phone just rang until his damn voicemail picked up, as usual. He was probably in his office fucking some girl.

"No problem. Better if we're all on the same page anyway."

Kane showed up quickly but had no idea where Stefan was. It didn't matter. It wasn't like he had any real part in anything that involved Shank anyway. Taking a seat next to the cop, Kane looked across my desk at me and gave me a knowing smile. We'd been through enough of these meetings that he sensed my distaste for them and Shank.

"Stefan is out at the moment, John, so let's get started. Can we still count on your help with the police?" I asked, figuring it was best to take the bull by the horns. If he wanted more money or some other perk, we might as well get it all out on the table now.

"That reporter bitch could have made things difficult for me, Cassian. Thank God it disappeared so quickly."

I smiled at my half-brother, agreeing for once with Shank. "That was Kane's handiwork, thankfully."

Shank turned his head and looked at Kane. Chuckling,

he said, "Well, thank Kane then. You work fast, son."

"I know my job."

"So how are things looking on your end, John? Can we still count on you?"

Shank twisted his hideous face into an expression that made it seem like he was thinking for a moment about what I asked. I had a feeling he might want an increase in the twenty thousand we gave him every month, but he'd stick to our agreement.

"I think I can see my way to making sure my fellow cops don't have this place on their radar, but you need to make sure things like that article don't happen. I think it's going to be slightly more to make sure things stay cool, though."

I shot Kane a glance and then turned my attention back to Shank. "How much?"

"Another five grand will do it, I think."

Five thousand more wasn't exactly good news, but we needed Shank's protection, and until we found some other means of keeping the police off our backs, whatever he wanted would be what he got.

"Fine. Five thousand it is."

Shank got up to leave and clapped Kane on the shoulder. "Good to see you two again, and Cassian, thank you for giving my little girl a job. She tells me she loves it already."

"She does?" I shot a look at Kane to see if he'd met Shank's daughter yet and he shook his head. I hadn't met her, so how could she be working for us already?

"Oh yeah. She tells me Stefan is taken good care of her."

The idea of Stefan's brand of taking care of someone sent a chill down my spine. Fucking around with Shank's daughter was the last thing I needed him to do. Plastering a smile on my face, I nodded and prayed that my brother wasn't doing anything that would cost us more money or worse, our lives.

"Good to hear it. Until next month, John."

"Until next month."

I waited until he left the building and turned to Kane. "I didn't hire his daughter. Did you check her out?"

Kane shook his head. "No. I would have noticed someone with the last name Sheridan."

"Fucking Stefan! We need to find him now."

Kane took out his cell phone and called him, but like his office phone, there was no answer on his cell either. Only God knew where he was or what he was up to.

"I don't know, Cash. If he's fucking around with Shank's daughter, we're going to have bigger problems than some minor league reporter."

"Have you seen anyone new behind the bar?"

"No, but then again, I haven't been paying attention. Have you?"

Rubbing my temples to ease the headache already making my eyes hurt, I admitted, "No. I've been a bit preoccupied."

Kane smiled at my allusion to Olivia. "Making any progress? Has she at least agreed to come back to work?"

"Yeah, she'll be back on Monday."

"Just as your assistant?"

Nodding, I tried to make it seem like that was good enough. "Yeah. I think it'll be fine."

He said nothing, but I saw in his eyes that he knew having her back in my life as my assistant would never be enough for me. With all that I had to handle with Stefan and Shank and everything in the club, I never needed what Olivia offered more. I just had to hope someday soon she'd take me back.

* * *

I entered Olivia's office and found her busy at work on her laptop like she'd been every day since she returned to her position as my assistant a week before. Each day I watched her arrive at eleven and thought about finally talking about what happened between us—not the Ciara Danson bullshit but how I'd stupidly jumped to the wrong conclusion and shut her out like only I could. But I hadn't said a thing about it, instead letting each day pass with not a word between us other than work talk.

She looked up from her computer and gave me a forced smile that never reached her eyes. "Do you need something, Cassian?"

Her tone told me she could do icy as well as I could. Fuck, being shut out stung. My walls shot up around me, like they always did when I sensed I could be hurt. I should have fought to say something to her, but I just shook my head and walked away back into my office.

I couldn't go on like this much longer. I spent every waking minute thinking about her. I missed the sound of her voice, the smell of her perfume, everything that made her so different from everyone else in my life.

But whatever I did to get her back had to be right. It had to show her how much she meant to me since telling her wasn't going to be enough after what I'd done.

Just before nine, I heard Olivia close her office door. Unlike so many nights before, she didn't peek her head in to say goodnight. I watched from my desk as she walked into the club and my chest ached from how empty I felt without her in my life.

Stefan came in just as she faded from view. As always, he was the last person I wanted to see. Before he could sit down, I held my hand up to stop him. "I'm leaving, so whatever you want will have to wait."

He ignored my warning and sat down anyway. Leaning forward to rest his forearms on my desk, he said, "I know. I just wanted to say I'm sorry."

A parade of ideas as to what he was sorry for marched through my mind. With Stefan, I never knew. "What are you talking about, Stefan?"

Looking down at the floor, he answered quietly, "Rachel. I'm sorry, Cash."

A flash of rage tore through me. Now he wanted to apologize? "What's this about, little brother? For five years you didn't seem to need to apologize. Now you feel the need to?"

Stefan looked up at me and grimaced. "I never meant to hurt you. I don't know why it happened. I know it should have never happened."

"Why are you telling me this now? Because Rachel and I are getting divorced? You want her? Feel free."

He shook his head. "No. We were never anything permanent. By the time you two fell apart, we were done. I just saw how this Olivia thing affected you and wanted to say I was sorry for what I did."

I moved from behind my desk to stand in front of him. "Stefan, Rachel and I didn't fall apart. You and she tore us apart."

Looking up at me with the same look he always gave our mother to get out of trouble, he nodded. "I know. There's nothing I can do about it now, but I thought you should know I'm sorry."

He stood to his full height, still two inches shorter than my six foot two inches, and stuck out his hand. I stared down at it in amazement, unsure what he expected me to do. "So we're going to shake on it and then what? We're all good?"

"Jesus, Cash. How long are you going to let this eat you up? I fucked up. I know. You'll never trust me again. I get it. But Christ, you're moving on with Olivia. You can't move on with me?"

Ignoring how wrong he was about Olivia, I snapped at him, "You sleep with my wife and I'm supposed to move on. Is that right? Let me guess. You have some bullshit excuse like our father never loved you like he loved me. Was that it?"

"Says the son who the sun rose and fucking set on. You get to be Cassian March IV, the heir to our father's name, and I get to be Stefan, the spare."

"So this is your apology for sleeping with my wife and ruining my marriage? You felt unloved by our father, so you thought fucking my wife would make up for that?" I barked at him, not believing what I was hearing.

"Whatever. You wouldn't understand. You're the son who always got everything."

I cocked back my arm to finally pummel the fuck out

of his face, to finally live out that dream I'd had night after night for months after finding out what he'd done to betray me. I'd played out in my mind over and over what I wanted to do to make him suffer like he'd made me suffer. Now, though, other than wanting to lay him out like I used to when we were teenagers, I couldn't bring myself to keep my anger at him alive anymore.

I didn't hit him. Even though I hated his bullshit "Daddy never loved me enough" excuse, I stopped myself. Instead, I gave him the forgiveness I hoped Olivia would give me. Lowering my hand, I said, "Maybe it is time to move on, Stefan. You're my brother, my blood. I can't go on hating you."

"See? I knew you couldn't stay angry at me forever," he said with that stupid smile on his face. "Don't worry. I won't ever do it again."

Leveling my gaze on him, I let my anger out one last time. "I swear to God if you ever try anything with Olivia, I'll kill you, Stefan."

The smile slowly slid from his face, and he raised his hands in front of him as he backed up toward the door. "I get it. I won't fuck up again. "

I walked around to sit down behind my desk, exhausted by Stefan's need for confession and Olivia's unwillingness to forgive me. Closing my laptop, I thought about what I could do to get her back. Day after day, the pain of missing her had grown until my chest felt empty and hollow.

"Cash, you okay?"

Looking up, I nodded at Stefan and forced a smile. "Yeah. I'm fine."

"If this is what love makes a man look like, I don't ever want it. You look shit, big brother."

"Thanks."

"She still won't forgive you? You know, you have this coming. You do that shut everyone out thing that you don't realize how much it bothers people."

"Don't you have a club to run or some bartender to molest?"

"I was just trying to give some brotherly advice. Thought I could help."

This was the second time in a week my brothers thought their advice was warranted. "You too? First Kane and then you with the advice on my personal life."

Stefan twisted up his expression. "Don't listen to Kane, whatever you do. What would he know about love?"

I thought about everything I knew about my half-brother's life before we'd begun working together at the club. "I'd say a whole lot more than you. The man did time for a woman he loved. I don't think you can make the same claim."

My younger brother snorted his disgust at Kane's chivalry. "Thank God! Like I'd ever go to prison for any reason, especially love. And if that's what love does to a man, fuck that. Look at you and him. He's done time and you're more miserable than I'd ever seen you. You two should do what I do—avoid love like the plague. It's does nothing but ruin a man."

At that moment I remembered Shank's daughter and the real possibility that Stefan was already fucking her and endangering our very livelihoods. "Speaking of that, did you hire a new bartender without telling me or Kane?"

"Yeah, a couple."

Slamming my hands on my desk, I exploded with anger. "Jesus Christ, Stefan! We have policies for a reason. You didn't think you should tell the other two owners of this club that you hired new people?"

Confused, he shrugged. "What's the big deal? One used to work for us. You remember Shelley. She came in and asked for her job back, so I said yes. She was one of my best bartenders. The other one said she'd been told the job was hers. I figured you'd already met with her in one of those fucking meetings I hated. Lola's doing fine."

"Lola Sheridan?"

"Who's that?"

"The person you hired."

Stefan shook his head. "No. Lola's last name is Markess."

"Does she look like her father?" I asked, unable to contain my curiosity.

"How the fuck would I know? I just met her. It's not like we're doing the meet the parents thing. I don't do that dating shit, remember? Fuck 'em and forget 'em, although I might keep her for a while."

Stefan's grin told me he'd already slept with the woman who was likely Shank's daughter. Nothing fucking good could come of this. "Please make sure to give Kane her information so he can check her out."

"Okay. I'm out. I have a bar to run."

As he turned to leave, I yelled after him, "And do me favor. Don't fuck around with these two."

He waved my suggestion off and laughed. "Yeah, yeah. I know the routine. All work, no play. Got it."

He left me sitting there with more worries than I'd had when he came in. And I still had no idea how to win Olivia back. All I knew was I had to. I couldn't go on like this.

I waited a few minutes before I headed out, determined to convince her not to give up on us. After stopping for flowers, I climbed the stairs to her apartment and had to admit I was in totally new territory. I'd never tried to win Rachel back after finding out what she'd done. The walls went up and that was it. We were done, and whatever feelings I'd had hardened over.

But now I had to be the man I'd been before Rachel broke my heart. The problem was I didn't even know if he existed anymore. I'd pushed him so far down inside me I couldn't be sure he was still in there.

I stopped in front of her door and stood with my hand up in front of me ready to knock for a moment as I told myself the same thing I'd said every day since offering Olivia her job back.

Don't lose her. Do whatever you have to, but don't let her go.

My heart pounded at the sound of her footsteps coming toward the door. I squeezed the stems of the roses in my palm and waited in anticipation. The door opened, and our eyes met for the briefest moment before she slammed the door closed again.

"Olivia, please open the door. I just want to talk."

Silence.

I leaned forward and pressed my forehead to the door. "Olivia, please…"

She said nothing, and my heart sank as I heard the sound of her footsteps walking away.

Every night I knocked on her door, and every night she refused to speak to me. Some nights she opened the door and stared at me with those beautiful brown eyes so full of pain. Other nights she didn't even open the door, ignoring me as I stood on her doorstep pleading my cause. The florist near the club either thought I was the world's biggest player or the world's saddest man in love. Each night he gave me the look that told me he was sure it was the latter.

Then each day I'd see Olivia at work and it was as if nothing ever happened the night before. With each time she called me Cassian and each cold glance she shot my way, I grew more miserable without her. I'd had no idea how much stubbornness lived in her. Day by day, she seemed to grow stronger in her choice to never speak to me again other than at work, and every minute I spent with her at the club was more painful than the next.

I loved her. I wanted her. I needed her. And nothing I did mattered if I couldn't convince her of those things.

Two weeks into my torture, I couldn't take it anymore. This double life of tepid professionalism by day and ignoring me by night had to end. Late Friday afternoon, I walked into her office to let her know.

She sat behind her desk focused on her work on an upcoming club event I'd handed over to her when we were still together. I stood watching her, remembering how happy she'd been then when I'd come to see her.

Looking up at me, she said coldly, "Did you need something, Cassian?"

God, I hated when she called me that. I knew it meant she was keeping me at arm's length. "I wanted to let you know I plan to knock on your door every night until you let me in. I don't care if it takes a week, a month, or a year, I'm going to be there every night at nine."

"What happened to you working until midnight each night?"

"This is more important. So just know we have a standing date every night at nine."

"And if I never let you in again?"

I wanted to think she was joking, but the stern look in her eyes told me she was serious. It didn't matter. She might believe she'd never let me in again now, but I wasn't going to give up.

"Then every night I'll knock on your door and hope that's the night you finally remember what we were."

Olivia said nothing in response, but it didn't matter. Someday she would.

EPILOGUE

Cassian

The gala at the Florida Museum of Photographic Arts kicked into high gear, but even as I schmoozed and glad-handed with the organizers to thank them for being club members for years and local politicos to ensure the safety of the club, my attention never really left my watch. No matter how much I needed to be at this event for Club X, I needed to be at Olivia's apartment by nine for a far more important reason.

In a room full of gorgeous women in expensive designer gowns, there wasn't one that even made me look twice. None of them were the woman I wanted, even if she hadn't opened her door for me in three days.

I took the last drink of my champagne and placed my glass on a nearby table. Nearly eight-thirty, if I didn't leave soon I'd be late. I made my way over to say my goodbyes, but a woman in a red gown stepped in front of me, blocking my way.

"Cassian March?"

Quickly scanning her face, I didn't recognize this woman who seemed to know me. Giving her a brief smile, I nodded and made a move to escape, but she wasn't having that.

"I hoped I'd get to see you here tonight."

I stopped and studied her face. Beautiful, she had striking blue-green eyes and brown hair, but she was no one I knew. Why was she speaking to me like we'd met before? "Do we know each other?"

Offering her hand, she smiled. "Josie Tellow. We have a shared acquaintance. Olivia."

"Oh. Are you a friend of Olivia's?"

Josie took a sip of champagne and nodded. "I am. You know at first I thought she should kick you to the curb. I didn't tell her this, but I knew what kind of player you've been for years. I've seen you at these events with a different woman on your arm each time. I figured you would only break her heart. Then you did, and I wanted to kick myself for not telling her to drop you. But then she told me what you do every night, even after weeks of her not giving you even the slightest bit of hope, you're still there every night."

"Then you know I have to leave now. It was nice meeting you, Ms. Tellow."

I moved to leave, but she grabbed my arm to stop me. "Don't give up on her. I know you're probably just about to, but don't. Don't be like most men."

"I'm not most men."

"Then show her that. Be that man she thought you were when she told me she could find another job, but she couldn't find another Cash."

The way she said that gave me hope, so I made my goodbyes and raced over to Olivia's apartment, arriving ten minutes late after practically having to beg the florist around the corner to stay open long enough to let me get flowers. Completely out of the roses I brought with me every night, all he could offer me was a bouquet of wildflowers.

Like every other night for weeks, I knocked on her door and waited, prepared to be ignored but hoping tonight would be different. Not a sound came from inside her apartment, so I knocked again and waited as the knowledge that tonight would be like most other nights with me standing there alone not getting the chance to say what was in my heart.

Discouraged, I leaned my body against the door and closed my eyes. "Olivia, please open the door. I can do this for the rest of my life, but I'd rather us do something together."

She said nothing. I wasn't even sure she was there. Pressing my ear to the door, I strained to hear anything that would tell me Olivia heard what I'd said. Nothing. Not a sound.

"Olivia, I'm sorry. I never meant to hurt you. I know that doesn't make up for what I did, but give me another chance."

Listening for any sound on the other side of the door, I heard nothing. Disappointed, I hung my head and knelt down to place the flowers on her doorstep, like I had every night before. As I stood to leave, I saw the door open. Olivia stood there in her black yoga pants, a pink T-shirt, and for the first time in so long, she had a smile on her face.

"Taking to wearing a tux for these nightly visits, Cash?"

I straightened my jacket and held the flowers up for her. "I thought maybe a suit wasn't enough. Is the tux working?"

She took the bouquet and held them to her nose. "These are pretty. Thank you. As for the tux, I'm not sure what it's supposed to do, but you do look nice. I'm afraid I'm a little underdressed, though, for whatever you had in mind."

I smiled at her teasing and looked into her eyes. "You look beautiful, especially now that you're smiling at me. I missed that."

"Do you know why I opened the door, Cash?"

I shook my head. "No. I have no idea. I'm just happy you did."

"It's because of what you said. Tonight, for the first time, you said you were sorry."

"I've been sorry since the moment I realized what I did. I am sorry, Olivia."

"That's what I've been waiting all these weeks to hear. It's all I ever wanted you to say."

"I guess I've been a bigger fool than I thought. All this time, I thought you knew I was sorry. I figured you wanted me to say something big or impressive and I just hadn't thought of the right words yet."

"So why did you say I'm sorry tonight?"

"I met your friend Josie at the museum gala, and something she said about me not giving up made me think there was a chance for us. I don't know why I said I was sorry tonight and not before this. I just said what was in my heart."

The smile she gave me made me happier than I'd

been in weeks. Her hand slid down the door and then she stepped back. "Why don't you come in instead of standing out in my hallway so all my neighbors can know my business?"

The sound of a door shutting behind me down the hallway made me chuckle. "I think it's too late for that. I'm pretty sure all your neighbors know more than they ever wanted to about us."

She flashed another sweet smile. "Then I better let you in before they insist on knowing how this all turns out. I think it's time we talked."

I followed her into her living room and sat down next to her. "I really am sorry, Olivia. I've been going crazy without you. I can't think about anything but you, and work has been nearly impossible knowing you're right there in the office next door but you won't even talk to me, except for ice cold answers when I ask a question."

"Why did you do it? I guess I can understand that you might think I could do something to you out of anger. I would never do that, but I can see why you might think that. But why did you shut me out like that? That hurt more than anything else."

"As soon as the thought of you betraying me settled into my mind, I shut down. It felt the same as when I found out Rachel cheated on me with Stefan, and I didn't want to feel that pain again, so the walls went up."

Olivia took my hand in hers and squeezed it gently. "I'm not like her, Cash. I wouldn't do that to you. I can't be with someone who I'd always be worried would shut me out, though. That hurt too much."

Pulling her close, I felt her meld to me and for the

first time in weeks, I was truly happy. I didn't want to risk losing her or feeling this way again. "I know. I'm sorry. I don't want to be without you. I know that now. I love you, Olivia."

I hadn't said I love you to a woman since Rachel, but those three words had never felt more right coming out of my mouth.

She looked up at me and smiled one of those Olivia smiles that never failed to touch my heart. "I love you too, Cash. But no more lies, okay? That includes the truth about the club."

"The truth?" I knew what she meant. I just didn't want the reality of my life to ruin everything.

"The truth, as in Club X isn't what you said it was when you hired me. Legal and all?"

I searched her eyes for any sign that what my life was could be something she'd accept. "Does it bother you what I do?"

Olivia shook her head and took my hand in hers. "No. I found the greatest guy in the world because of what Club X is."

"I wish I wasn't the kind of man I have to be at the club. You deserve better."

She knitted her eyebrows and cradled my face. "I must still be giving off that good girl vibe. Let me tell you something, Cassian March. You're not doing anything immoral or wrong there. People come to Club X to live out their fantasies. There's nothing wrong with that. I got to become someone I wanted to be because of your club. I've always wished I could be that sexy woman a man like you would want, and that happened at Club X."

"You've always been sexy, Olivia. That men like me didn't see that was our fault, not yours."

"Cash, you should be proud of who you are and what you and your brothers have accomplished. There's nothing for you to be ashamed of. I'm proud to say I'm with you."

Pressing my forehead to hers, I closed my eyes. "I love that you can accept everything I am. I never thought someone good like you would. I love you, Olivia."

I kissed her and as I held her in my arms, I felt like no matter what the world threw at me, I could handle it as long as she was mine.

Three Months Later

Olivia

Shaking Cash's shoulder, I whispered in his ear, "If you don't get up, you're going to be late to the club again."

He pulled me close and mumbled, "I don't care. Kane and Stefan can handle things without me for one day. I want to stay right here with you."

"Didn't you say you had at least one interview today?" I gently reminded him.

Opening his eyes, he looked up at the ceiling as he ran through his schedule in his mind and sighed deeply. "I really want to stay in bed with you."

I nuzzled his jawline, loving the feel of the stubble as it scraped across my lips. "I can't. Remember? I'm meeting with the event planner today at noon. You could stay and join us."

Rolling me over onto my back, he nudged my thighs open and settled in between my legs. Already hard, his cock pushed against my clit, sending strings of arousal through my body. With a sparkle in his blue eyes, he moaned, "This is what I want to do."

"You know what I mean, Cash. You could come to the meeting with me. I'd love your input, you know."

He kissed me softly on the lips in that way that never failed to make me melt inside. "You know I'd do anything to make you happy, Olivia, but I doubt any of my suggestions would be helpful. I don't know a centerpiece from a..."

Quickly, I finished his sentence. "Centerfold?"

"Not exactly what I was thinking, but you get my point. I have no idea what an engagement party is supposed to be like." Kissing my left hand, he added, "I figure that's your thing since I didn't need any input on the ring."

I ran my palms over his back, loving the feel of his taut muscles under my fingers. Holding my hand out to stare at the stunning two caret diamond engagement ring on my finger, I had to admit he'd done well with it. "You're lucky you're cute and that I love this ring. Okay, I get it. Not exactly what a man wants to spend a few hours talking about. Go to your interviews. Who's on the schedule today?"

He buried his face in the space between my neck and

shoulder and planted kisses across my skin. "Some dancers for Kane's area."

"Should I be worried? Those dancers are pretty hot."

Lifting his head, he smiled down at me. "Not in the least. I have no interest in dancers, or for that matter, any woman but the one about to make love to. But I can go with you to your meeting, if you want."

I cradled his face, looking deep into those gorgeous blue eyes, and shook my head. "No, go to work. Somebody's got to make sure Stefan doesn't sexually harass the girls in the interview. I'll be fine on my own."

Cash kissed me again. "Good point. But you don't have to ever worry about me with another woman, Olivia. I'm happy with the one who shares my bed and in a few months will share my life."

"Are you scared?"

"About what?" he asked, knitting his brows.

"Getting married. It's a big step."

A smile spread across his lips. "No. Some men are meant to be married."

I couldn't help but giggle at his response. "Says the man who up until recently was one of the city's most eligible bachelors. I thought players hated the idea of marriage."

"I never wanted that. All I ever wanted was someone to come home to after spending my days at the club."

"Pretty boring stuff for most men, Cash."

"I'll leave the other stuff for guys like Stefan, although he seems to be like a lost puppy these days."

"What's wrong with him?"

"I think he likes one of the bartenders, but she wants nothing to do with him."

"Oh, the poor thing!"

Cash's eyebrows raised in surprise. "Poor thing? Every time he sleeps with one of our employees, we end up paying more money. I'm happy she doesn't want to give him the time of day. I'd like to think it's because of my stern explanation of the non-fraternization clause in the contract, but that's never worked before."

"Maybe she has a boyfriend already."

"Again, that's never stopped Stefan. I think Kane has something to do with it. I've noticed he seems to be suspiciously around a lot when she's around."

I was surprised to hear anything about Kane and a woman. "Really? He never seems interested in anyone at the club."

"I don't think he's interested in her. Something tells me he's blocking Stefan for some reason."

I gently jabbed him in the side. "You brothers are so bad."

"What's bad is Stefan constantly costing us money. If Kane is blocking him, I'll have to take him out for a nice steak to say thanks."

"You are so bad, Cassian March!"

"Mmmm…enough about my brothers. I'm more interested in you, Olivia Lucas soon-to-be March."

Cash slowly slid his hand down my right side to cup my ass as he leaned in to kiss me. Raking my fingernails over the soft skin of his back, I moaned, "You're going to make it impossible for me to leave this bed."

"Good," he groaned in my ear as he made quick

work of my skirt and panties. "If I could, I'd have us stay here forever. No club, no brothers, nothing but you and me naked in bed for the rest of time."

As he eased into me, I looked up and smiled. "I like the way you think."

"I like this. No, I love this." He kissed me sweetly. "I love you, Olivia."

I whispered I loved him too as we made love, and later as I watched him dress in his usual suit and tie look that never failed to make me want him, I thought about the chance I'd taken reserving that fantasy room that first night. All my life I'd played it safe, and all I'd gotten in return was a safe, boring life. For the first time ever, I'd taken a risk, and even though things hadn't gone exactly the way I'd thought they would, I'd ended up right where I wanted to be.

Like he did every day since we got back together, Cash went to work late that morning after making love to me. As for me, I had our engagement party to plan.

Temptation Extras

Visit Pinterest to check out the **Club X board** to see Cassian's Maserati, Kane's Mustang, and other great pics related to Temptation and all the Club X series!

Want to know the music that influenced the writing of Temptation? Check out the book's playlist below.

Temptation Playlist

Caught Up – Usher
Missing – Everything But The Girl
Say It Right – Nelly Furtado
Linger – The Cranberries
All Of Me – John Legend
Days Go By – Dirty Vegas
I Won't Give Up – Jason Mraz
Clarity – Madilyn Bailey
Let Her Go – Passenger
I Won't Let You Go – James Morrison
Do I Wanna Know? – Arctic Monkeys

Sneak Peek

COMING SOON

SURRENDER (CLUB X #2)

Stefan March, the manager of Club X, loves the single life. Women are his playground, and this man lives to have fun. Committed to never settling down, Stefan may have met his match in Shay, a bartender at Club X who seems immune to his charms. Stefan loves nothing more than a challenge, but will this player lose when it matters most?

EXCERPT

Cash's office door opened and a knockout brunette walked out right past me on her way toward the front door and out of my life if I didn't stop her. Quickly following behind, I caught up to her and tapped her on the shoulder. "Hey, where you going? If you're here for a job, you'll probably be dealing with me."

She turned around and looked me up and down, her gaze settling on mine after she'd thoroughly checked me out. "Yeah? Well, if I get the job, we can talk then."

"I'm part owner here, so you'll definitely get the job. What's your name?" I asked, dying to find out who this woman with as much nerve as I had was.

"Shaylene Callahan, but everyone calls me Shay."

"Well, Shay, whatever job you want, it's yours."

Despite the fact that I'd just assured her she could have a job at the hottest club in town, her expression screamed she was unimpressed. What was with this girl?

"Well, that's good. Guess I'll be starting when your boss calls me."

"Brother, and he's not my boss. He and I own this place, along with our other brother. My name is Stefan March. I manage Club X. What job were you interviewing for?"

I silently prayed to God it wasn't one of Kane's dancers because while I would fight him for her, dealing with that miserable fuck was difficult on any day but especially recently. I didn't know what his problem was, but he'd been downright surly for the last week.

Shay pushed her right hip out and smiled. "Bartender. I need some good money and I've heard this place is where to get it."

"Then you'll be working under me," I said as I licked my lips in anticipation of her being under me in more ways than just at work.

Her green eyes flashed anger. "Under you? Well, bossman, this is the twenty-first century and this act of yours is straight out of chapter one in the how to sexually harass your employees handbook. Perhaps we should say I'll be reporting to you during my working hours. And that's it."

Her words were like a hard slap to my face. I couldn't decide if she was the world's biggest bitch or what could be my greatest conquest yet. Either way, she had sharp tongue in that beautiful mouth of hers. This kitten had claws.

"You don't sound like any bartender I've ever had…working for me."

"That's probably because you don't often get microbiology grad students serving liquor to your guests."

God, every word out of her mouth was a jab, but I liked a challenge. "Do you have any experience bartending, Shay? I mean, you're nice and all, but I don't have the time to train a newbie."

Her eyebrows shot up, and her eyes flashed her anger once again. "I think you'll see by my application that I have more than enough experience for you. I've been bartending since my second year in undergraduate school. That's the first four years of college, by the way."

Ah, now I understood. She was a smart girl. Normally, I stayed as far away as possible from that kind of female. They always had all the answers and never understood how to truly have fun. And worst of all, they always wanted a relationship. Of all the things I wanted in my next woman, intelligence was at the bottom of my list.

"College? Well, I guess that's a nice way to spend four years. I preferred earning money, but to each his own. Microbiologist, huh? Probably will never make enough to afford a membership here anyway. Good thing you're going to be an employee working for us. Employees get free memberships."

In truth, as a bartender, Shay wouldn't be given a membership since she wouldn't be an upper level employee. Only Cash, Kane, and I got them, along with his assistant, Olivia. But as part owner, I could give Shay a membership if I chose to.

At the moment, I couldn't think of anything I'd like to do less.

"I'm not interested in a membership, Stefan. I'm interested in making money at a job. Hopefully, you and your brothers will recognize my talents and hire me. Either way, I have to go."

Before I could say another word, she turned on her heels and marched out the door. Fuck, she was a feisty one. I stood there watching the door close while my brain played tug of war with itself. On the one hand, Shay was smoking hot and I had no doubt having her would be a good time. Long brown hair, a mouth that would have made me hard if it wasn't spewing such sharpness, and a body…fuck, her body was hot! My mind was already filled with thoughts of how incredible it would be to fuck her. What an ass she had! On the other hand, she was smart and possessed a level of bitchiness that even I had to admit I might not be able to overcome.

Might. But if I'd ever met a challenge, it was her.

"She wants a job as a bartender," Cash announced behind me. Turning to face him, I pretended not to care. "Yeah?" I said with a shrug. "I don't know if I need a new bartender, and we have a list a mile long of people who want to be one."

"Okay. I just wanted to mention it. She seemed nice in the interview. Kane liked her well enough, which says something, I guess. You would have gotten to talk to her if you bothered to join us."

Why I hadn't gotten to the interview on time had to do more with nursing a hangover from the night before than with not caring about Cash's precious hiring process. Not that I really cared to sit through hour after hour of interviews with him and Kane. "We have private investigators for a reason. I don't need to see every goddamn person who walks through the door for a job, Cash."

He put his hands up in surrender. "Okay, okay. Take it easy. You don't want her to work for us, she won't work for us. Case closed."

Cash walked away as I stood still stinging from Shay's barbed jabs. I didn't know if I wanted to bother trying to get with her. With all the women in the world, why take the time to overcome whatever defensive bullshit she had going on?

Kane came around me and stood with his arms folded across his chest. "She's a wild one, isn't she?"

"Wild? I missed the interview, so I wouldn't know."

"I heard how she took you down a few pegs before she left. Looks like there's at least one woman you won't be having."

I didn't enjoy Kane's smugness. Whether it was because he'd been pissed off about something recently or because he never had any women, he seemed to truly enjoy Shay's attitude with me.

"It doesn't matter how fucking wild she is. She's not going to be working here, so what do I care?"

"Seems to have struck a nerve there, Stef. I guess she's just out of your league."

He wasn't even trying to hide his joy over this. "Has nothing to do with leagues, Kane. If it did, we might be talking about how someone like that wouldn't even bother talking to the likes of you if you weren't part owner of this club."

"I'm not the one who thinks he can have any woman on Earth. I'm a little choosier and I prefer to keep my relationships a little more private. You prefer to have them displayed on the bar each night and then in lawyers' offices during depositions. But you're not going to get the chance with this one."

"That sounds like a challenge, Kane. I don't think you're up to it, though."

He chuckled and shook his head. "She's not my type, Stefan. I don't want her, and I won't fight for her."

"Not fight for her. It just sounds like you don't think I could get her."

His chuckle morphed into a full-blown laugh. "I know you can't. That woman is too smart for you. She saw your game coming a mile away. Accept it. Shay isn't a woman you can have. Move on and be happy with those cheap little playthings you prefer to spend your time with."

"You honestly don't think I can get her to go out with me, do you?"

"I honestly can't believe you'd want her. She's too much work for you, Stefan. You'd have to be more than the man whore you've always been. I just don't think you're up to it."

Was Kane serious? "You're saying you think there's a woman I can't seduce? Am I hearing you right?"

"I'm saying seducing her isn't something you know how to do. It's going to take a whole lot more than a few drinks, your charming smile, and whatever smooth lines you use to get with your usual type."

I couldn't believe what I was hearing. Kane, who I didn't think I'd ever seen with a woman, was doubting my ability to charm someone. Kane, who most females backed away from in fear, was saying I wasn't smart enough to get Shay Callahan, science nerd, into bed. He had to be kidding!

"Kane, you're coming dangerously close to insulting me. For a man who has so little success with women, you seem to not know how successful I've been."

"I've seen your conquests. Not impressed. It doesn't take much to get cheap sluts to fuck you. They're going to do it anyway, so if you're the nearest guy around, you luck out."

"Fuck you, Kane!" I spat out, sick of this conversation. It wasn't bad enough I was hung over, but now I'd had to deal with two people giving me shit.

"You know what they say. It's all about location, location, location. I'd bet that if you didn't have a constant stream of young ones wanting to work as bartenders here that you'd get far less ass."

The guy was taunting me. I knew it, but something in me snapped and made me want to force him to put up or shut up. Kane was much bigger than I was, though, and I wasn't stupid. I may have wanted to knock him flat on his ass, but the reality was that I'd likely get one or two shots in before he kicked me around my bar.

No, I couldn't beat him physically. But there were other ways to bring him down to size.

"Kane, I could stand here all day trading jabs with you, but I've got a better idea. Let's make a bet. That's if you're up to it, of course."

He stepped back and stared me down. "You want to bet what with me? That you can get with that girl?"

"Yeah. Take the bet or show you're all talk."

"I'm not interested in chasing after that girl. She's not my type. I don't even pretend she is. I'm not interested in her or your bet."

He turned to walk away, but I caught him by the shoulder and stopped him. "Hear me out. I'm not talking about a bet to see if you can get her before I do. I'm saying I'll bet you I can get her to fall for me."

"What's in it for me, other than seeing you make an ass out of yourself?" he asked with the sinister grin he wore so often around me.

"Name it. You set the terms."

He took a few moments to think about my offer and finally said, "Let me see if I got this straight. You're bothered that I don't think you have in it you to get this girl, so you want to make a bet that you can?"

I forced a nonchalant shrug. "If you don't think you're up to it..."

"Is this part of that Stefan charm that gets all the women to fuck you? I don't see it, but if you insist, I'll take your bet."

"Good. Name your terms."

"You have to get this girl to fall for you, and I don't mean just sleep with you. She has to be in love with you or you don't win."

The reality that making a woman fall in love was much harder than making one fall into bed with you was a real problem. Women like Shay didn't do either easily, I guessed, but sex was a whole lot easier than love.

"Fine."

"And you have only one semester to do this in. She made it clear in the interview that next semester she's not going to be able to work since she'll be studying abroad. That gives you maybe four months."

"Four months? What the fuck, Kane? How long does it take for you to get into a woman's pants? Jesus, I bet I can do it in a tenth of that time."

"You do realize she's not like the other women who work for you, right? She's smart, successful, and from what I already heard from her when she stood right there and dressed you down, she doesn't even like you."

"No matter. I'll take the four months, but I don't plan to need it. What else?" I bragged, secretly admitting to myself that it very well could take half that time just to get her to warm up to me. After that, though, it would be smooth sailing.

"You have to show proof."

I'd always suspected Kane was a kinky one. What did he want? Video? "Proof like what? You planning to watch me sleep with her?" I joked.

"Cash and Olivia are planning their engagement party for just around the time you'd have to get Shay to fall for you. You're going to have to show up to the party with her, and you're going to have to get her to say she loves you."

"As long as I don't have to be in love with her, we have a deal."

"The man whore in love? I'm not ready for Hell to freeze over just yet. No, all you need is her in love with you."

I chucked him on the shoulder. "I don't think I've ever seen you this cruel, Kane. It seems heartless to have the girl fall in love with me when I won't be in love with her."

Shaking his head, he smiled. "Not cruel at all. If I thought for a second that this one would even give you the time of day, I wouldn't agree to this bet at all. I don't think you have a chance, little brother. You've met your match this time."

"Yeah, yeah. Whatever. So what do I get if I win?"

Kane grinned. "A gorgeous woman you'd never deserve in love with you."

"Not good enough. I want something from you when I win. Put up or shut up."

"You can't want money. What else do I have that you want?" he asked, genuinely confused about what I could be angling for.

"Your Mustang."

A look of terror crossed his face and he shook his head quickly. "No."

"What's wrong, big brother? Chicken shit?"

"I'm not risking my car. There's no way in hell I'm letting you touch that baby."

I'd wanted to get my hands on Kane's 69 Mustang Boss 429 since the first time I laid eyes on it. Black, sexier than any vehicle I'd ever seen, it was the one car I hadn't been able to find for my own. I'd get that car and Shay too.

"Seems like you think I might win, Kane. All that talk and when push comes to shove, you're nowhere to be found."

Leaning down, he pushed his face close to mine. "I'm not betting my car, Stefan. I don't care if you fuck this girl or not. No deal."

"Then let me have it for a weekend. I win and you give me your car for a whole weekend."

He seemed to think about my concession and nodded. "And what do I get if you lose? I'm not risking the one thing I care about more than life itself if I don't get something pretty fucking incredible in return."

"My humiliation won't be enough?"

"I don't think you'll be humiliated. You won't really care for her, so your feelings won't be involved. This has to be something worthwhile if my car is on the line, even if it is only for a weekend."

"How about my apartment? You seemed to like it when you came over that one time."

Kane raised his eyebrows in disbelief. "You're going to give me your apartment on the bay?"

"Sure." I was pretty sure he'd never get to step foot into my place.

"So let me get this straight. If you don't get this woman to fall in love with you within four months, you'll give me your apartment. For how long?"

"For an entire year."

"And if you do get her to fall in love with you, you get my car for a weekend?"

"Sounds good. Is it a deal?" I asked, holding my hand out to shake on it.

Kane took my hand and shook it hard. "I'm going to enjoy that place of yours, and seeing you get shot down by a real woman will just be icing on the cake."

"Just get that Mustang ready for me. I plan to enjoy my weekend with it picking up women. If you had any skills, you'd use it to get chicks too."

Shaking his head, he mumbled something as he walked away, no doubt sure he would win our bet. I had no intention of losing this one. That car and my reputation meant too much to me.

About the Author

K.M. Scott writes sexy contemporary romance with characters her readers love. A New York Times and USA Today bestselling author, she's been in love with romance since reading her first romance novel in junior high (she was a very curious girl!). She lives in Pennsylvania with her teenage son and a herd of animals and when she's not writing can be found reading or feeding her TV addiction.

Be sure to visit K.M.'s Facebook page at https://www.facebook.com/kmscottauthor for all the latest on her books, along with giveaways and other goodies! And to hear about Advanced Review Copy opportunities and all the news on K.M. Scott books first, sign up for her newsletter today!

OTHER BOOKS BY K.M. SCOTT

Crash Into Me (Heart of Stone #1)
Fall Into Me (Heart of Stone #2)
Give In To Me (Heart of Stone #3)
The Heart of Stone Trilogy Box Set
Ever After (A Heart of Stone Novella)

Surrender (Club X #2) Coming Fall 2014
Possession (Club X #3) Coming Early 2015
Add them to your Goodreads shelf today!

Love sexy paranormal romance? K.M. writes under the name Gabrielle Bisset too! Visit Gabrielle's Facebook page and her website at www.gabriellebisset.com/ to find out about her books.

BOOKS BY GABRIELLE BISSET:

Vampire Dreams Revamped (A Sons of Navarus Prequel)
Blood Avenged (Sons of Navarus #1)
Blood Betrayed (Sons of Navarus #2)
Longing (A Sons of Navarus Short Story)
Blood Spirit (Sons of Navarus #3)
The Deepest Cut (A Sons of Navarus Short Story)
Blood Prophecy (Sons of Navarus #4)
Blood & Dreams Sons of Navarus Box Set

Love's Master
Masquerade
The Victorian Erotic Romance Trilogy

19894269R00187

Made in the USA
Middletown, DE
07 May 2015